P

"Gone is the surfer boy to be replaced by a hard, cold man that still has a heart of gold. Gunner will do anything for Adri including letting her go even if his other half is against it." —*Melanie, GoodReads*

"It isn't very often that I feel rewarded for waiting on a book. I have been pacing, waiting on more of the Sons of Sangue, Washington chapter. Needing a fix, I had recently read all of the Sons of Sangue books. It made me want more, more more. Gunner is that more." —*Trudy, GoodReads*

"A must read for anyone who love an adrenaline rush, passion kindling to flames, and the loyalty of family!" —*Annette, GoodReads*

"This story has a lot going on and is a page turner with lots of hot sizzles. I also like how some of the brothers from the Oregon chapter are brought in and of course Vlad! You can't go wrong with reading this book it's a keeper!" —*J Andrade, GoodReads*

"These books are so much fun to read. A true total escape for me. They help bring me to a happy place. I just love the love, drama and laughter these books bring out in me." —*Alys, Goodreads*

Other Books by Patricia A. Rasey:

Diablo: Sons of Sangue Washington (#1)

Viper: Sons of Sangue (#1)
Hawk: Sons of Sangue (#2)
Gypsy: Sons of Sangue (#3)
Rogue: Sons of Sangue (#4)
Draven: Sons of Sangue (#4.5)
Preacher: Sons of Sangue (special edition)
Xander: Sons of Sangue (#5)
Ryder: Sons of Sangue (#6)
Wolf: Sons of Sangue (#7)
Viper: Sons of Sangue (#8)

Love You to Pieces
Deadly Obsession
The Hour Before Dawn
Kiss of Deceit
Eyes of Betrayal
Façade

Novellas:
Spirit Me Away
Heat Wave
Fear the Dark
Sanitarium

Gunner
Sons of Sangue Washington

Patricia A. Rasey

Copyright © 2023 by Patricia A. Rasey.

All rights reserved. No part of this publication may be reproduced, distributed or transmitted in any form or by any means, including photocopying, recording, or other electronic or mechanical methods, without the prior written permission of the publisher, except in the case of brief quotations embodied in critical reviews and certain other noncommercial uses permitted by copyright law. For permission requests, write to the publisher, addressed "Attention: Permissions Coordinator," at the address below.

Patricia A. Rasey
patricia@patriciarasey.com
www.PatriciaRasey.com

Publisher's Note: This is a work of fiction. Names, characters, places, and incidents are a product of the author's imagination. Locales and public names are sometimes used for atmospheric purposes. Any resemblance to actual people, living or dead, or to businesses, companies, events, institutions, or locales is completely coincidental.

Cover design © 2023 by CrocoDesigns
Book Layout ©2013 BookDesignTemplates.com

Ordering Information:
Quantity sales. Special discounts are available on quantity purchases by corporations, associations, and others. For details, contact the email address above.

Diablo: Sons of Sangue Washington / Patricia A. Rasey – 1st ed.
ISBN-13: 979-839154503

In Loving Memory

Bernard Eugene Miller
Wanda Mae Rasey
Todd

Dedication

I don't like dedications because I feel like I'm always leaving someone out. So, for here on out … these books are for the readers.
Thank you for the patience and sticking with me. You are the reason I write.

CHAPTER ONE

MOTORCYCLE AND MAN SLID INTO THE CURVE AT A HUNDred miles per hour, narrowly missing the turn and skidding sideways into the guardrail. *This was going to hurt*, Gunner Anderson thought. Gravel kicked up in his wake and the bike slammed into the rail. The ass end flipped over the wood and steel, sending the Washington Sons of Sangue president face-first into the dirt and stone alongside the road.

Bones snapped, his chest compressed, and skin ripped, leaving bloody road rashes as he slid along the shallow ravine of State Highway 410. Hell, he had barely applied the brakes, hoping to beat the braggart son of a bitch from the Blood 'n' Rave in the stretch of dangerous curves near Chinook Creek.

The crotch rocket behind him made the curve, its tires squealing as the other rider no doubt saw Gunner flip ass-over-end in his rearview mirror. The guy likely thought Gunner was dead. But that was the benefit of being a vampire. It took more than mangled bones and peeled flesh to take him out.

The metallic flavor of his blood filled his mouth as he coughed up a fair amount. He'd heal. Already, he could hear his bones snapping back into place. Even so, it hurt like hell but he'd live to see another day.

The motorcyclist he'd been racing pulled along the guardrail and peered over the side. "Jesus! You're alive?"

Gunner laughed, spitting up a bit more blood. "Looks that way. I think I fared better than my bike. I doubt she's going to run again."

His Harley Davidson lay on its side, nothing but a tangle of metal and rubber. Good thing he worked for the Tepes twins at K&K Motorcycles, because he was going to need a new ride ... again. It would be his third bike in less than three months. Maybe he ought to stop challenging the locals to race along Highway 410. The spike of adrenaline was hard to resist, and thankfully, most times he was the victor. Humans usually didn't possess the balls it took to take the curves at the high rate of speed needed to beat him.

"Stay where you are. I'll call a squad."

"No need." Gunner coughed again, holding his chest. *Damn, that hurt.* "I'm sure my buddies will be along at any moment."

And as if right on cue, Gunner's vampire hearing picked up on the rumble of Harleys coming from a distance.

"You sure you're going to be all right? You don't look so good."

His grin had to be a bloody one. "Get out of here before the law shows up. They don't take too kindly to racing along these roads."

The man nodded. "I won't even bother asking for the couple hundred you owe me for winning. Looks like you might need it for the hospital bill."

Gunner chuckled and straightened his oddly bent leg, the snap of the bone no doubt picked up by the human's ears. The man's face paled, but instead of further engaging Gunner in conversation, he started his bike, kicked up his feet, and sped off down the highway. Gunner doubted the fool would take up another bet that required racing along these curves any time soon.

The sound of approaching motorcycles grew in intensity just before simultaneously silencing. It wouldn't be long before he was looking up from the ditch at his vampire brothers from the Sons of Sangue. They tended to keep a close eye on him the past few months as Gunner grew more brazen. Hell, his given name said it all. Gunner had an addiction to speed, so he hadn't even needed a moniker. Any time he crawled onto the back of his bike, he tended to gun it.

The winter thaw had allowed the Mount Rainier roads to reopen, and Gunner couldn't be happier about it. He felt right at home racing along twists and turns at a high rate of speed. Challenging people to a race? That was the new and brazen part. The truth of it, Gunner just didn't give much of a fuck. With life came death, unless you were frozen in time as a vampire. And Gunner had yet to weigh in on how he felt about that. He supposed it had its benefits, like now. But living forever? The way Gunner saw it, he had a long, lonely road ahead of him.

Not that he didn't see himself wanting to spend eternity with someone, much like Dante "Diablo" Santini had found with his mate, Angelica Hart. But Gunner feared the love of his life had already passed him up, for a dirtbag no less. He doubted there'd be another. Adriana Flores had been it for him, even if she hadn't felt the same way.

Life moved on.

"When the fuck are you going to learn?" Speak of the devil. Diablo peered down at him, his hands braced on the guardrail. The skull tattoo on the vampire's neck seemed to mock Gunner for playing with his immortality.

Gunner slowly sat up and rolled his shoulders. "Which one of you asswipes is giving me a ride back? I doubt my bike will make the trip."

Adrian "Smoke" Wellman and Brandon "Neo" McClure were next to look over the rail, neither appearing even remotely concerned with his wellbeing. He supposed unless he lost his head or somehow managed to stop his heart from beating, they knew he'd crawl out of the ditch of his own accord.

"As Road Captain," Neo said, "I think it's my duty to go get the paddy wagon and pick up that heap of junk. You realize you destroyed yet another fine piece of machinery, P." Neo ran a tattooed hand through his long brown hair, pushing the tangled mess from his face. "You can ride back with Smoke."

"Hell, no." Smoke chuckled, shaking his head, his overlong, deep-brown bangs momentarily hiding his vivid green eyes. "As club VP, I'm passing that off on Diablo. You can ride bitch with him. I'll ride back with Neo and get the truck. You two figure it out."

Gunner attempted to chuckle, holding his aching ribs. No doubt Diablo, newly promoted to club Sergeant at Arms, wasn't too happy about the given order. Nonetheless, he knew Diablo would adhere to the directive and respect the hierarchy of the motorcycle club.

"Take my hand." Diablo reached down and gripped Gunner's outstretched one, slowly easing him to his feet. "When you going to stop this nonsense, P?"

Gunner shrugged, letting go of Diablo. He easily hopped over the guardrail, already feeling much better than he had moments ago. Smoke and Neo turned their bikes and headed back down the road.

"What you call nonsense, I call living. Nothing like a good ol' adrenaline rush to make you feel alive."

"I think the idea, though, is to stay alive, man. Sometimes I think you got a death wish. You're an adrenaline junkie."

"Can't disagree, but I didn't ask for your opinion, Diablo."

"No, but we're the ones scraping your ass off the asphalt and stone. One of these days you won't stitch back together."

"Hell, I have at least a hundred lives left."

"Maybe." Diablo placed a hand on Gunner's shoulder and led him over to his motorcycle. "I'm remembering a time not all that long ago when you offered an ear. I'm doing the same thing now, bro. You need someone to talk to, I can be a good listener."

"It's all good, but thank you anyway."

"You got that head screwed on straight?"

"Maybe not the helmet." Gunner righted the askew skullcap on his head. "But trust me, it's just about the rush."

"If you say so."

Diablo stepped over his bike seat and sat down on the worn leather. Gunner crawled on behind him. "I say so. Now, let's get the hell out of here."

Turning on the ignition, Diablo pushed the start buttons and the engine roared to life. As Diablo pulled away from the guardrail, Gunner couldn't help but look back. He had been lucky, yet again, not to stop his heart on impact. Maybe Diablo was correct. He did have some sort of death wish. *When the hell had he stopped caring?*

About the time Adriana walked out of his life, confessing to love a cartel kingpin. Fuck, how bad did he have to be for Mateo Rodriguez to be the better choice?

"You seem to be in yet another mood today."

Adriana Flores ran a hand through her hair that now barely brushed her shoulders and glared at the man stopping just inside the door to her room. Months ago, she'd shorn her waist-length hair knowing Mateo Rodriguez would hate it. She might have returned to Mexico with him of her own accord but it was for no other reason than to protect the Sons of Sangue from the murdering bastard and his army.

More specifically, to protect Gunner Anderson.

Adri wouldn't have been able to live with herself had Mateo ordered him dead. Mateo, her ex-fiancé, had sworn he meant to get her back at all costs, proving so when he'd torched her best friend Gabriela Trevino Caballero's beach home while several people, including her, had been at the residence. Luckily, no one had been harmed. Adri forced Mateo to reimburse Gabby for the loss, even though she and Ryder Kelley had plenty of money to rebuild. Which in no way meant that Adri forgave Mateo for his malfeasance.

Offering him a fake smile, Adri stepped away from the third-story French doors that opened onto a terrace overlooking the expansive acreage. "You know how to fix my mood."

Mateo returned her grin with a malice-filled one. "I've told you many times, you're my guest until I say otherwise. Are your accommodations not to your liking?"

She glanced around the lavish room at the high-end style furnishings which must have cost him a small fortune. The old Trevino Caballero estate had been built and furnished for no less than a king, or in this case a kingpin. But the home had been completely gutted and remodeled after Gabby's uncle Raúl had been slain by the Sons of Sangue. Adri had taken care of selling the estate for Gabby to an unknown bidder, allowing Gabby's lawyer to complete the details before moving north to Oregon. Adri found out at a later date that the home had been purchased by none other than her criminal ex.

"Of course, not. You've provided well for me."

His dark eyes blackened with anger. "Then I fail to see the fucking problem."

"Because I'm little more than your prisoner."

"You can come and go as you please. I've not once stopped you from leaving."

Adri bit back the retort on the tip of her tongue. Instead, she said, "Not without an escort."

"That's for your own good. No one would hesitate to use you to get to me."

"I understand perfectly, Mateo. I'm a possession. And as such, I have no rights." Her hand did a sweep of the room. "Your wealth can provide me with anything I need, but it won't give me what I desire."

"And what is that, *darling*?" His sarcastic tone wasn't lost on her.

"My freedom."

Mateo chuckled, then wiped away his smile as he ran a hand down his chin. Mateo Rodriguez was a man without conscience. Adri had once thought Gabby's uncle Raúl Trevino Caballero depraved when Mateo had first gone to work for him. The mentor had trained Mateo well, for he now transcended the master. Gone was the handsome boy who had first wooed her years ago, leaving behind only the shell of the person he'd been as a teenager.

"My darling fiancée¬—"

"Don't." Heat radiated up her spine. "You don't get to refer to me as such."

"Then what shall I call you if not my *esposa para ser*?"

"I am not your wife-to-be or otherwise. Nor will I ever be. Saying it will not change that."

His jaw hardened and his face streaked red. "Do you not know how lucky you are?"

"To be caged like an animal?"

"I could make that happen with a snap of my fingers. Don't tempt me, *mi pequeña reina*. You live here, free to roam the compound as you please." Mateo's gaze narrowed. "What the hell has brought on this hostility?"

She was no one's *little queen*, certainly not his, and she hated that he referred to her as such. Adri couldn't tell Mateo her sour mood came from a dream, one in which Gunner had come for her. If Mateo was any other man, she would've never left Oregon or Gunner. Maybe eventually she would've even moved to Washington to be with him. His feelings for her had been transparent, but acting on them would have been foolhardy on her part, putting him in danger.

"I miss my best friend."

Mateo chuckled cruelly. "I'll get you a new one."

Rolling her eyes, she scoffed. "You can't just order me up a new friend like you would a piece of furniture, Mateo. I want to see Gabriela. Bring her here."

"No." Adri knew arguing with him would be futile. "Gabby is lost to you. She's the one who's shacked up with the enemy."

Tears gathered in Adri's eyes even though she had already known the consequences of her actions when she left Oregon for Mexico. "You must hate me."

Mateo closed the distance. His icy gaze warmed as he gently gripped her shoulders. She resisted the urge to step away, knowing doing so would only bring back his fury. If Adri was ever to win any favor, she'd need to appeal to his softer side. There was never any doubt that Mateo had loved her once. But when she'd moved to Oregon, breaking their engagement, he had been crushed, his affection eventually turning to rage. Hell, he had burned down Gabby's house. It was only by the grace of God that Adri and her friends had all escaped before it was fully engulfed.

Now, seldom did she see this tender side.

"*Mi pequeña reina*, I could never hate you. I would give you the world. My wealth, everything I own, could be yours, too."

A tear slipped down her cheek. She had at one time given him her heart ... until the ugliness in him surfaced after taking over Raúl Trevino Caballero's empire. His ego had flourished. Now, Mateo was no better than Gabby's murderous uncle.

"All I ever wanted was to be happy."

"You used to think I made you happy. What happened, Adriana?"

She turned from his touch, giving him her back as she walked over to the open French doors, stepping through them and onto the veranda. She stopped short of the railing, her gaze taking in the many men, heavily armed, guarding the estate. Footsteps padded against the tile and onto the concrete, telling her Mateo had joined her, his calloused hands returning to her shoulders.

"This is not freedom, Mateo. Not surrounded by soldiers twenty-four-seven. This is the life you chose, not the one I did."

"My love means nothing?"

Adri turned in his grasp, another tear slipping. He brushed it away with the pad of his thumb. Adri resisted the shiver of revulsion it caused. "I'm your possession. This is not love."

He swore beneath his breath, dropping his hold and sticking his hands into the pockets of his trousers. Gone was the tenderness. "You belong to me, *mi pequeña reina*. The sooner you realize, the better. I'm tired of waiting. We will be married. I had hoped you'd come around. I'll tell you what, *esposa para ser*, you agree to marry me within a month and I'll see that Gabriela can come to your wedding."

Mateo didn't wait for her reply. He turned on his heel, strode back into her room and through the door, slamming it in his wake. Adri's knees weakened at the thought of his demand. No doubt he'd expect her to share his bed as well. Her breath stuck in her chest as she turned back to the expansive lawn and the soldiers patrolling it. There would be no escape.

She was doomed.

Even the promise of allowing Gabby to come to the wedding didn't soften the blow of his words. Her dreams of a life with Gunner were effectively over the minute she stepped aboard Mateo's yacht months ago, leaving the port. Adri knew Gunner would never forgive her for that betrayal.

The thought of Gabriela telling Gunner that she'd be coming to Adri and Mateo's wedding sickened her. She hadn't seen Gunner in months. But regardless of the time and separation, her heart had never stopped loving him.

CHAPTER TWO

GUNNER LEFT THE PRIVATE LOUNGE AT THE BACK OF THE loft at the Blood 'n' Rave and entered the second-floor bar reserved for members of the Sons of Sangue. Massive windows overlooked the dance area, drowning out the loud, industrial music pumping through the club below. Thankfully, other than the bartender, the upstairs room was empty. Gunner's current disposition didn't warrant company.

Mei, a beautiful young Asian blood donor, had followed him from the lounge but took the stairs down to the club alone. Gunner hadn't been in the mood for chit-chat or extracurricular activities; hadn't been for the past couple of months. Oh, he had put on a happy face when in mixed company. But ever since Adriana's phone call a few months ago, he couldn't get the dark-haired minx off his brain.

His broken bones, scrapes, and bruises were nearly healed from his trip over the guardrail, thanks to his vampire DNA and the pint of human blood donated by Mei. But what was it going to take to heal his damn heart? Adri chose the La Paz cartel kingpin and it was high time he got the hell over it.

Thankfully, Mei had offered him the sustenance he needed and nothing more. Donors were a society of women gifted to the Sons by the club's owner, Draven Smith. He and his pretty mate, Brea Gotti, ran a couple Raves providing humans willing to feed vampires, and giving the Sons complete anonymity when doing so. The donors were easily spotted by the black cord circling their necks, a tiny vial of vampire blood and a red crystal dangling from it. Those who wore them, like Mei, were sworn to keep the vampires' secret.

Sliding up to the bar, Gunner tapped the wooden top to catch the bartender's attention from the television suspended over the back wall. The bartender grabbed a bottle of Gentleman Jack and set it in front of him.

"On the rocks?"

Gunner nodded. Within seconds, a short glass containing a large ball of ice was set in front of him. Picking up the bottle, Gunner helped himself to the amber liquid, filling the glass nearly to the top. It wasn't as if he could become an alcoholic, not with his blood cells regenerating at the speed of light.

"Anything else I can get you?"

"Nope." He withdrew a hundred from his pocket and laid it on the bar. "Keep the change."

"Thanks, Gunner."

He turned and headed for the drink rail situated in front of the bank of windows. He placed a palm on the cool glass and looked down over the crowd. The Blood 'n' Rave had once again drawn a packed house. Ravers gyrated to the music as strobe lights pulsed around the room. What must have started out as a speakeasy of sorts for vampires had turned into quite the lucrative business for Draven. Both of his Raves never lacked for business.

Usually, Gunner was more than happy to mingle among the crowds, being more of a people person than a loner. But he'd had enough action for one night. Rolling his shoulders, the stiffness in his muscles remained from his earlier tumble, even if the consumed blood had helped him to heal. Diablo's remark from earlier hadn't been far off. Gunner wasn't moving on from Adri and he could probably use someone to unload his shit on. Otherwise, this crap might just consume him.

Following Adri's phone call a few months ago, warning him that Mateo Rodriguez and the La Paz cartel were planning to descend on the Sons of Sangue, he had meant to write her off. After all, her call verified she was still romantically involved with the kingpin. But the aching hole left in his heart proved he was far from over her.

Diablo's scent drifted to him, long before his MC brother spoke. "What's got you all pensive?"

His vampire scent could always detect another vampire in the vicinity, making it damn near impossible to sneak up on one. Even though his mind had been a million miles away, his sense wouldn't leave him vulnerable. Still, he needed to get a handle on this shit and fast.

"Nothing you'd care to hear about."

Diablo pointed at the half-filled glass in Gunner's hand. "Let me get one of those and I'll be all ears."

"You're going to need more than one glass for the boatload of crap going on in my head."

He heard Diablo's answering chuckle as he turned and headed for the bar, pouring himself a tumbler of the whiskey. He returned, clinked glasses with Gunner's, then said, "Spill."

"What brings you here?"

"Angel was busy at the house."

"I thought you didn't have anyone in residence at the moment."

Diablo shrugged. "We don't, but Lisa stopped by. I thought I'd give the women some privacy. I didn't need to be around to hear the gossip. How'd you get here? Last I saw, your bike wasn't drivable."

"I took Smoke's ride. He said he and Neo weren't going out. Something about inviting a few ladies to the clubhouse. Good enough reason for me to get the hell out of there."

"You must be going through some shit if you weren't willing to stick around for the festivities."

"Yeah, well…" He took the glass to his lips and took a sip.

"What's got you all tied up, Gunner?"

Hell, there was no skirting the issue. "Adriana Flores."

"I figured as much. You hear from her again?"

"Nope." And that was the problem. He sure in the hell hoped Mateo hadn't found out about her phone call to him. The man didn't seem the forgiving type. "That and we haven't heard one word from the cartel since sending Juan's head back to Mateo in a potato sack a few months ago."

"Pretty sure they haven't forgotten."

"When the hell are they going to act? Viper and Hawk, as well as the rest of the Oregon Sons are on high alert, but it's been crickets since her phone call. Had it not been for Adri, we wouldn't have even known if the motherfuckers cared. I'm also worried Mateo may have hurt her."

"You still have the phone number she called you from?"

Gunner nodded.

"Then call her."

He jammed a hand through the waves at the top of his head. Apprehension clawed up his spine. "I can't."

"Why?"

"Because what if Mateo answers the damn phone?"

"Then hang up, man. It's not rocket science." Diablo tipped his glass, finished the whiskey, then set it on the wooden rail in front of them. "I'm betting if she used a cell to call you, it's not one she'll let Mateo have access to, just in case you were to ever call the number back."

Gunner took a deep breath. "I don't know what I'd say to her anyway."

"You could start with asking her what's going on with Mateo's plans where we're concerned."

He supposed Diablo was right.

"At least then you'll know if she's okay. Once you get an answer to your question, you can lead into how she's doing."

"And if she's not okay?"

"Your call, man."

"What would you do if it were Angel?"

Diablo scrubbed his short-cropped hair with his hand. "Nothing would've stopped me from going after her."

Gunner left the bank of windows, grabbed the bottle of whiskey and refilled his glass, which he quickly downed. He should just drink the fucking bottle. Going after Adriana was foolhardy at best. He couldn't fight an entire army of soldiers. But not doing anything?

Diablo walked up behind him and placed a hand on his shoulder. "Give her a call, Gunner. When you do, and if you find out you need to go to Mexico, I'll have your back."

Setting his empty glass down on the bar, Diablo turned and headed for the exit. No doubt giving Gunner the time and privacy to do what was right. Call Adriana.

ADRIANA STOOD ON THE TERRACE, the slight breeze rustling her hair. Soldiers patrolled the meticulous lawns, garbed in military vests, automatic rifles in hand. The day was otherwise beautiful, not a cloud in the azure horizon.

If only she had no care in the world.

Even though Mateo had thankfully left the estate hours earlier, there would be no escaping for her. No way to slip away unseen. He rarely made her privy to his affairs, not that she cared. But his confession of returning well after nightfall had given her a bit of a respite. Not that she didn't desire human interaction, just with anyone other than Mateo. After his earlier bombshell of their looming wedding, Adri needed time to come to terms with the unwanted course her life had taken.

She was his captive.

And had been since her return to Mexico.

Doomed to marry the murderous son of a bitch unless she came up with a solid strategy to avoid it. Her gaze traveled the lawns again. Breaking out of his stronghold wasn't going to be easy. If her plan of escape failed, though, it would undoubtedly spell her death.

Adri heard a muffled ringing. Turning her head toward the door, the barely audible sound continued. Her gaze landed on the bedside table where she had hid her cell from Mateo. Moving swiftly over to the stand, she pulled open the drawer and rifled through her undergarments. Picking up the cell, Adri silenced the ring while noting the number on the glass she'd committed to memory. She nearly dropped it in her fumbling.

Answering the call and taking it to her ear, she whispered, "Gunner?"

"Can you talk?"

"Hold on." Her heart fluttered hearing his voice for the first time in a few months. Adri placed a hand over her rapidly beating heart as she crossed the tiled floor to the en suite and closed herself inside. Lord, she couldn't believe how good it was to hear his voice again, but she couldn't let him know. "The last time we spoke, you told me to lose your number. Apparently, you didn't heed your own advice."

"I never said I was losing yours, babe."

"Don't." Her heart ached at the term of endearment she used to love hearing tumble from his lips. "You don't get to call me that."

"Why? Is it because Mateo calls you that while he's fucking you?"

His question damn near brought her to her knees, cutting her deeper than any misspoken words from Mateo. She supposed she deserved it. After all, she had lied of her love for the bastard to Gunner, even though Mateo could never hold a candle to him. Since their meeting, it had always been Gunner that her heart sought. But to tell him so now would only put him in further danger.

"Why are you calling, Gunner?"

"Does Mateo still plan to come North?" Not to hear her voice. Not to see how she fared. How much more hurt could her heart take? "Last we spoke, you said he was bringing down an army on the Sons. So, where's the army, Adri? Or was your earlier call nothing but bullshit?"

She sucked in a deep breath, feeling as if he had slapped her. Adri's warning had been for the sole purpose of sparing Gunner and his brethren from being blindsided. Dealing with Gunner's animosity now was nearly more than she could take. Mateo's plan to make her his bride within the span of a month was a much easier pill to swallow than realizing that Gunner abhorred her.

"Don't let his non-action fool you, Gunner." Lord, she wanted to bridge the distance, to have him hold her and tell her that all would be okay. "Mateo wants every last Sons of Sangue member dead."

"So, what's the hold-up?"

She rubbed her forehead, attempting to stave off the oncoming migraine, and took a seat on the edge of the oversized jetted tub. "It's not like Mateo tells me his plans."

"You're okay with his chosen career? He's a murderer, for fuck's sake."

Not in a million years would she be okay with anything Mateo did. It wasn't as if she didn't know the things Mateo was guilty of. Adri was far from blind. "What do you want from me, Gunner?"

"The truth."

"I've been nothing but honest with you."

"Then you do love him?"

Adri couldn't utter the words a second time, to knowingly wound Gunner again. Instead, she mocked him. "Mateo isn't here. Would you like me to ask him when he plans to head your way upon his return?"

Gunner chuckled. The cruel sound carried through the speaker. "No. I don't expect to be the topic of your next pillow talk."

"Lord, Gunner" ¬—she massaged her brow again¬— "I don't sleep with him."

Adri nearly groaned at her mistaken admission, hoping it would slip Gunner's notice.

"You have separate bedrooms?" he asked, to her chagrin.

"That's not what I said."

"You said you don't sleep with him. Then what did you mean, Adri? Same room, separate beds? I highly doubt you're sleeping in the same room with the man and he's not fucking you."

"Do you have to be so crude?" Lord, Adri wanted to tell him the truth. Hell she was already teetering on an admission of loving the man she had left behind. "It's not like you and I slept together."

"No." He chuckled again. "But I sure as fuck wanted to."

Adri opened her mouth to respond, but she had no words. The idea of making love to Gunner sent an arrow of desire straight between her thighs.

"Cat got your tongue, babe? Or is the thought of fucking me truly that distasteful?"

"Gunner…" What was she to say? Gunner had been the only player in her frequent dreams since leaving Oregon.

"I don't need to hear how you prefer a sick fuck like Mateo. I don't think my ego could take it a second time. I called to see if Mateo still planned to come North, to send his army to take out my brothers."

"That's never changed."

"Then when?"

"I don't know." Adri bit back the rise of tears. Even if she couldn't tell Gunner, she'd never stop loving him. She'd go to her grave knowing what she had left behind. "I overheard him saying he'd give the Sons time to let down their guard. It could be tomorrow or next year, for that matter. I'm sorry, Gunner. I don't know anything more."

"Will you call when you do?"

Adri couldn't stand the idea of Mateo and his band of soldiers slaughtering Gunner and his brethren. "As soon as Mateo makes plans to send soldiers North, I promise you'll be the first to know."

"Will Mateo come as well?"

"If it's soon, Mateo will likely just send his army."

Gunner went silent for a moment, then asked, "What aren't you telling me, Adri?"

"Please, Gunner. Let it go." Her voice shook with the sound of tears she tried desperately to keep at bay.

"You're holding out on me. I can hear it in your voice."

Adri bit her lower lip to still the trembling. "I'll call when I know more."

Before she had a chance to end the call, the door to the bathroom suddenly opened. Startled, Adri nearly fumbled the phone. "Who the fuck are you talking to?" Mateo asked, his cheeks reddened with his mounting anger.

"No one."

He drew back his lips and snarled. "Who?"

"You're home early."

"Because I forgot to ask you your dress size."

Her brows pinched. "What for?"

"I'm having your wedding dress custom made and I need the size to give the seamstress."

The phone fell from her slack hand to the floor, clattering as it hit the tiles. Spider-vein cracks filled the glass screen.

She bent to retrieve it, but Mateo snatched the cell up and took it to his ear. "Who the fuck is this?"

Adri waited for his fury. What would Gunner say? Would he even answer?

Looking back to her, Mateo demanded again, "Who were you talking to and where did you get this phone?"

She refused to cower, no matter what he heard before entering her en suite. "I stowed it in my suitcase when I boarded your yacht. Am I not allowed a way to communicate?"

"Who were you talking to, Adri?"

"Gabby." The lie quickly left her lips. "You told me I could have her at my wedding. I wanted to ask her to be my matron of honor."

"And did she agree?"

"Of course. She's coming."

Mateo tossed the broken cell onto the granite vanity top. "Do I need to have your cell replaced?"

And monitor her calls? She'd find another way to get a hold of Gunner. "If I need to call Gabby, I'll use yours."

Mateo hadn't likely heard any of her conversation with Gunner or there would've been no placating him. But had Gunner overheard anything said before the phone shattered?

"What size dress, *mi pequeña reina*?"

"Thirty-two." Adri spoke her Mexican dress size, placing her hand on his chest. "Can't I have a say in the design? After all, it is my wedding, too."

Mateo narrowed his gaze. "What, no argument from you now? Why the sudden change in attitude, Adriana?"

She drew her lower lip between her teeth. If she were to escape, then she needed to get Mateo to let down his guard. "Gabby helped me see how foolish I was being."

"Gabriela Trevino Caballero?" He laughed. "I'm having trouble believing that she'd talk you into anything concerning me."

"Gabby reminded me that I once had feelings for you and that maybe I owe you the chance to prove yourself again." The lie soured her stomach the minute it was spoken. Never would he own her heart.

"Truly?"

Adri stood on her tiptoes and forced herself to lightly brush her lips against his. "Let me get my shoes and I'll go with you. You can drop me off at the dress shop."

Mateo rubbed his clean-shaven chin, cautiously eyeing her, obviously not taking her at her word. Adri would need to keep up the ruse if she had any hope of escaping. She had one month.

"I suppose it wouldn't hurt to leave you with a couple of my men while you visit the shop."

Adri's sickening sweet smile came easier than she thought possible. "What will you do while I visit the seamstress?"

He grunted, closing himself off. Back was the cold, calculated man she had become accustomed to the past few months. "I'll be meeting some of my men at Salazar's. Would you like me to order you takeout?"

Adri knew this might be her chance to overhear any future plans. "I'd rather eat it while it's fresh. Can't the men you leave with me bring me to Salazar's when I finish? I promise not to be long. It could be a date."

"A date?" Mateo looked at her queerly. "Up until now, you could barely stand my company. One call to Gabby and you now want to go on a date? Please excuse my skepticism, *mi pequeña reina*, but I'm finding this sudden change of heart hard to believe."

Adri had likely flipped too easily, making him mistrustful. She'd need to be more careful in the future. "Then you'll just have to trust me."

His smile didn't reach his eyes. "Get your shoes, *mi pequeña reina*. We leave in five minutes."

CHAPTER THREE

"What the fuck?" Gunner grumbled, leaving his bedroom, slamming the door in his wake.

His boots struck the pine flooring, the sound echoing about the vast room. Cursing beneath his breath, he tossed the cell phone onto the wooden L-shaped desk just off the hallway. He strolled over to the wet bar lining the back wall of the clubhouse, grabbed a bottle of Jack, and quickly downed half of it. The resulting buzz would be fleeting at best.

What the hell? A wedding dress?

The idea of Adriana… Fuck, his Adri marrying the murdering son of a bitch cut him straight to the heart. Lord, he couldn't begin to stomach the concept of Mateo putting a ring on her finger, let alone sleeping with him. Adri admitted to not having done so since her return to Mexico, which helped alleviate some of the pain. Gunner doubted, though, that would continue to be the case once she walked down the aisle.

Adriana was about to seal her fate.

Fuck, he shouldn't care. But damn it, he did.

Gunner tipped back the bottle and swallowed another good portion.

Nothing would change that fact. She should've been his. He should have asked her to be his mate when he had the chance. However, Gunner had wanted to give her time to put her past to rest. Hell, Adri didn't even know about the monster that lived inside him. Instead, he had given Mateo an opportunity to swoop in and take her back.

Gunner bit down on his molars, feeling the ache clear to his skull. Allowing his fangs to emerge, he didn't bother stopping the oncoming transformation. He growled, frustration and resentment sizzling up his spine.

Finishing the whiskey, he was about to launch the bottle against the white shiplap wall across from him when he heard the chuckled words, "Angry much?"

Gunner had scented Diablo's presence through his tirade, but hadn't cared as he was too caught up in his rage. He turned on his heel and faced his MC brother. Diablo smirked, adding nothing more to his sarcastic remark as he sat on the arm of the sofa on the opposite side of the room.

"Don't you have something better to do?" Gunner glared at him, setting the bottle on the counter.

"Thought maybe you could use someone to talk to. Stopped by to see if you had called her yet." His lips thinned. "Want to talk about it?"

"Not really." Gunner gave Diablo his back and grabbed another bottle of whiskey. He twisted the cap and took a swig.

Diablo's booted feet thudded against the floor in his approach from behind. "You mind sharing? Or you going to down that one by yourself as well?"

"Get your own bottle."

"Doesn't matter how fast or how much you drink, bro. You still won't get the desired effect."

Gunner turned and scowled. "Fuck you, Diablo."

Diablo grabbed the bottle from Gunner's hand and took a pull, then set it on the counter. He straddled a nearby chair, sat on it backward, and rested his arms along the back. "What's going on, Gunner?"

Leaning his backside against the bar, Gunner crossed his booted feet at the ankle. "The cartel, they're like a dog with a bone. They don't give up. We knew they'd eventually make good on their word. The question, though, was when."

"Did Adri know anything?"

"No clue when he'll make his move. Apparently, he's been silent on the matter."

"We figured as much. That isn't what brought out your other half, though." Diablo aimed a finger at Gunner's lips, indicating the emergence of his vampire. "What's really going on?"

He shrugged. "Adri likely only answered my call because Mateo wasn't around. She feels he's still planning to try to take us down, promised to give us a heads up."

"Then we'll know when they make a move North." Diablo scratched his slightly whiskered cheek. "So, what's got you bent?"

Gunner took a deep breath, trying to calm his vampire into remission. "Mateo caught her on the phone."

"How do you know?"

"I heard him, dude. He requested her dress size right before he asked who she was talking to."

Diablo's brow furrowed. "What for?"

"The fucker said he was having her wedding dress custom made. I can't believe she's going through with it. Jesus!" He jammed his hand through his hair and started pacing. "Why the hell would she marry the son of a bitch?"

"That's tough. What did she say?"

He shook his head and looked down at his boots. "I don't know. I heard a clatter, then the line went dead."

"You think she's okay?"

Gunner didn't know a damn thing and that frustrated the hell out of him. She acted as though she didn't want to hear from him again. Why she'd take the murdering bastard over him, he had no clue.

"You want to try calling back?" Diablo asked.

He raised his head and glared at him. "Hell, no. I can't chance getting her further in trouble. What if he found out it was me on the phone?"

"Can we have someone else call?"

"Maybe Gabriela? Ryder Kelley's mate was her best friend."

"It's worth a try."

Gunner grabbed his phone and tapped Ryder's name on the screen, then put it on speakerphone.

"Hey, Gunner. What's up?" Ryder answered.

"Dude, I need a favor. I have Diablo here with me." Gunner quickly filled Ryder in on the situation. "You think Gabby could give her a call, find out if she's all right?"

"She hasn't talked to Adriana in a long time. Gabby no longer had a working phone number for her. But if you have a new one, it might be worth a shot."

Gunner rattled off the digits. "Call me back as soon as you know anything."

"Give me a few minutes. Gabby's just in the other room," Ryder said, then the line went dead.

Gunner and Diablo stood in silence, waiting for the return call. He hadn't felt this powerless and agitated in a long time, causing him to pace the floor. Thankfully, it hadn't taken long before the phone rang.

He grabbed the cell and hit speaker. "What'd you find out?"

"The number goes straight to a voicemail, one that's not set up, so no way to leave a message," Ryder said. "You want to hop on a plane? I can take time off from K&K and go with you. We can be there tomorrow if you know where Mateo lives."

"Raúl Trevino Caballero's compound. Adri told me once Mateo had been the one to purchase it."

"No shit? Then no one knows his compound better than I do."

"Thanks, Ryder." Chasing after her might not be the right move. Adri didn't sound as if she needed, let alone wanted, him there. "I'm not sure that's what's best. Besides, she made her choice. I'll let you know if anything changes or if I hear Mateo and his soldiers are on the move."

"Thanks. You need anything, Gunner, call. Gabby said she'd try to get a hold of Adri in the meantime."

"Thanks. Take care, dude." Gunner tapped the END and set the phone down next to the bottle of Jack. "I guess we wait."

"You sure you don't want to hop on that plane?" Diablo asked.

Gunner shook his head. "I'm not even sure if Adri is in any danger, Diablo. And unless I have proof, I have to assume she knows what she's doing."

ADRIANA STOOD BAREFOOT, draped in white lace, on a plush carpeted pedestal. Unshed tears blurred her vision as two women measured, pinned, and stitched material for what would soon be her wedding dress. Not that she didn't think the result would be beautiful. On the contrary, Mateo had chosen the finest seamstresses La Paz had to offer. The quality of the silk currently bunched around her spoke volumes.

Only the best for *Señor* Rodriguez.

The A-Line lace dress Adri had picked from several sketches had elegant embroidery and seed pearls stitched to the bodice. A deep V-neckline and high waist was meant to accent her slender figure, while appliquéd roses would embellish the flowing skirt and short train. The gown would be perfect for her and Mateo's upcoming beach nuptials.

Adri had always imagined being married in such a dress, the white lace standing out beautifully against her deep complexion and black hair. Now? She wanted to rip off the yards of lace and run from the boutique. Too bad Mateo hadn't trusted her long enough for the fitting. Instead, while he waited in the air-conditioned, bulletproofed SUV, one of his men stood just outside the fitting room door in the lobby.

There would be no escape. Not from here. Not today.

A fluttering began in her chest, telling Adri she was about three short breaths away from a panic attack. She needed to get a hold on her runaway thoughts. Gunner might now be very well lost to her.

"Are you nearly finished?" she asked.

The shorter, heavier of the two women looked up and smiled, unaware of her agitation. "This takes time, *señorita*. You will be beautiful on your wedding day. No?"

"I have no doubt." Adri attempted a smile, swallowing back the tears nearly clogging her throat. "How many more fittings?"

"At least two more, *señorita*, before you see the final version."

The other seamstress, an elderly woman, stepped back and dusted her hands on her apron. She smiled in appreciation. "*Muy bonita*."

"Yes, it's very pretty." Adri worried her lower lip, wishing Gunner could see her in the finished dress. That it would be him, not Mateo, waiting at the end of a rose-strewn sandy beach aisle. "*Gracias*. We are done for today?"

"*Si.*" The younger of the two helped her out of what seemed to be miles of lace. "We will call *Señor* Rodriguez when we are ready for a second fitting."

"*Muy bien.*"

Adri stepped down from the platform and walked over to the antique, green-painted room divider decorated with an angel motif. She'd need divine intervention if she were ever to get out of her current situation and away from Mateo. Grabbing her blue jeans from the high-backed chair, she shimmied into them, then pulled a white handkerchief-style tank over her head. She slipped on her espadrille high-heeled wedges and tucked her clutch beneath her arm before heading back around the divider. After thanking the women again, Adri headed for the front of the shop where Mateo's soldier now waited.

She waltzed past him, out the door, and into the late afternoon heat. Sweat immediately pooled between her breasts. Adri much preferred the cooler weather in Oregon over the stifling humidity in Mexico. Mateo's driver leaped from the vehicle, circled the rear, and opened the back door for her. Adri slid onto the smooth, black leather next to Mateo. Keeping her gaze trained on the windshield, she hoped to avoid conversation, unsure she could be civil at the moment. She had one month to come up with a plan or find herself married to this man holding her captive.

Shortly, the SUV traveled along Federal Highway 1, heading for Salazar's. Seafood, not to mention several glasses of wine, might go a long way in bolstering her for the night before her. She'd much rather spend it in solitude, locked inside her bedroom. But that would not produce the information she was listening for, or rather, that Gunner needed.

"How was the fitting?" Mateo asked, breaking her blessed silence.

"Fine."

"The dress will be to your liking?"

Adri turned, raising a brow. "How could it not be when you offered them more *dinero* for one dress than most here in La Paz make in a year?"

His chuckle rumbled through the tight space of the vehicle. "You make it sound as if having wealth is a bad thing."

"Extravagant spending is. A dress off the shelf would have sufficed."

"Not for my *esposa para ser*."

Adri hated that he referred to her as his wife to be. *Not if she could help it*. Looking out the window at the Gulf of California and the passing coastline, she said, "I'm not used to having money. And I'm quite okay with that."

"Most women would die to be in your position."

"I'm not most women. I'd rather have my freedom than be followed around like a common criminal."

"You have freedom. Do I deny you anything?"

"Yes." She turned and glared at him. "I can't go anywhere without having one of your men nipping at my heels."

"We talked about this. Some enemies wouldn't hesitate to come for me through you. I protect what's mine."

"I need space, Mateo."

He took in a deep breath, looking to the front of the vehicle. Adri could see a muscle ticking in his cheek. She had angered him. *Good.* "Do you not know that soon what is mine will be yours? You can have anything your heart desires."

Adri needed to somehow gain his trust if she were to get him to let down his guard. Fighting would accomplish nothing. "Anything?"

"Within reason, of course."

"Then I want Gabriela at my wedding, as my matron of honor."

"Adriana…" His tone spoke of warning.

"It's who I want, Mateo. I'll not budge on this."

His lips thinned; his gaze narrowed on her. "And her husband?"

"Would you not allow her to bring him?"

He chuckled again. "You can't be serious, *mi pequeña reina*. You can have anything but that. No Sons of Sangue member would be welcome in Mexico, let alone La Paz. If Gabriela can't come without him, then you must pick another."

Adri turned her head, looking out the side window. Could she somehow use Gabby to her advantage? If anyone could aid Adri in her plan, it would be Gabby and Ryder since no one knew Raúl's compound better with Gabby having lived there. Mateo had purchased it from Gabby's inheritance when her uncle had been taken out by the Sons. Adri, though, would need to secure another phone if she was to communicate with her best friend. Using Mateo's wasn't going to be an option.

She glanced back at Mateo. "I need a new phone."

"You can use mine to call Gabriela."

"I could, but then you're not always home. I don't suppose you could leave your phone with me when you leave?"

"Of course, not." He sighed heavily, shaking his head. He appeared to ponder her request, then said, "I'll have one of my men procure you one."

"Thank you."

Adri turned her head back toward the front of the vehicle and smiled, riding the rest of the way to Salazar's in silence. Getting a hold of Gabby would be her first plan of action. If she let her best friend know that she needed a way out, Adri had little doubt Gabby and Ryder would move Heaven and Earth to make that happen. She had hesitated to involve them before now. But with only a month before sealing her fate, Adri was left with little choice.

The SUV rolled to a stop in front of the seaside tavern. The name Salazar was brightly lit in neon green, lending a soft glow to the outdoor tables sporting similarly colored umbrellas. The building had been recently renovated, Mateo having footed the bill. His ego couldn't allow him to be seen at a club that was anything but top rate. The outdoor wall along the alley had been painted with a seascape mural covering the old stone blocks, while the front was now a wall of glass and steel. It now looked more like a nightclub than a seaside shanty that specialized in not only seafood, but Mexican cuisine as well. An outdoor balcony had been added to the roof, a cable railing surrounding the space. Only Mateo and his men were allowed on the rooftop. The view of the Gulf from the upstairs dining tables was unmatched.

The driver opened the door and Adri alighted, taking Mateo's hand as they approached the large glass steel-edged doors. Once inside, she followed Mateo over to the corner staircase that led to the roof and onto the deck. The sun had started to set, lending an orange glow across the horizon and softly rolling waves. Several boats dotted the landscape, including Mateo's large yacht, moored just offshore. The evening couldn't be more beautiful ... unless she had been with anyone else.

Taking a seat near the back of the rooftop, Adri ordered a sangria from a waitress who had followed them to their table. Once the woman had returned with the drinks, she took their food orders. Adriana sipped her sangria, looking out over the water, as though she paid little attention to the men. It wasn't long before a plate of shrimp chilaquiles verdes was set in front of her. Just as she was about to take a bite of the egg, shrimp, and tortilla goodness, Adri overheard the name Sangue.

Mateo's second in charge, Joseph continued. "We still haven't paid back *hijo de puta* who cut off Juan's head. We need to retaliate."

Mateo nodded, taking a large bite of his carne asada taco. He chewed for a bit, then wiped his lips on a napkin. *"No me jodas, amigo*. If I tell you it will happen, then it will."

Adri continued to take bites of her meal while watching the sun further set over the horizon, not wanting Mateo to believe she was listening in on their conversation.

"I would never fuck with you, Mateo. But when?" Joseph asked. "*Mi compadres*, they are starting to talk. We don't want those guilty to think we are weak."

Mateo set down his fork and knife with such a clatter it made Adri startle. "You dare question me, *amigo*?"

Adri glanced at Joseph, who nervously wet his lips. "Never. I would like a timeline is all, to give my men."

"Tell them the week following my wedding. Only then will we make a move." He took another bite from his taco, then said around a mouthful, "Now please, I would like to enjoy my meal with *mi esposa para ser*."

Picking up her sangria, Adri took a large gulp, hoping to calm her now rattled nerves. Gunner waited for word of when the cartel meant to make their move. And now that she had it, she no longer had a cell phone on which to call him.

Adri finished her wine, then set down her glass. Placing her hand on Mateo's forearm, she said, "I need to use the restroom. Could you order me another glass of sangria?"

Mateo paid her very little mind. "Certainly."

Heading for the stairs, Adri was aware of the foot soldier tracking her to the lower level where the restrooms were located. The man walked into the room ahead of her, making sure it was vacant, then held open the door for her to enter. Adri walked past him and allowed the door to close softly behind her. Pacing the floor, she tried to think of a way to get a hold of Gunner. Her gaze stopped on the door. Surely, Mateo's man carried a cell. He no doubt had overheard Mateo saying on the ride over that she didn't have a phone and that she could call her friend Gabby.

Adri walked over to the door and opened it, smiling sweetly. "Can I please borrow your phone?"

"I would need to ask Mateo for such a request."

"He gave me permission on the ride over."

His brow pinched. "He did?"

"Yes, when he said I could call my friend Gabriela, did he not?"

"*Sí.*"

"I'll only be a second. There's no need to bother Mateo's meal."

He appeared in thought before digging out his phone and unlocking the screen. "Be quick."

Adri grabbed the phone from his hand. "*Gracias.*"

Closing the door, she punched in Gunner's number. Thankfully, the call was quickly answered.

"Gunner," she whispered when the line was picked up.

"Adri?"

"I have news."

"What is it?"

"Mateo and his men will be making their move in about a month."

The line went silent for a moment. Then he said, "Tell me exactly what was said."

"Mateo was talking to his second-in-command. He told him the week following the wedding. Only then will they make a move."

"Your wedding?"

Adri took in a deep breath, knowing she was hurting him. "Yes, Gunner. My wedding."

"What the fuck is taking so long?" Adri heard Mateo's voice over the din of conversation just outside the door.

"I have to go," was all she got out before the door opened and Mateo stepped in, followed by the guard who had helped her. Mateo ripped the phone from her hand.

Mateo frowned, then hit the speakerphone button. "Who is this? Gabriela?"

Silence greeted him.

Mateo let the phone hang from his left hand while pulling the Ruger from his holster with his right. He aimed the gun at her chest. Adri gasped, her life nearly passing before her.

Her heart damn near stopped when Mateo turned to the man in charge of guarding her and fired. Adri screamed. The man jerked backward seemingly in slow motion, then slid slowly down the wall, leaving a trail of blood. Joseph opened the door to the restroom following the blast, his gaze going to the dead man on the floor.

Phone still in hand, Mateo grumbled, "See this mess gets cleaned up and that no one out there heard or saw a damn thing."

Bile rose up the back of her throat. Blood and brain matter stained the wall. Mateo pulled Adri from the room, causing her to squeal and stumble along in his wake. Not one person in the tavern bothered to look their way. Mateo might as well own the place. Adri sucked in a sob as they headed out of Salazar's and made their way to the SUV.

"Why?" she whispered.

"He gave you his phone. He didn't have permission."

The driver quickly started the car as Mateo opened the rear door and shoved her inside the dark interior. Her hands shook, her breath faltered as Mateo climbed in beside her.

"Who were you talking to, Adriana?" When she didn't answer, he took the phone off speaker and placed it against his ear. "I'll ask you one more time who the hell this is. Speak now or she's next to die."

CHAPTER FOUR

"Your worst nightmare," Gunner, in full-on vampire, growled into the phone. "You touch one hair on her head and I'll make sure you don't live to see another day, motherfucker."

Mateo chuckled, further enraging Gunner. Lord, he'd make him suffer long and hard before he drained the son of a bitch of every last drop of his blood. Gunner had heard the earlier gunshot, which damn near stopped his heart before he heard Adri's questioned, "Why?" over the open cell line, reassuring him she had not been the one injured. The quickest he could get to her would be a four-hour long flight, not to mention the additional time being stuck at the airport and possible layovers. If he took the bike, it would take him two days to drive the distance to La Paz, Mexico.

"You don't have much of a say, *amigo*. *My esposa para ser* is none of your business. If you want to live, I'd say you best mind your manners and your interest in my fiancée."

"You just made it my business, *friend*," Gunner spat the final word, right before he hung up. Anything more and he feared Mateo might take it out on Adri, if he hadn't already subjected her to harm.

The rest of the Sons had gone to the Blood 'n' Rave for a little nutrition. Gunner had gone home long before their arrival, not wanting to party. Following Diablo's earlier departure, Gunner had sat in the brown leather chair overlooking Coal Creek and pondered what he was going to do, if anything, about Adriana Flores. Her latest call had solidified what he had known he needed to do all along.

Get her out.

Now, he knew that to be the right decision. Grabbing his phone, he to tried to secure a flight to La Paz International. Very few commercial planes flew in and out of the small airport. The quickest any airline could get him there was twenty hours due to the layovers. Gunner didn't want to leave her alone with the psychopath for four more, let alone twenty.

Theodore "Tag" Jones came to mind. Gunner had gone to the same school as Tag, but hadn't really kept in touch. After graduating a couple years ahead of Gunner, Tag enlisted in the United States Air Force. Last Gunner had heard, Tag had become an Adjutant General in charge of training before retiring from the military, hence his nickname.

A quick search on his phone pulled up a Theodore Jones in connection with a privately owned general aviation field called the Training Wing. Gunner crossed his fingers and dialed the number. It was already past nine and Gunner wasn't sure if anyone would still be at the hangar.

"Hello," came a gruff greeting.

"Tag?"

"Yeah. Who wants to know?"

"Gunner Anderson."

"Well, I'll be damned." Gunner could hear the smile in Tag's tone. "I haven't heard from you in a few years. How are you? Still crazy as hell, I assume."

"My friends might agree with that." Gunner cleared his throat and hoped he'd get Tag's cooperation. Adri's life no doubt depended on it. Mateo wasn't going to be happy that his fiancée had been calling another man. "You still flying?"

"You wanting a lift somewhere?"

"I do. Flying commercial won't get me there fast enough, Tag."

The line went quiet for a few seconds. "Involving anything illegal?"

"No. Someone needs my help." Which was an understatement.

"A woman?"

"Yeah." Gunner heavily sighed. "She's not asking for help because she hasn't admitted to needing me yet."

"Most women don't." Tag chuckled. "Where to?"

"La Paz."

"Mexico?" His tone raised an octave. "You got a death sentence, man?"

"Maybe." Gunner rubbed the back of his neck. "Look, dude, I can get another flight. Fly commercial."

"Then why not do it?" Tag asked. "My price tag is a lot heftier than a commercial flight."

"Because the woman in question could be dead by the time it takes me to get there. Time isn't on my side."

"How soon you looking to leave?"

"How soon can you get me there?"

"Do I even want to know who this involves?"

"Nope."

Tag laughed again. "I'll be fueled up and ready to go in a half hour. That soon enough?"

"Right on time," Gunner said. Lady Luck had just smiled upon him. He hoped like hell it would continue. "See you in half that time."

Disconnecting the call, Gunner made note of the address for the Training Wing. He headed for his bedroom suite, grabbed a backpack from his closet, and stuffed a couple pair of shorts and tees into it. Bending on one knee, he entered his five-digit code on the safe he kept there and opened the door, withdrawing a few thousand dollars and a credit card, just in case things went south and they needed a lot more than the cash on hand. He wouldn't require much as he planned on getting in and out of La Paz as fast as possible. This trip wasn't about a showdown with Mateo. That would have to wait. Gunner might be able to take on the son of a bitch one-on-one, but he didn't stand a chance in hell of taking on the whole cartel. Thinking otherwise would not only get him killed, but likely Adriana as well.

Gunner scribbled a quick note for his MC brothers about being gone for a few days, grabbed his backpack, and headed for the kitchen where he tossed the paper onto the island. Telling his brethren any more meant they'd try to stop him, or worse yet, follow along. Getting the Sons involved at this point wasn't going to be an option. First, he needed to extract Adri. When Mateo and his men came North, and there was no doubt they would, they'd then be on the Sons' territory and Adriana would be out of harm's way.

MATEO OPENED THE DOOR TO Adri's bedroom and shoved her inside. She stumbled over the area rug and to the bed, tears streaming down her face. Would he kill her? He had ranted for a solid fifteen minutes about her betrayal while she remained silent, following their departure from Salazar's. My God, she had watched him turn and fire upon an innocent man who had done nothing more than lend her his phone.

His death, his blood, was on her hands, the horrifying image now burned in her brain.

She looked up at Mateo, his face contorted with rage. The handsome man she had met many years ago, had nearly grown up with, now turned hideous. Foam gathered at the corners of his lips like a rabid dog. Wiping the back of his hand across his face, he glared at her. His chest rose and fell with each deep breath. His cheeks mottled red in his rising anger.

"I'll not ask you again, *esposa para ser*, who the fuck was on the other end of the phone? Don't lie to me. I will know if you do."

Fortifying her resolve, Adri squared her shoulders, even though her insides trembled like a junkie suffering from withdrawal. She swatted away the tears that had fallen. "Will you kill me like you did your loyal soldier?"

"Loyal?" His cruel chuckle matched the darkness in his eyes. "If he were, you wouldn't have been given a phone to call your boyfriend."

"He's not my boyfriend," Adri whispered, dropping her gaze to the floor. Lord, if she would've just stayed in Oregon…

"You're lying, *mi pequeña reina*. Look at me when I ask you a question."

Adri brought her gaze back up, steeling her jaw. "He's not my boyfriend, though he is twice the man you are."

"But you're engaged to this one," he spat in fury as he pointed a thumb to his sternum. Had she been anyone else, Adri had no doubt Mateo would've already put a bullet in her as well. "You're to be my wife in less than a month. Maybe that's too long to wait. Either way, you're sequestered here until you answer my question."

"You'll starve me?"

"My servants will bring you meals, *mi pequeña reina*. But, otherwise, you will be locked in here until I see fit." Her gaze drifted to the patio doors, the locks being on the inside, causing Mateo to chuckle. "I'd think twice about jumping. It's a long way down."

"Breaking a bone or two would be preferable to being your prisoner."

"If you survived the fall, my men would detain you the minute you hit the ground."

"Then give me your phone, Mateo. I need to call Gabriela back. She's already planning on coming here for our wedding."

Adri had yet to call her, but hoped Mateo bought her bluff. Because if he didn't, without Gabby and Ryder, she had no means of escape.

"You can't be serious." He ate up the distance between them, gripped the hair at her nape, and forced her to lock gazes with him. "Your chance for Gabby to come here left the minute you called your boyfriend. You lost your freedom, *mi pequeña reina*."

"And when we marry?"

One of his brows quirked upwards. "Not even then. Not until you prove to me that you're trustworthy."

"You're a tyrant." Adri's heart plummeted at her chance to flee being ripped away. "I hate you."

Mateo let go of his grip, stepped back, and smiled cruelly. "That may very well be. But once we marry, I'll be the one fucking you every night regardless. Not the man you spoke to on the phone."

Adri gasped. "Not willingly."

"You think I care?"

"You bastard."

Adri shivered at the thought of sharing his bed again, forced to let him touch her. At one time she had done so willingly, loved him even. That was before he showed her his true colors … before she'd fled Mexico. Before Gunner.

Now? The thought turned her stomach. She'd never survive it.

Lord, did she have no recourse?

Gritting her teeth, Adri glared at him. "I will not marry you. I'll tell the priest no."

Mateo looked upon her thoughtfully. "You'd rather be my whore?"

She approached Mateo and placed a hand on his chest, hoping he'd see reason. "I'd rather you let me go. Don't you want to marry someone who loves you?"

"You loved me at one time. You will again."

"No, Mateo, I won't. I've changed … we've changed."

The ugliness returned to his face and he growled. "Because of him?"

She shook her head. "Because I don't belong here. Oregon is my home. Not Mexico."

He sneered. "You belong to me."

"No, I—"

He backhanded her, cutting her words short and snapping her head back. The sting traveled up her cheek and rang in her ear. The metallic taste of blood filled her mouth. Tears stung the back of her eyes but she refused to let them fall. The man in front of her had become no better than an animal.

"We will be married. I own you. If you recall, I paid your ransom."

Her brows pinched. "How do you figure?"

"When you asked that I send Gabriela the money to rebuild their home."

"You burnt it down!"

"Show me the proof." He smirked, raising a brow. "You best prepare yourself, *mi pequeña reina*. There is one guarantee and it's that you and I will be married."

Mateo turned, stormed from the room, and slammed the door. Adri heard the snick of the bolt on the outside as it slipped into place. Mateo had ensured she'd never again ask one of his men to disobey him. He had shown the consequences of betrayal should any of them think to help her. Now, she had no means in which to aid her in escape.

CHAPTER FIVE

Gunner ducked beneath low-lying branches in the thick brush, swatting away a swarm of mosquitoes buzzing his ears. About twenty feet ahead of Tag, he trudged through the dense foliage that flanked the ten-foot stone walls surrounding Mateo's manor. Cartel soldiers carrying assault rifles secured the front gate. Luck was on their side, because the back of the estate had not a soldier in sight, most likely due to the security cameras mounted atop the walls and aimed at every angle.

Hence the reason Gunner and Tag stayed close to the insufferable brush.

Sweat dripped into Gunner's eyes and rivered down his back, making his shirt stick to him like a wet fucking shower curtain. He'd only been in the unbearable heat for a quarter of an hour and already he couldn't wait to be somewhere else.

But not until he had Adriana in hand.

Gunner wasn't about to leave her behind.

His last stint in Mexico had been short-lived, ending with him being left for dead and buried in a shallow grave. He hadn't exactly taken the time to get the lay of the land. Nor, at the time, had he cared. That mission had been Ryder Kelley's, ending with the death of his mate's crime boss uncle, Raúl Trevino Caballero.

Upon landing the jet at the La Paz airport, Tag had asked the airline attendant manning the gate for directions to Raúl Trevino Caballero's estate, purposely not using Mateo's name. The man had chuckled, mumbling something sounding like *stupido gringos*, then pointed to the road ahead and told them which way to go.

"Señor, everyone from these parts knows Mateo Rodriguez now owns La Paz."

The attendant hadn't said estate or home, but rather the city name, telling Gunner they best be careful to whom they speak with. The town and many of its people were likely owned by Mateo. He no doubt generously showered the locals with his money, making him more of a hero than a villain in their eyes.

Being on foot, Gunner was pleased the airport was a few miles away. Not that the distance would bother him; his vampire DNA could eat up a couple of miles in no time, but he had Tag to contend with. Tag, being human, slowed down the pace. Though Gunner had suggested he stay with the plane, Tag had refused. Even now, the man plowed through the foliage like a true general, keeping up with Gunner's stride.

Gunner stopped a few feet ahead, looked back to Tag, and pointed at a section of uneven rocks that could be used to scale the wall. Any rock climber would have no problem and he'd bet Tag wouldn't either. Gunner, on the other hand, could easily leap the ten-foot wall due to his vampire DNA. But that wasn't the problem. Where they now stood, they were far enough from the cameras at the corners of the property to go undetected. But on the other side? Gunner had no idea what they'd be getting into, even if his vampire senses didn't pick up any humans nearby.

Before Gunner could suggest that Tag let him go first, the pilot reached up, his fingers grasping a rock about a foot above his head, then easily hefted himself up to the next rock. Before long, Tag scaled the wall and looked down on Gunner with a smile. Seconds later, he slid his leg over the top undeterred and landed on the other side. Gunner listened intently, thankfully hearing nothing but the wind rustling through the brush. It appeared Tag had dropped from the wall unexposed. Gunner hoped to hell the cameras hadn't caught Tag's descent either. Wasting little time, Gunner leaped to the top of the wall, then quickly slid down the other side, next to the retired general.

A quick scan of the area told Gunner their luck continued. The cameras didn't seem to swing far enough in their direction to be seen and none of the foot soldiers patrolled the grounds behind the house. A couple of them stood chatting on a balcony three stories up, but otherwise paid no mind to the vulnerable rear of the manor. Mateo apparently felt the back side of his fortress was impenetrable.

Well, guess what, motherfucker?

"You know which of those windows belongs to Adriana?" Tag asked quietly.

Gunner shook his head. "I wasn't planning on making the trip. Like I told you on the way here, she's engaged to this piece of shit. Now? I feel she's in danger."

"The cameras appear to be on a rotation, scanning the yard. I think if we make our move at the right time, we might be able to reach the back of the house undetected."

"Which leaves the likelihood of an alarm."

"I have an idea." Tag's smile bespoke his confidence. That or he was as much of an adrenaline junkie as Gunner. "I'll make a run for the back of the house. When I spot a foot soldier on his own, I'll put him to sleep and borrow his clothes."

"Sleep?" One of Gunner's brows arched. "For a short period or for good?"

"No sleeper hold will give us the time we need. But I'll be quiet about it. I'll signal you when I'm finished."

"I'm not waiting behind. You work on someone on the ground. I'll find one on a balcony with an opened door. Hopefully, that will give me a bypass to any alarm system."

"How will you get up there?"

"You leave that to me. Be smart. If you need an assist after you take out your soldier, I'll let you in. Otherwise, see you inside."

Gunner took a quick look at the cameras that appeared currently focused on the east and west side of the grounds, then took off on a run. He didn't look back to see if Tag followed, but heard his footsteps not far behind telling him as much. Although he hated to leave his human comrade on his own, Gunner had little choice.

Getting Adriana out was the main objective.

Stopping beneath one of the large cement verandas facing the back, he heard a door slide open and footsteps just overhead. He had no way of seeing if the person who exited was alone. He stepped forward, looked up, and saw a man's large hand wrapping the railing. Gunner didn't give him time to retreat. Easily leaping the one story, he landed softly next to him. The soldier had no time to alert others before Gunner, with his inhuman like strength, easily twisted his head, hearing the bones in his neck snap, then dropped him to the cement. Too bad he had been short on time, he would have preferred to drain the poor bastard.

Gunner hated to kill him, but Tag was right, a sleeper hold wouldn't give him the time he needed. There were casualties in war, and as Gunner saw it, this was war.

Quickly undressing the guard, he donned his clothes before situating him in the dark corner of the porch and out of sight. Grabbing a large potted plant, he moved it in front of the dead man, further concealing him. He pulled the man's hat low over his face and quickly entered the estate, hoping Tag was having similar good fortune. Gunner hadn't heard a ruckus from the ground, so he had to assume Tag's operation was also being successful.

Slipping into the cool interior, Gunner didn't need the time for his eyes to adjust to the darkened room. His vampire sight worked as well as night-vision goggles. A quick scan told him he stood alone in what looked to be an upstairs library. The walls were lined floor to ceiling with books, moving ladders attached to rails. Leather chairs flanked a fireplace, looking as though it hadn't been used in years. The entire space smelled of cigar smoke. Mateo must use the place as a den. Wasting no more time, Gunner stealthily moved to the cracked-open double wooden doors leading into the hall, coming face-to-face with another soldier.

The man spoke to him in Spanish. Gunner, a bit rusty on the language, wasn't exactly sure what he had been asked. He replied in a deeper than normal tone, "*Sí*," hoping it fit the entirety of the question.

The man simply nodded and walked away. Gunner headed down the long hallway in the opposite direction, approaching a large stairway that looked as though it opened onto a grand front entrance. Just as he reached the railing, he spotted another soldier, but this time he heard Tag's whispered, "It's me."

Gunner waited for him at the top. "You know any Spanish, dude?"

"Sure."

"Then if we approach anyone else, you do the talking. I haven't used it since the last time I was in Mexico. My luck, I'll stumble over my words and get us killed before we even find Adri."

Tag chuckled.

"Not funny, dude. I just had a soldier ask me a question back there. Thankfully, my replied '*Sí*' worked."

Taking the stairs up another flight and reaching the end of the long hall, Gunner peered around a corner, seeing a lone soldier standing in front of a door. He wasn't sure what or who was being guarded, but someone appeared to be a prisoner, possibly Adri, based on what Gunner overheard before their last phone conversation that had been cut short.

"She might be down there. Mateo seemed pretty pissed off with her."

"Then follow my lead."

Tag squared his shoulders and headed in the soldier's direction. Gunner fell in beside the retired general.

"*Soy tu reemplazo,*" Tag said.

The guard cleared his throat. "*Pero tengo dos horas más.*"

"*Cambio de planes.*"

"Mateo… *el te envio?*" The soldier questioned Tag, eyeing him suspiciously.

"*Sí.*"

"*Pero el se fue hace horas.*"

"Mateo *me llamó, estúpido.*"

The soldier stood for a moment longer, then shrugged and headed down the hall. Gunner picked up a little on what was said. Surely, it couldn't have been that easy. "Telling him Mateo called and told you to replace him. Smart thinking."

Tag chuckled. "Lucky he didn't pull his gun on me for calling him stupid."

"True." Gunner placed a hand on Tag's shoulder. "Let's hope he was guarding Adri, dude. If it's the wrong damn room, we could be in for some serious trouble."

Sipping on a glass of rosé, Adri lounged on a lavender-colored, overstuffed chaise, facing the double doors that opened onto the veranda. A warm breeze fluttered the alabaster voiles hanging from the rods on either side of the exit. But not even the light wind could cool her sweat-glistened skin as anxiety threatened to choke her.

How had her well-meaning decisions turned her life into catastrophe?

Less than thirty days and she'd be married to a man who was nothing short of a mass murderer. A man she'd once thought she loved, but no longer. Had she stayed in Oregon, she'd likely be drinking wine with Gabby while giggling like schoolgirls over her secret crush on Gunner. Instead, because she tried to do what was best for him and the rest of the Sons of Sangue, she sat inside Mateo's estate as much a prisoner as if there were iron bars on her doors and windows instead of silk curtains. There would be no escape. Mateo had lost his damn mind.

A four-car motorcade had left the manor hours ago with the promise Mateo wouldn't return until well after nightfall. Not that she cared. Any time she didn't have to endure his dreadful company was a blessing. Now, looking across the well-kept, expansive lawns and clear azure skies, Adri couldn't help but wish for the home she left behind. To feel the refreshing breezes of the Pacific Northwest across her heated skin. To enjoy the company of Gabby and her friends. Loneliness threatened to swallow her. Adri missed Oregon. Washington too, if she were being honest. Lord, she missed Gunner's kindness and sunny nature. He was the opposite of Mateo.

Unshed tears blurred her vision as she thought of the life she could've had with Gunner, if she'd only had the courage to reach for it. Instead, she faced an existence of misery and despair with a man she detested.

Voices from the hallway caught her attention. Not that it was unusual for soldiers to relieve one another from their post, but the timing seemed off. The exchange normally happened around bedtime. A glance at the clock told her it was just past the supper hour.

Setting her glass down on the gold-trimmed side table, Adri swung her legs from the lounge and stood. She slid her feet into a pair of high-end designer slippers and padded to the door just as it opened inward, startling her. She gasped, placing her hands over her rapidly beating heart. Two soldiers, hats pulled low, stepped into her room. Her pulse quickened. The guards never entered her quarters and certainly not without Mateo present.

Adri squared her shoulders, though her knees threatened to give out. *Never show your fear.* Surely, these men wouldn't blame her for Mateo's assassination of one of their own. With Mateo gone, she had no way of protecting herself. What if they killed her, stashed away her body, and told Mateo she had escaped? She wouldn't put anything past these crude soldiers, who killed for no other reason than *dinero*.

"I'm sorry. I don't recall asking for anything. If you wouldn't mind, I'd prefer to be alone until Mateo returns. Please relock the door on your way out."

The taller of the two men grunted at her request, drawing her attention. Something about his stance seemed familiar. Adri stepped forward, stopping just out of reach, looking into his darkened, down-turned face. "Is there a problem?"

"Would you rather I was Mateo?" came the deep-throated response.

"I… I'm not even sure how to respond to that."

The man growled, grabbed the bill of his hat, and removed it. Adri's breath stuck in her throat, instant recognition setting in. Gunner's curls had been shorn over his ears and close to his head, leaving the top with unruly waves. His once dirty-blond hair was now a shade darker. Gone was his boyish appearance, leaving a man even more handsome than she remembered.

"Gunner? What are you doing here? Mateo¬—"

He stepped forward, his large hands encompassing her shoulders. "Is he here?"

Adri shook her head.

"Then pack your bags."

"Are you crazy?" Her gaze widened. "I can't leave with you. Mateo will have you both killed."

"Let's go," Gunner's companion spoke up. "We don't have long before the soldiers we borrowed these clothes from are discovered."

"And who are you?"

"Most call me Tag, ma'am." He stepped around Gunner. "I hate to break up this little reunion, but if you wish to get the hell out of here, you best grab what's most important and follow us. I have a plane waiting to head north."

Adri's head swam with the possibility of regaining her freedom, perhaps her last chance at it. Mateo would no doubt use all his resources in his attempt to hunt her down again. Last time, they had gotten away with no one getting hurt. Next time, they might not be so lucky.

Dare she put everyone in danger a second time?

Gunner placed his fingers gently beneath her chin and raised her gaze to his. "We don't have time to think about this, Adri. Mateo do this?"

She didn't respond, moving her hand to her swollen lip. The decision to leave with Gunner and Tag would be hers and hers alone.

"If he hasn't done worse," Gunner snarled. Moving her fingers, his gaze darkened with anger. "I do not doubt that he will."

"He's a dangerous man, Gunner. If I leave with you, he has an army of men that would come after you both."

"Let them."

Tears welled in her eyes. "They'll kill you next time. I couldn't live with that."

Gunner's jaw tightened, a muscle ticking in his cheek. "Trust me when I say I'm far more dangerous, babe. This is your last chance. That is, unless you wish to marry the son of a bitch. Do you?"

She shook her head, a tear slipping from her lashes, which Gunner caught with a sweep of his thumb. "Then let's get the fuck out of here while we still can."

Adri didn't hesitate a moment longer. This was a last chance staring her in the face. If she didn't go with them now, Gunner was likely correct. She'd be subjected to a life of abuse from Mateo. Grabbing a pair of lace-up boots from her closet, she took off her slippers, slipped on a pair of socks, then stuffed her feet into the boots, tying them securely. The peasant-style shirt and blue jeans she wore would suffice. Everything else she could leave behind.

"I'm ready."

Gunner's smile and outstretched hand were all she needed. Clasping his fingers, she followed him and Tag through the door. Tag slipped the bolt back into place before leading them down the hall.

"Let's blow this place." Tag grinned, then jogged the short distance to the stairs with Gunner and Adri not far behind.

Once they left the manor via the rear exit, the three ran like the hounds of Hell nipped at their heels. Reaching the wall, Tag scaled the stone first, then leaned down and gripped Adri's hand. Gunner helped boost her to the top. Once the three landed on the other side, they kept to the brush. Adri could hardly hear anything other than the blood rushing through her ears. Keeping a firm grip on Gunner's hand, they navigated through the foliage for some time before hitting a clearing. A quick look back told her the few soldiers Mateo left behind likely hadn't yet noticed her missing. They'd no doubt suffer Mateo's wrath once he found her gone.

Adri was free.

Not only that, but she was with Gunner. He had come for her, and dear Lord, she hadn't even asked. How would she ever repay him? Adri hoped that her love for him would be enough, because she knew with every beat of her heart that this was far from over with Mateo.

CHAPTER SIX

"How ... much ... farther?" Adri pulled up, placed her hands on her knees, and attempted to draw deep breaths. How far had they gone? Surely, it wasn't but a couple of miles, though it felt as if she had run a marathon. Her rubbery legs seemed incapable of taking another step. Slowing down was not an option. But she was out of shape, her short-windedness a testament. It wasn't as if she got a lot of exercise the last couple of months. Mateo had kept her mostly under lock and key. On a good day, he might allow her to take an escorted stroll around the grounds.

"About a half-mile," Tag replied, his breath slightly labored. "Do you need to take a break?"

"No," Gunner grunted before scooping Adriana into his arms, earning him a squeal. "We need to keep moving."

"You can't possibly carry me the rest of the way. I'm too heavy."

"You let me worry about what I can handle." Gunner looked down at her. The tenderness in his brown eyes warmed her as he gave her a wink. "You're light as a feather. Now, let's stop the small talk and get back to the plane. I'm sure by now the two dead soldiers have been found along with Adri being missing. We need that jet in the air before Mateo can make a call to the airport or we're fucked."

Adri tried not to focus on the word dead. She had seen enough death already at the hands of Mateo. Surely, Gunner and Tag had no other choice. Without another word, Tag turned and sprinted down the dirt road, faster than before, making it obvious she had been holding them back. Gunner had no problem keeping the pace either, even though he held her tightly in his embrace. Despite his heart beating rapidly against her cheek, his breathing wasn't the least bit labored. Almost as if he hadn't jogged the last couple of miles.

It wasn't long before they arrived at the entrance leading to the airport. Gunner placed her back on her feet, probably as not to draw unwanted attention. Gunner and Tag still wore their borrowed soldier garb, which worked in their favor, allowing them to pass without being challenged. In La Paz, Adri was sure Mateo's men came and went without question, as he was no doubt the law of the land. No one would dare stand in his way. Adri's thoughts immediately went to the poor man who had loaned her his phone, filling her heart with remorse. Shaking off the gruesome image, she quickly fell into step beside Gunner. Now was not the time to harbor guilt for him or the two Gunner and Tag took out. They needed to get in the air.

Once through the main airport, they made their way out the rear exit and onto the tarmac of a smaller hangar situated to the back of the lot. A single jet was positioned for takeoff, while a second plane sat a ways behind its tail. Tag jogged in the direction of the smaller aircraft and pulled down a set of steps. Gunner ducked beneath the rounded doorway and assisted Adri into the interior. He indicated she should take one of the six empty seats, before taking his own beside her. Tag turned toward the front of the plane and dipped his head beneath the doorway leading to the cockpit.

Gunner helped her strap in before securing his belt. It wasn't but seconds later Adri heard the soft roar of the engines. Tag put on a set of headphones and began speaking in Spanish into the headset. She glanced at Gunner, her heart swelling even though he had his back to her, peering out the small port window. Good Lord, he hadn't forgotten her or left her alone to deal with Mateo. Even if that's what she deserved.

He had come to rescue her, to set her free from the nightmare of the past few months. How could she ever repay him? Gunner and Tag would be on Mateo's most wanted list for taking what he believed belonged to him. And yet, even though Gunner knew that to be the risk to his bravery, he had come anyway.

"Christ," Gunner muttered. "How long before you get this thing in the air?"

Tag looked back from the cockpit. "I'm next out after the jet."

"Then you best drive around it. We got company with guns."

Adri gasped, her hand going to her chest as she looked out her window. Other than the opened door of the hangar, there was nothing that would cause alarm on her side. Turning in Gunner's direction, she spotted the approaching vehicles through his porthole. Three black SUVs sped in their direction, men standing through the opened sunroofs, guns at the ready.

Before she could unlock her belt to get a better look, the force of the plane jetting forward pushed her back against her seat. The aircraft that was lined up to take off before them passed quickly by her window as Tag swerved to miss it. He was no longer speaking into the headset but pushing buttons and pulling back on levers. The plane moved swiftly down the tarmac, past the oncoming vehicles and taking to the air.

Small pops could be heard beyond the roar of the engine, what could have only been the rounds of bullets Mateo's soldiers had fired upon them. Lord, she prayed the bullets hadn't reached the aircraft and caused any damage. Holding her breath, she briefly closed her eyes and tightly gripped the armrests. Her heart damn near stopped in her chest as she counted the short minutes it took them to get above the clouds. Breathing a sigh of relief that they weren't plummeting from the sky and that the engines sounded normal, she glanced at Gunner.

"You going to be okay?" he asked.

"Are we?" she managed to squeak out.

He reached over and gripped her hand, giving it a reassuring squeeze. "It will take them time to get a plane ready to follow us. Tag will soon fly under the radar … after we point them in the wrong direction."

"So, we fly home to Oregon? Washington?"

"I don't think that's wise. Tag says he has an old military buddy that has a hunting cabin near Helena, Montana, he's used before. Said the place is damn near in the middle of nowhere, has its own plane hangar and landing strip. We'll go there for now."

"Is Tag from Montana? Or will he then fly home?"

"Washington's his home. But he'll stay with us. By now, they'll also know about him. The airport won't keep the details of his plane or our flight a secret from the cartel. He's in danger now, too."

Tears fogged her vision. She turned from Gunner, not wanting him to see her at her weakest, and looked out her window. His bravery had cost both him and Tag far too much. Adri should've refused his help and stayed in La Paz, accepting her fate. After all, she had been the one to stupidly fall in love with Mateo years ago. Maybe, once they landed to refuel, she could return to Mexico, convince Mateo this was her doing, that Gunner and Tag had fallen victim to her deceit.

Swiping away a stray tear, she looked back at Gunner. "Take me back. Or at the very least, let me go once we land so I can return to Mateo."

Gunner grunted. "You can't be fucking serious?"

Adri undid her belt, left her seat, and knelt in the aisle by Gunner's knees. "You have to see that Mateo will never stop looking for me."

His feral gaze blackened almost unnaturally. "Mateo needs to be worried about me. Not the other way around. I look forward to the day he comes looking for me. He won't stand a chance with me one-on-one, or ten-to-one, for that matter. But for now, I'll hide away you and Tag, keep you both safe. I'm not about to get reckless and chance losing you again."

"Take me back, Gunner." She placed her hand on his thick forearm. "It's not worth the chance of losing you forever."

"Fuck that. I'll protect what's mine with my last breath." He gripped her fingers and took them to his mouth, placing a tender kiss on her knuckles. "You'll just have to trust me for now."

"But Mateo—"

"Do you love him?" Gunner's tone deepened and his gaze narrowed. "Tell me the truth, babe. Be straight with me."

"I used to… But no longer." Her gaze dropped to her feet until the slight tug of her fingers brought her attention back to Gunner.

"And now?"

"Ever since moving to Oregon, I realized the monster he'd become. I abhor him."

"We're now under the radar," Tag hollered from the cockpit. "We're going to need to stop to refuel, but otherwise we should be there in about ten hours."

"You think we'll have trouble when we refuel?" Gunner asked.

"Not if we make it to the U.S. border first. I have an old military buddy with a hangar in northern New Mexico. I'll be contacting him shortly."

"Will he log our flight?"

"Not when I tell him what we're up against. No worries. I'd trust him with my life."

Tag turned back to the front of the plane, punching more buttons. When Adri looked back to Gunner, he was smiling. "What?" she asked.

He ran a knuckle down her cheek, warming her. It wasn't fair to Gunner to ensnare him in her screwed-up life.

"I'm glad you're here ... with me," he said.

If the situation were different, she might even tell him what her heart truly felt. That it had been only him since Oregon. Falling in love with Gunner had been incredibly easy.

"Believe me, I'm thrilled to be out from under Mateo's tyranny. But I'm scared, Gunner. For you ... for Tag. I involved you in my mess."

Gunner unbuckled his seat belt, then lifted her off the floor and onto his lap. He wrapped his arms around her and tucked her head beneath his chin. Adri could hear the heavy beat of his heart, feel the security his arms offered.

"You needn't worry about me, babe. I'll be fine. And Tag, he's a grown man capable of making his own decisions." He kissed the top of her head. "Go to sleep. We've got hours ahead of us."

Adri snuggled fully into his embrace, feeling truly safe for the first time in months. She stifled a yawn with the back of her hand and thought, "*Mi amor*," right before her heavy lids drifted closed and she fell sound asleep.

ADRI HAD SLEPT IN HIS ARMS through most of the flight until Tag requested they buckle up for landing. Nothing felt more right than having her there. Just the two of them in the passenger area seemed intimate. Gunner couldn't begin to regret his risky decision to fly off to enemy territory and snatch Adri from the stronghold of a madman. She belonged with him, and he'd fight to his death to keep her safe. He wasn't sure how the rest of the Sons of Sangue would see his actions, but at the moment he didn't fucking care. Judging by the cut to her lip, he did not doubt that Mateo would've hurt Adri again. The coming showdown would be between him and Mateo; he'd make sure the rest of the Sons understood that.

The moment Adriana left his embrace and strapped into her seat Gunner felt the cold loss. If he didn't succeed in his mission, he'd rather die than live without her.

No more playing around.

He wasn't about to let her go a second time.

They rode the rest of the way in companionable silence until the aircraft touched down. Gunner couldn't help but wonder what was going through her mind. Surely, she felt the connection between them. But to have any kind of relationship with her, he knew he needed to come clean. Mateo wasn't the only hurdle he faced. His being a vampire wasn't likely going to be an easy pill to swallow. Maybe Adri would view him as much of a monster as Mateo. The thought sobered him, knowing it could easily mean losing her for good.

Tag exited the cockpit, then lowered the hatch so they could descend, stopping Gunner's troubling thoughts. Rosy-cheeked and beautiful as ever, Adri said she needed to freshen up. He doubted a trip to the bathroom would make her more so. Tag pointed her in the direction of the hangar's lone restroom.

Gunner leaned back against the side of the small plane and crossed his arms over his chest. Watching her walk away, he pondered her last words before falling asleep. *Mi amor.* Had she been referring to him? His blood had heated the moment the whispered, "My love," left her lips. Good thing she hadn't felt his hardened response nestled against her hip. Not that he didn't want to fuck her. Hell, he did in the worst way. But now was not the time.

The truth of it, he had been enamored with Adri since the moment she'd asked him to dance when he'd first laid eyes on her in Mexico. Because of a mission he'd been involved in with Ryder Kelley and the Sons at the time, Gunner'd had no choice but to leave Adri behind and head back to Washington. He never thought he'd see her again. That was until the mission had been completed and Ryder moved his mate, Gabby, north with her best friend, Adriana. Explaining to Adri that Gunner had needed to fake his death to the cartel in order to get Ryder close to the kingpin had been asking a lot. Asking her to accept that he was no longer human wasn't going to be any easier, but he had no other choice.

No more secrets.

Once they reached the hunting cabin, a part of him knew he'd need to be straight with Adri, removing the elephant from the room. If he told Adri he sported fangs, though, would she feel differently about him?

Circling the front of the plane, he approached Tag as he refueled. "Got a question for you."

He looked up, hand on the nozzle. "What's that?"

"*Mi amor—*"

Tag chuckled. "I hate to burst your bubble, but I don't swing that way."

Gunner rolled his eyes. "Not you, dude. I was asking what you'd think if a woman inadvertently said that to you?"

"Thanks for clearing that up. I'd hate to think I'd have to leave your dumb ass here in New Mexico." He shrugged. "I guess it would depend on who was doing the talking."

A smile itched up Gunner's cheeks. "I was just surprised to hear—"

"Hear what?" Adri asked upon her return.

A stray hair blew across her cheek. Gunner reached out and tucked it behind one ear, feathering his knuckles across her downy cheek. "Nothing. All set?"

"I'd feel better with a shower, but for now it will have to do."

The idea of her wet and under the showerhead had him thinking thoughts he shouldn't be entertaining, at least not at the moment. As a vampire, he wasn't used to denying his baser instincts. And right now, he wanted to fuck her in the worst way. But Gunner needed full disclosure before going down that road. The Sons of Sangue had rules about telling their secrets to humans. Hell, he was the damn president. They were to stick with the donors for all their needs. Though he had managed to learn hypnosis, he wasn't about to erase her memories of him to keep their damn secret. So, unless he was ready to be straight with Adri, there would be no horizontal mamba or anything close to it.

"You could never look bad." Gunner needed to clear his thoughts and steer the conversation away from his carnal ones. "By the way, I love the new hairstyle."

Her gaze warmed with her smile. "Mateo hated it."

"He's an idiot."

"That's putting it mildly." Adri laughed. "And I like yours as well. It matures you."

He brushed a hand through the unruly curls and smirked. "Because we all want to look old."

She batted the back of her hand against his sternum. "Not old, silly. Mature in a good way. You lost that surfer-boy vibe."

"Ready?" Tag asked, hanging up the nozzle. "We best get back in the air."

Gunner dug out a roll of bills from his pocket and handed several hundred to Tag. "This enough?"

Taking the cash, Tag counted out the bills, handing a couple back, though Gunner refused. "Tip him the rest."

"I'll make sure he keeps this one off the books. Be ready when I get back."

Gunner watched Tag disappear through the office doorway of the small hangar. Had it not been for Tag, Gunner wouldn't have been able to pull this off. He owed the man his life. Now to figure a way out of the mess without getting them all killed. The first order of business would be to call his VP, Smoke, once they arrived at the cabin and fill him and the rest of the Sons in on what went down in La Paz. Mateo would no doubt waste little time heading north. The last thing Gunner wanted was the Sons blindsided. Gunner hated involving his brethren in his mess. But with Mateo's hatred for them, he saw no other way.

"We best get back onboard." Indicating the steps with his outstretched hand, he said to Adri, "After you."

Gunner followed her up the steps and helped her strap in before taking his own seat. A few minutes later, Tag alighted the steps, then pulled closed the hatch. Without a word, he headed for the cockpit. It wasn't long before he heard the soft roar of the engines starting.

Tag called back to them, "It will be another five hours before we get there. You might want to catch a little more shut eye. I'll keep us off the radar."

"Thanks, Tag. How will I ever repay you?"

"No repayment needed. Always glad to help out a friend in need."

"Even if it might get us all killed?"

"We'll get it figured out, Gunner. Let's first get to the cabin. We'll come up with some concrete plans there."

Tag slipped on his headphones, then started the plane down the short runway. Gunner turned to Adri, her hands gripping tightly to the armrests. "Nervous flying?"

"Smaller planes freak me out a bit. When we left La Paz, I was so fixated on getting out of there alive, I hadn't had time to worry about the takeoff. I'll be fine once we level out."

"You want to sit on my lap again?" he asked, earning him a chuckle and the slight relaxation of her hands. "I wouldn't complain."

Her laughter was like a balm to his soul. Gunner should've never let her leave months ago. Instead of nursing a broken heart, he should've gone after her. Damn it, but he had been a selfish prick.

Her smile sobered. "Why did you do it, Gunner?"

"Do what?"

Tears welled in her eyes but did not fall. "Come after me? You must know Mateo will not stop until he finds me again. He'll kill you."

"He won't get the chance, babe."

"How can you be so sure?"

"Because if he comes after you, I'll kill him first."

CHAPTER SEVEN

Ryder Kelley pocketed his phone, anger radiating from every pore as he paced the floor of the Oregon clubhouse. His booted heels struck the wood, filling the silence. Christ, he'd like nothing better than to wrap his fingers around Mateo Rodriguez's throat and squeeze until his head popped off. That or drain the motherfucker of every drop of his blood. Nothing would give him more satisfaction. The piece of shit didn't deserve to walk the face of God's green earth. Hell, Mateo was the devil himself. And here he thought Gabriela's uncle, Raúl Trevino Caballero, held that title.

How wrong he had been. Mateo had surpassed even him.

It was time to involve all the Sons of Sangue, Oregon and Washington. The Oregon Sons had taken out Raúl some months back; Ryder had no doubt they could take out his apprentice, Mateo.

Gabby approached, likely detecting his drop in mood, and placed her small hand across his forearm. He'd never tire of her beauty, inside and out. How the hell could something so beautiful carry the genes of one so deeply ugly as Raúl?

"Who was it?"

Ryder growled his displeasure. "Mateo."

She gasped. "Did it have anything to do with Adriana?"

"Yes and no. Apparently, she somehow managed to escape last night and Mateo thinks we're involved. He swore vengeance."

"But we haven't heard from Adri in months."

"I told him as much, though I doubt he believed me. He's holding us personally responsible. If we don't want hell to rain down on us, his words, not mine, then we'll find her and return her. He's giving us fourteen days."

Her warm brown eyes iced over with concern. "The last time Mateo came after us, he burned down our house, trying to take those of us inside with it."

"I still owe the motherfucker for that, even though Adriana forced him to give us the money to rebuild." His gaze heated as his vampire simmered just beneath the surface. The idea he could have lost Gabby that day still infuriated him. "He's a coward who hides behind his army."

"We should tell Viper and Hawk. They need to know what's going on."

He tilted his nose upward. "Well, we won't have to look far, Viper's on his way in."

Seconds later, the door to the clubhouse opened and the large vampire strode through. "Did I hear my name?"

Ryder chuckled. "Always there when we need you. Sometimes, I swear you're all-knowing."

"Just on this side of God, but don't let Preacher know I said that. He'll think I'm being blasphemous." Kane "Viper" Tepes, Oregon club president, chuckled. "So, what's got you up in arms?"

"Gabby's friend, Adriana, escaped from Mateo Rodriguez's stronghold. He's blaming us."

"You call the Washington chapter? Ask them if they have any idea where she might have gone?"

"Why would they know?"

"There's bad blood there since Gunner took the head of one of Mateo's soldiers. Sent it back to them in a potato sack."

"That and Gunner had a thing for Adri," Gabby added. "You don't think the Washington chapter would risk heading for La Paz, do you?"

"Hard telling." Viper rubbed his large hands together. "Maybe we should give them a call, see if Mateo contacted them, or if he just gave us the heads up. Either way, we'll need them on board with this."

Ryder couldn't agree more. They'd need numbers if they were to come out of this with their heads intact. Pulling his phone from the pocket of his jeans, he slid his finger across the glass and touched Gunner's number. The vampire's voicemail picked up. After the beep, Ryder growled into the phone, "Call me, asswipe."

He hit the END, then looked back to Viper. "Want me to call one of the others?"

"You got the VP's number?"

"Smoke? Sure do."

"Call him."

Surfing through the names in his phonebook again, he found Adrian "Smoke" Wellman's name, touched it, and sent the call through.

Seconds later, Smoke answered. "What's up, Ryder?"

"You're on speaker, Smoke. Viper's here with me. We're looking for Gunner. You have any idea why he's not answering his phone?"

Smoke heavily sighed. "We haven't been able to reach him in over a day. I have no idea where he took off to. He hasn't exactly been himself the past few months."

"How's that?" Viper asked.

"Just doing stupid stuff. Like we picked his ass up last week when he wrecked his bike going way too fast around a curve. It would have killed anyone else. Almost like he has a death wish or something."

"Enough so he might head for Mexico?"

"Why the hell would he do something that stupid?" Dante "Diablo" Santini asked, telling Ryder they were also on speaker. "Although maybe…"

"What do you know, Diablo? Spit it out," Viper grumbled.

"Gunner talked about Adriana a lot the past few months. He spoke with her on the phone recently. Maybe he was worried, went off half-cocked, and headed south."

Ryder rubbed his chin, not liking where this was going. "None of you have spoken with him?"

"Nope," Smoke replied.

"Anyone else from your crew unaccounted for?"

"All here, Viper. That is, except Gunner. We were just talking about him when Ryder called. Thought maybe the damn adrenaline junkie was off testing his immortality again or something. Figured we'd be rescuing him from another scrape soon. Looks like we might've been correct."

Ryder laid his cell on the wooden bar and braced his hands. Damn it. "I suppose that rescue is going to be a bit trickier this time, if my intuitions are correct. The problem is, unless he calls, we have no idea where he's at, or if Adriana is even with him. All I know is Mateo is livid and is giving us fourteen days to produce her or all hell will break loose."

"He doesn't stand a chance against us," Diablo quipped.

"No," Ryder grumbled. "But they have a big army. They outnumber us by a large margin. So, unless we come up with a solid plan, we could be looking at our numbers decreasing. Losing even one of us isn't an option. That motherfucker isn't playing, but neither are we."

"Get a hold of Gunner, Smoke." Viper's jaw tightened, telling Ryder that the club P was good and pissed. "When you do, you let me know straight away. I'm not about to lose one of my men to this psychopath. We'll need to be on the offense."

"I'll find him, Viper. When I do, you'll be the first person I call."

"Thanks, Smoke. Make sure you guys are well prepared to go to war on this."

"Ready and willing."

"We'll be in touch." Ryder ended the call and looked at Viper.

His eyes had blackened unnaturally. Razor-sharp fangs appeared just beneath his upper lip when he next spoke. "I'll apprise Hawk of the situation. Call a church meeting, Ryder. Looks like we have fourteen days to get prepared. Less, if my assumptions are correct. I don't trust Mateo to hold to his word."

It had been a damn long time since he had all of his brothers under one roof. It would be good to see everyone again, including Viper's twin, club VP, Kaleb "Hawk" Tepes. Although, he wished the circumstances were different.

Gripping Gabby by the shoulders, he pulled her back against his chest and wrapped his arms firmly around her, kissing the crown of her silky brown hair. Damn, but he could get lost in her heavenly scent. Now was not the time to be thinking about slipping between the sheets with her, though, not when he could sense fear for Adriana sluicing through her.

"We'll find her, *ángel*. That I promise you."

Gabby took a deep breath. "I just hope we find her within fourteen days. Otherwise, Adri will be the least of my concern."

GUNNER TOOK A GANDER AT his surroundings as they headed for their temporary digs. He had finally shed the cartel soldier's uniform for shorts and a T-shirt. The log cabin was well-sheltered by dense forests on three sides, with a short asphalt runway leading toward a small hangar at the back of the property. Tag had stored his plane inside before closing the large metal doors. When the plane had descended onto the tarmac moments ago, Gunner noted there weren't many neighboring houses. The closest appeared to be about a mile down the country dirt road.

All the better.

Tag led Adriana up the steps to the back porch running the length of the cabin. The deck looked to be in good condition. No peeling paint or rickety stairs. Whoever owned it, took great care. It wasn't overly large, but being that Gunner had expected a run-down, backwoods shelter, this was a nice surprise. He wouldn't have wanted to take Adri from the lap of luxury only to offer her mouse-infested cabinets and flea-ridden sheets. Thankfully, this place was not at all what he pictured a hunting cabin to be.

He followed Adri, noting how well her blue jeans cupped her ass. No matter the peril, his vampire's immense hunger wasn't far from the surface. Add to the fact he hadn't fucked anyone in a long time, his libido was in overdrive. All he could think about was getting Adriana out of those damn jeans. Lord, he needed to keep his focus on her wellbeing. Food and rest were what she needed most, not appeasing his appetites.

Speaking of vampire needs, the remote cabin was about to become problematic. He hadn't fed in a while himself. Another day or so and his skin was going to take on the death chill, making his flesh appear a bit translucent. He'd need to find a willing donor soon, before Adri and Tag began to wonder about his sudden strange condition.

"How far are we from town?" Gunner asked as Tag pulled a spare key from beneath a nearby terra cotta pot then used it to open the thick oak door.

"There's a small town we can get supplies from about ten miles east." Tag flipped on a few lights, illuminating the cabin. Unfinished pine tongue-and-groove walls provided a bright interior. "There's a car in the garage that Bud uses when he flies in. I think the keys are hanging by the back door. If you guys give me an idea of what you might like, I'll go to the store."

Gunner couldn't have Tag running for supplies, even if he desired some alone time with Adri. He needed to go by himself if he were to find someone to snack on. He certainly didn't want to use his hypnosis skills on Adri or Tag unless necessary.

"How about you two get to know each other a bit, and I'll run to town." Gunner rubbed his nape. "I could use a bit of fresh air. Being cooped up in that small plane has me on edge."

Adri looked ready to offer to ride along when Gunner's phone rang, saving him. He pulled the cell from his pocket. "I have to take this. Be back shortly."

He strode toward the back door, grabbed the keys, and headed out. Not until he was out of earshot did he answer the call. "What's up, Smoke?"

"You tell me what the fuck is going on. Where the hell are you? And don't fucking think to lie about it. Ryder called and it seems Adriana Flores is missing. You wouldn't happen to know anything about that, would you?"

Gunner swore beneath his breath. He knew it was only a matter of time but had hoped for a few more days to figure this shit out. "Mateo called?"

"Who else would be wanting to slay a den of vampires over the loss of his fiancée? He called Ryder, likely because of Gabby's connection to Adri."

"You told Ryder you had no clue, right?"

"What the hell else was I supposed to tell him?"

"The less you know, Smoke, the better. Stay the hell out of it."

"Look, P, he's given Ryder fourteen days to produce her. Doesn't sound like we have an option to stay out of it. If you know where she is—"

"Even if I did," Gunner's voice rose in pitch, "I sure in the hell wouldn't give her back."

"Oh, for fuck's sake, P. Why the hell would you go and do something like that? Better yet, how the hell did you pull it off?"

"How I did it isn't important. It was only a matter of time before he'd hurt her. You know that. The man is a sociopath. When he calls back, tell him I have her. He can damn well come and find me. The Sons have nothing to do with what happened."

"Am I supposed to give him your whereabouts too? Because I have no fucking idea where you are."

"Tell him I'm AWOL and that I acted on my own. Let Mateo do his own damn research." Gunner lifted the door on the unattached garage and found a tiny blue car. "What the hell?"

"Excuse me?" Smoke asked.

"I'll call you later, Smoke. Right now, I'm in need of finding myself a bite."

"Gunner—" was all he heard before he hit END and pocketed the phone. Of course, he'd find a car fit for a child. Gunner had half a notion to run into town on foot, and likely would have, had it not been for the cabin's occupants. Hitting the button on the remote, he watched the lights blink, briefly spotlighting the interior. He opened the car door and squeezed behind the wheel, moving the seat back, though it did nothing to keep his hair from brushing the top liner of the roof.

It would have to do.

Using the push-button ignition, he started the car, put it into drive, and headed out of the garage. At the end of the long driveway, he turned east. Sooner or later, he'd have to run into the small town Tag spoke of. Flipping on the radio, he hit the gas and spun gravel on the dirt road. If the town was ten miles away, then he planned to arrive in half the time it would normally take. His shriveling veins screamed for some fresh blood and Gunner was done denying them.

THE DIRT ROAD GUNNER HAD traveled the past five minutes ended with him having to turn onto a highway. A sign across the asphalt read Highway 282, while a second one sported an arrow, designating Montana City two miles to the right. He supposed it was the town Tag had referred to.

Seeing no other traffic, he eased the car onto the road and hit the gas.

It didn't take long to find the place, population 2,056 according to the sign. *Perfect*. All he needed was one of the 2,000-plus residents. Gunner pulled into the parking lot of *Ralph's EZ Stop*. It appeared the store was a bit of an all-in-one from gas pumps to groceries. A neon sign in the window flickered, indicating fresh 'Hot Pizza.' Before heading back to the cabin, he'd be sure to order a pie for Adri and Tag. They had to be hungry as well. The flight and been long with nothing but a few snacks stored on the plane to hold them over. He'd also grab some staples to stock the cabin for several days.

The first order of business, though, was finding himself an unsuspecting donor.

Gunner opened the door and slid out of the car, stretching his cramped muscles. A glance around produced only one other vehicle at the back of the lot. *Good*. The store was nearly empty. He certainly didn't need an audience.

The bell above the door dinged as he opened it and strode in. A young man with a top knot stood behind the counter. Tattoos littered his forearms and several steel hoops hung from his earlobes. An *EZ Stop* badge pinned to the left side of his T-shirt read 'Justin.' Glancing up from the tablet Justin had been perusing, he simply nodded at Gunner's approach.

The young man laid the tablet on the counter behind the register before asking, "What can I do for you?"

"You the only one here?"

"Why?"

"I was wanting a pizza and you're obviously working the register."

Justin shrugged. "Consider me a multi-tasker. What'cha want on it?"

Gunner had no idea what Adri preferred on her pizza. Most women seemed to like vegetables. "Veggies."

"Peppers, onions, broccoli, and mushrooms okay?"

"Perfect."

"What size?"

"Large."

"You got other shopping to do?" he asked. "It will take about ten minutes for the pie."

"Not a problem."

Justin took the key from the register, pocketed it, and headed for the rear of the small building. Gunner waited by the counter to make sure no one else popped up to help the young man. Satisfied they were alone, he walked over to the glass doors and turned the thick metal lock. He didn't need any surprise company while partaking of communion.

Gunner walked to the back of the store where he found Justin starting the order. Tossing a crust into the air a few times, the young man then placed the dough on a paddle. He quickly ladled on pizza sauce, a couple of handfuls of cheese, and a good helping of vegetables before sliding it into a small brick oven.

Before Justin could turn, Gunner banded an arm around him, bringing him flush against his chest, and covered the man's mouth with his free hand.

"Not even a squeal or you die," Gunner whispered against his ear. "Understood?"

Justin nodded, sucking in a sob.

Gunner wasted no time sinking his fangs into the soft flesh of the man's neck. Rich, warm, metallic-flavored blood slid over his tongue and down his throat. Though he preferred the sweeter blood of a female, being in Montana, he'd have to take what was available. Not wanting to harm the poor man, filled with enough to sustain him, Gunner withdrew his fangs with a pop and sealed the twin holes with a swipe of his tongue. Turning the man in his embrace, he looked down on him with his unnaturally black eyes.

"What the hell?" Justin's wide gaze looked up at him. "Please … please, don't kill me."

"Not my intention." Gunner held tight to his shoulders. "Hear me now, Justin, you won't remember my fangs, nor the fact I fed from you."

Justin stumbled back a few feet, blinking, his gaze seemingly unfocused. "What just happened?"

Gunner smiled. "I'm not sure what you mean. My pizza?"

Rubbing his neck, he turned to the brick oven. "It's almost done."

"Great, I'll meet you up front with the rest of my items."

After gathering a few days of supplies, Gunner met Justin back at the register when an elderly woman knocked on the locked doors. The clerk looked to the door strangely. "That wasn't locked—"

"Let me get that." Gunner walked over to the door and turned the lock. "I must have bumped it after I came in."

After paying for his groceries and pizza, Gunner left the small carryout and loaded the items into the trunk. He slammed down the lid, walked around the car, and slid in behind the wheel, feeling much better than when he had arrived.

CHAPTER EIGHT

Dumping the uneaten portion of her pizza into the receptacle, Adriana then carried her plate over to the counter and placed it into the stainless-steel sink. The vegetable pizza had been decent coming from a convenience store, but only she and Tag had eaten any of it. Gunner had brought in the pizza and groceries from his trip to town, then disappeared just as quickly.

Had he regretted his decision to rescue her?

Adri had given him ample opportunity to let her go and wash his hands of her when they refueled the plane. But he had outright refused, even adding that he'd personally kill Mateo if he came after her. So, why had they barely spoken since their arrival? She had no clue. When Tag suggested they get supplies, Gunner had jumped at the opportunity to leave. Something had changed between New Mexico and arriving in Montana.

Mi amor came to mind, her thought right before she had slipped off to sleep in his lap on the plane.

Had she been so tired she'd actually whispered the words?

If so, it was no wonder Gunner avoided her. He had come to Mexico to rescue her, no doubt as a favor to Ryder and Gabby. Adri had been foolish to think there had been ulterior motives behind his heroic actions. Why would Gunner want to be with someone who was tangled up with a cartel kingpin? Many months ago, she'd likely misread his feelings for her then, just as she did now.

Gunner's gallant decision to rescue her, though, would come with drastic consequences. Mateo, having by now found her missing, was likely rounding up troops. And unless Mateo was taken out as Gabby's uncle Raúl had been months ago, Adri doubted he'd ever stop looking for her. It wasn't an inflated ego that had her thinking as much. No, Mateo thought of her as a possession. And as such, he wasn't about to let anyone take from him what he thought of as his. He came for her once, he'd do so again.

"Are you okay being alone?" Tag asked, interrupting her troubling thoughts. Tag's dark hair had been shaved nearly to the skull. Add in an icy-blue gaze, strong facial features, and a square jawline, and he looked nearly savage.

"Of course. I don't need a babysitter. I'm sure you have better things to do than sit with me. I'll see to these groceries."

His warm smile was the only thing that made him appear approachable. "I didn't mean to imply you needed to be watched over. I meant it simply as offering my company."

Heat filled her cheeks. "I'll be fine."

"The television works. Not many stations come in this deep into the woods, but there might be a few channels to keep you from getting bored."

Adri couldn't help but ask, "Are you going out to find Gunner?"

"He's a big boy." Tag opened a cabinet by the back door, pulled out a rifle, and pocketed some bullets. "I thought I'd go hunting deer. We're going to need to stock up on meat. Hard telling how long we'll be here."

"Oh." His answer caught her by surprise, as did the idea of eating deer. She opted not to offend her host by mentioning the latter. "I thought this was to be short-term lodging. I guess I should've packed a few clothes then."

"Gunner can take you into Helena, get you a few outfits. You won't need many. There's a stacked washer and dryer behind those folding doors next to the bathroom. We can wash when we need to."

With that, Tag headed out the rear door of the cabin. Best to busy herself with putting away the groceries. Adri's thoughts, however, refused to be reined in and headed down a path she'd rather not entertain. Her feelings for Gunner. They had intensified since his showing up on Mateo's compound back in La Paz. Only someone extremely brave or foolish would've taken on the stunt he and Tag had pulled off. Adri had no business placing him on a pedestal, whether he'd been her knight in shining armor or not. Gunner had made no such declarations that she was anything but a friend. Worse yet, he might just think of her as a friend of a friend.

Pulling out several cans from the paper sacks, Adri stacked them in the pantry alongside a few packages of dry goods. The rest she added to the refrigerator. Carefully folding the bags, she laid them on the counter next to the empty pizza box. Most of what Gunner had purchased were non-perishable items that could stand time. She couldn't help but wonder how long he planned to stay. Surely, someone would be wondering about his whereabouts, which brought her to his earlier phone call. Had it been Ryder or Gabby? If so, she had a right to know and intended on asking him as much upon his return.

Pouring herself a glass of milk, she put the carton back into the refrigerator and closed the door. Tag had suggested she turn on the television, but Adri doubted she could focus on anything other than the answers she hoped to get from Gunner.

The back door opened a bit later as she was about to add her empty glass to the dishes already in the sink, causing her to fumble it. The glass shattered at her feet. Gunner was quick to her side. He picked her up, and set her next to the room's small table away from the breakage.

"Let me clean it up so you don't cut yourself."

Adri winced, embarrassed to have him acting savior again. She couldn't help the sarcasm from slipping into her tone. "I could've gotten that, Gunner. I'm not an invalid."

His dark gaze dropped to hers. "I wasn't insinuating you were."

But instead of allowing her to clean up her mess, he quickly picked up the pieces and dropped them into the garbage. Adri spotted blood welling to the surface on his palm.

Before he could wipe it off, she crossed the wood floor and grabbed his hand. "You're bleeding."

"I'm fine."

"There could be glass embedded in the cut."

He yanked it from her hold. "Christ, I said I was fine."

Gunner turned his back and washed away the blood, dried his hands with a paper towel, then threw it into the garbage. His rigid back indicated he might somehow be angry with her, though she had no clue as to why. Moisture gathered in her eyes. Instead of allowing the tears to fall, she squared her shoulders. She wouldn't cower, even if this entire situation was because of her. Gunner had made the trip to Mexico on his own. Adri hadn't asked him to.

Gunner braced his hands on the counter, bowing his head. His back rose and fell with his deep breaths. She was at a loss, having no idea how to even approach him. Did he truly hate her? Or was he just angry at the situation? Either way, she was baffled as to what she had done to displease him.

"You want to talk about it?"

Other than the tightening of his hands on the counter, he didn't move.

Adri paced the distance, placing her hand on his back. "Gunner, tell me what I did."

He turned, looking down on her, his brown irises deepening in color. "You didn't do anything. It's me."

She raised her hand to his whiskered cheek. "Then help me understand. I feel like I've upset you in some way."

He shook his head, saying nothing.

"If I'm a problem, then give me the keys to the car. I'll go. If Mateo comes after you … lie. Tell him you haven't seen me."

A muscle in his cheek ticked. "I won't leave you on your own to fend against that monster, Adri. And I sure in the hell won't let you return to him."

"I have no intention of going to Mexico, let alone to La Paz. I'll find someplace else to go."

"And if he finds you?"

"He won't."

Gunner chuckled, though his eyes held none of the humor. "Mateo has people everywhere. He'll find you, babe."

Adri raised a brow. "Then how exactly do you intend to stop him?"

"I already told you, I'll kill him if he comes anywhere near you."

"And if he brings an army?"

"I'll take out anyone who thinks to harm you." His gaze further blackened almost unnaturally. Surely, it was the lighting playing tricks. His jawline became more severe; his cheekbones raised. "You underestimate me."

Gunner tried to give her his back again, but her hand on his biceps stopped him. Adri wasn't about to allow him to retreat. She wanted answers. Her breath hitched. Gunner no longer looked even remotely human. *What in the world?*

"Don't," he growled, attempting to hide his face from her.

"You're one of them?"

His thick brows came together. "What?"

Adri raised her hand, gently lifting his upper lip with her fingers, clearly seeing the elongated fangs, just like those she'd spied on Ryder months ago. She hadn't told anyone, had even tried to pass it off as her overactive imagination. But now … as she faced the same anomaly in Gunner?

"Are you a vampire?"

His gaze narrowed in uncertainty. Did he fear what she would now think of him? Lord, did it change anything?

His lips turned down. "Gabby told you about us?"

Adri shook her head. "I saw it with my own eyes in Ryder, looking the way you do now. I thought to tell Gabby, but then she entered the room, not seeing me spy them through the window. I lived in their pool house at the time. I was about to enter through the sliding glass doors into the main house when I saw Ryder's eyes, his fangs. Gabby didn't even flinch at his appearance. She walked right over and kissed him. She knew what he was."

His gaze grew weary, his brows meeting over the bridge of his nose. "Who did you tell, babe? Mateo?"

"No!" Adri would never put Ryder or Gabby in harm's way. "No one. Especially not him."

"Why not confront your friends?"

"I don't know." She shrugged. "Ryder treated Gabby like a goddess. I knew, whatever he was, that he loved her and would never harm her."

Gunner's features slowly returned to human. He looked upon her in compassion. "Knowing that I'm a vampire, does it change how you feel about me?"

"What is there between us, Gunner? Why come rescue me when it could've gotten you killed? Did you do it as a favor to Gabby?"

"No one knew I went to Mexico."

"No one? You did this on your own?"

"I had to. I was afraid Mateo would hurt you after our last phone call. I wasn't sure what I'd find when I got there. But my brothers now know what I did." He took in a deep breath. "That phone call I took earlier? Was Smoke. He said Mateo had called Ryder. He's given them fourteen days to return you."

Adri gasped. "But by your admission, your friends don't even know where we are."

"My actions are my own. I take full responsibility for them." He framed her face between his palms. "We'll figure it out, babe ... together."

"You have to take me back, Gunner. Your friends will die because of me."

"I don't have all the answers just yet. But I'm not letting you go back to Mateo."

"But your MC brothers—"

"—would agree with me. When Mateo calls again, they'll tell him they don't know where I am, and if I did anything, that I acted on my own." He released her, feathering his knuckles across her cheek before dropping his hands. "It will buy us some time to put together a plan. Mateo won't expect my brothers. Only me."

"So, Ryder, Viper, Hawk ... they'll be coming here?"

"I'm counting on it, once I give them my location. The Sons of Sangue are family. You're part of that family. We take care of our own."

"Speaking of taking care, you need a Band-Aid." Adri gripped Gunner's wounded hand and turned it over. The cut on his palm had disappeared. "The cut? Where did it go?"

"There's a lot you don't know about me. For one, I heal quickly due to being a vampire. Does that scare you to know what I am ... a vampire?"

A shiver passed down her spine. Knowing Ryder might be inhuman had been Gabby's business. Not hers. Not to mention, she'd hoped it had been a hallucination. Now?

"Vampires are real?"

He nodded. "We keep our secret carefully safeguarded."

"Tag too?"

"No. He's not one of us, nor does he know about me."

She dropped his hand and rubbed the side of her neck. "Now what? You bite me?"

Gunner tilted his head back and laughed. "No, babe, not unless you want me to. I promise if I do, though, you won't forget the pleasure you derive from it. But I took care of my needs earlier."

"You bit someone? Are they dead?"

His smile flattened. "We only take what we need. We don't harm humans. They're our food source."

"Then how do you keep this secret if you feed on people?"

"We normally feed on what we call donors. They're part of a secret society that are aware of us. They provide what we need and we never harm them. Today, though, I had to hypnotize the young man I fed from so that he'd forget what had taken place. He had no more than an ache at the side of his neck as a reminder. I promise I didn't harm him."

Her head swam with the idea of Gunner being a vampire, the man she'd been in love with for months, standing in front of her. Was he ever human? If so, how had he been turned? It was nearly too much as she swayed on her feet. Gunner gripped her by the shoulders to steady her. "Are you okay?"

"I just have so many questions." She bit her lower lip to steady the sudden tremble. "You said you could hypnotize anyone? Does that include me?"

"If I needed to."

"Meaning?"

"I could make you forget ever seeing Ryder as a vampire." He released his hold and tucked her hair behind one ear, causing her to shiver again, but not out of fear. "Or me, for that matter. I could make you forget everything you just learned. And rightfully, I should."

Adri raised her gaze, holding it steady with his. "What if I didn't want you to?"

"Are you freaked out even a little by what you've seen?"

Adri wasn't sure how to answer that without offending him. "I'd be lying if I said I wasn't."

Gunner's gaze darkened. "And how would you feel if I did this?"

Lowering his head, he slanted his lips over hers. Adri's heart beat heavily against her chest, causing desire to pool low in her abdomen. Her thighs trembled and her knees damn near gave out. She gasped. *Lord, she was being kissed by a vampire.* But all she felt was Gunner, her love for him, and the need that nearly swept her off her feet. Gunner took the opportunity to deepen the kiss, sweeping his tongue deep inside her mouth. She touched her tongue to his, causing him to groan and crush her against him. His kiss was soul-deep and all-consuming. Adri felt the hot flames of desire nearly stealing her very breath.

She wanted to relish it, to hold him tightly against her and take all he had to give. But the word vampire came back to her like a flashing neon light, causing her to push against his chest and step back from his all-consuming kiss.

"Just as I thought," he whispered, Adri barely detecting the words.

She swept her tongue over her lips, relishing the heat of the kiss. Had she not known what he had become, she'd no doubt be begging him to carry her to the lone bed of the cabin. Part of her still desired as much. But her saner part warred against getting too close, fearing the feelings she had developed for him might get her hurt in the long run.

His mouth flattened, his blackened gaze holding hers. "I'm sorry, Adri. Please know that I'd rather not do this."

"Do what?"

"Hear me now..."

Adri blinked, unsure why his words had trailed off or why he now looked queerly at her. Had she somehow missed what he was trying to tell her? "Hear what? You didn't finish your sentence."

"You don't remember what I said? Did you have a moment of blackness?"

Adri frowned, feeling oddly confused and unstable on her feet. "I'm not sure. Did I black out for a moment?"

"You wobbled on your feet. Are you feeling better now?"

"I believe so." Weirdly, it was as if she were missing something that her brain couldn't quite pick up on. "What were we talking about?"

"Contacting Smoke, letting him know where we are."

Her thoughts seemed somewhat scrambled, like opening her mouth to say something, and yet she couldn't remember what it was. "They're coming here to help?"

"I believe so, but Mateo won't expect to find them here. Not if they tell him that I made my bed and I must lie in it. He'll hopefully believe the Sons left me to fend for myself since I acted on my own and that way he won't bring his whole fucking army."

"I hope you're right. I'd hate to be the reason that any of your friends got killed." Adri placed her palm against her forehead. "I'm sorry, Gunner. I'm feeling a bit lightheaded."

Gunner leaned down, and for a moment she thought he might just kiss her, hoping that he would. Instead, he placed a lingering kiss upon her forehead. Lord, although she wished otherwise, she had to remember he had offered nothing more than friendship.

"Go lie down a bit. I'll make my phone call to Smoke."

Feeling out of sorts, she said, "Maybe I should."

Gunner stepped away, looked back at her with what appeared to be regret, then walked out the back door. *Odd.* Unless he, too, had misgivings over the missed opportunity for a kiss. Her heart skipped a beat at the idea that he might feel more for her than just a friendship.

CHAPTER NINE

*S*ELF-LOATHING. THAT PRETTY MUCH SUMMED UP HIS CURrent mindset. Gunner had hit an all-time low. Hypnotizing someone in the past had not once left a bad taste in his mouth ... until now. Hell, it had been for Adri's own good and that of his MC. So, why was he so damn troubled over his actions? The Sons of Sangue had rules. Humans weren't allowed to know of their existence. He was the president, and as such, he had a responsibility to his club.

Adriana had dumbfounded him when she had noted his untimely vampire emergence and wasn't entirely shocked over his appearance. According to her, she'd witnessed the same from Ryder months ago, clearly the reason Gunner's turning hadn't startled her. During the passing months, she had not once disclosed to anyone what she had observed. Gunner's secret would've no doubt been safe with her as well.

And yet, feeling shameful, he had erased it all anyway.

Right along with the kiss he had purposely done before taking away her memories, knowing that too she wouldn't remember. Kissing her before he hypnotized her had been a cheap shot, one that had seriously backfired. Because he sure in the hell wasn't going to be able to forget it.

Fuck, that kiss had stirred him to the very core.

Her hot little body plastered against his chest, her lips melding with his, had him ravenous. Never had someone fit so perfectly in his embrace. There was no doubt where the kiss would've led, right before she stepped back and ended it. Gunner hadn't missed the scent of her desire. The bouquet of her blood was like a fine bourbon and damn if he didn't want to drink every drop.

Even now, his dick remained hard. His raging libido wasn't about to go without appeasement if they had to share the cabin's only bed. There was a pullout sofa in the living area, which Tag had already called dibs on, probably thinking there was more to his and Adri's relationship. After all, he had asked Tag to fly him into cartel territory just to retrieve her.

The hammock swaying in the light breeze caught his attention. He supposed he could sleep on the back porch. But the idea of crashing outside with nighttime temperatures still reaching the low forties wasn't something high on his wish list, not while wearing a pair of shorts. Thankfully, Gunner didn't require a lot of shuteye, due to his vampire DNA. Maybe he could forgo it altogether.

Sleeping next to Adriana every night would no doubt make his good intentions fly right out the fucking door. Rescuing her from Mateo wasn't about getting into her pants, no matter how badly he wanted her.

He was a monster and he'd do well to remember that.

Even though his vampire was famished for her, Gunner needed to put a lid on it, even if it was getting harder to ignore. It wasn't just her red blood cells he craved; that hot little body of hers drove him to the brink of madness. Gunner could easily imagine his hands spanning her model-thin waist and lifting her onto his cock.

Just the idea left him groaning. His willpower was better than that, damn it. He needed to man up and stop acting like a horny teenager who had just discovered the opposite sex. Going out behind the woodshed to single-handedly take care of his itch wasn't about to pacify him either. Instead, he pulled out his cell and punched in his VP's number.

"What's up, Gunner?" Smoke asked. "Tell me you're already on your way back to La Paz, returning that little package to Mateo. Fourteen days, man. Tick Tock."

"You really think I'm going to do that?"

He heard Smoke's chuckle. "Nope."

Even the idea Smoke might think as much irritated him. He growled, "You believe I should?"

"Fuck that. Just getting a rise out of you, man. We all know that if Adriana goes back to Mateo he'll harm her, if not outright kill her for her disobedience. That's not an option we're entertaining."

Gunner paced the small wooden porch, shoving a hand through his hair with his free hand. He knew he couldn't do this alone. But what right did he have to ask? This was his doing.

"I can't ask you to come here, Smoke. This is my mess. I acted on my own."

Smoke chuckled again. "I can't argue with you. You're always running off and doing foolhardy shit like crashing your motorcycle, leaving us to scrape your dumbass up. Even had you asked before you ran off, I wouldn't have stopped you. I probably would've gone along. All of us in Washington feel the same way. We're brothers, through and through. You should've confided in us."

"I didn't want to get anyone killed."

"Look, I've been in touch with Viper and the Oregon crew. We all agree. Adriana is one of ours. Whether through you or Gabby. We protect our own. If she is with you, then we'll come there, fight this war with the cartel together."

"I'm not sure I want to bring the fight here."

"How far are you from Seattle?"

"About an eight-hour drive."

"Text me the address and Diablo, Neo, and I can be there by tomorrow. It won't hurt to have a few extra pairs of eyes on the grounds. I'll call in Blade and Sting to keep an eye on the clubhouse."

"They're Devils, dude."

"Not for much longer." He could hear the smile in Smoke's voice. "They both want in and Viper's given the Oregon crew's blessing. We took a vote and as long as you're cool with it, we'll be patching them over."

Gunner couldn't help but be surprised. Last he knew, Cy "Blade" Moon might be interested in returning to Washington. But he thought Sawyer "Sting" Barnett was all Santa Barbara, California. "They know about the vampire DNA?"

"They will when you sign off."

"Let's not muddy the water unless we have to. Get them back to Washington, with the intent to patch them over to Sons. When we get out of this mess, we'll deal with making them members and vampires."

"Got it, P."

"I'll text you the address, but it will take two days to get here if you wait on Sting and Blade. I don't foresee a problem with that. We're well hidden. Make sure Viper and the Oregon crew know what's up. They'll need to keep an eye out in case Mateo makes a move for Seattle. I don't want to hang Sting and Blade out to dry."

"I'll get a hold of Viper and Hawk. We'll come up with a plan and get back to you. Otherwise, I'll see you in a couple of days, man."

"Stay safe, dude."

"You as well," Smoke said, then the line went dead.

Gunner's heart warmed at the prospect of his brothers coming out. Not that he didn't expect them to. After all, brothers to the end. Just the fact that Smoke offered without him having asked, though, went a long way in securing their brotherhood. Regardless of how Gunner had gotten himself into the mess, his brethren were ready to take up the gauntlet.

ADRIANA STARED AT HER REFLECTION in the small circular mirror hanging over the vanity in the cabin's lone bathroom. She braced her hands on the countertop to still their trembling. Washed up and free of makeup, she found herself self-conscious about what she viewed in the reflective glass. Not once had she shared a bed with Gunner. The cabin's only mattress was small in comparison to his large body, a body she wouldn't mind exploring. Adri couldn't help but be aware of him lying next to her. Just the thought had her heating in places that had long been dormant.

A shiver passed through her.

Too bad Gunner wasn't of the same mind. Since their arrival, he had acted as if they were merely friends, spending very little time in her company. But with Tag claiming the sofa for the night? That left Gunner and her sharing the bedroom.

Adriana stepped back, looking at her slender curves adorned with a white lace bra and panties. The pristine color stood out in contrast to the warmth of her skin. She couldn't help but hope that Gunner might find her sexy. Her clothes had been neatly folded and left on the side of the tub. She couldn't think to sleep in them, nor had she brought any others with her. Tag had mentioned earlier that Gunner could take her shopping, but that wouldn't be until the following day.

What would Gunner think, dressed as she was?

Did he prefer women with more curves?

She covered her small lace-covered breasts with her hands. Maybe even these he'd find lacking.

A sound outside the door caught her attention. The cabin had been empty when she had gone to the bathroom to wash up. Someone moved about the interior. Grabbing a towel from the rack, she wrapped it around her middle. The bathroom wasn't connected to the bedroom, so she had little choice but to pass the person rummaging through the living area.

Squaring her shoulders, she opened the door expecting to find Tag since Gunner had gone MIA. Instead, she spotted Gunner poking through one of the closets. "Looking for something?"

Gunner turned and looked at her. His Adam's apple bobbed in his throat as he quickly turned his gaze. "I'm sorry, I didn't realize you weren't dressed."

"Relax. I'm not naked. I still have on my bra and panties." Adri tugged on the shoulder strap as proof. "What are you looking for?"

His eyes returned to hers, seemingly darker than when he first looked at her. "Blankets."

"There are covers on the bed and Tag already threw one on the sofa for himself."

"The bed is yours, babe. I'm looking for blankets for the hammock on the back porch. It's likely to get damn cold tonight."

Her brow creased. "What on earth for? You'll catch your death."

"I'll be fine."

"And so will I, Gunner Anderson." She shook her head in dismay. He'd rather sleep in freezing weather than next to her. So much for wondering what he'd think of her state of dress. "You're a gentleman. I'm not afraid of sleeping next to you."

His gaze darkened even more. "Am I?"

"Part of me hopes not." She smiled, then headed for the bedroom door, dropping her towel just before entering the room. Gunner's curses followed her through the door.

Pulling back the covers, she slipped between the sheets and nervously waited. A blatant invitation. Adri hoped Gunner saw it for what it was and didn't finish his search for a blanket to sleep outdoors. He had traveled a great distance, placed himself and Tag in grave danger, and for what? Because Gabby had asked him to? Adri doubted that to be the case. She saw the way Gunner looked at her just now. He could deny his interest, but the sudden thickness of his groin pressing against his shorts told another story. If he accepted her invitation and followed her to the bed, she didn't plan on getting a lot of sleep. She had waited a damn long time to be in Gunner's arms and she wasn't about to deny herself a moment longer. Gunner was the man she was supposed to be with. Always had been. Not Mateo. Adri felt it in her bones the night she asked him to dance months ago in Mexico. She might have followed him then, had she not thought he had been murdered by the cartel.

Now she meant to show Gunner exactly how she felt.

She wasn't about to lose him a third time.

Slow and sexy, he walked through the door, slamming it behind him. He pulled his T-shirt over his head and tossed it to the floor, then flipped the light switch on the wall, cloaking them in near darkness. His shadow self slowly approached the bed.

"Do you know what you're asking for, babe?" he asked, his voice deep, raspy, and sexy as hell.

Oh, but she did.

Adri grabbed the covers on his side of the bed and tossed them back. Gunner didn't hesitate as he stepped out of his shorts, answering the question if he went commando. Even in the darkness, she could see his thick cock jutting out from his groin, hard and long. The mattress dipped beneath his weight as he filled three-quarters of the bed. Adri damn near gulped, wondering if she were even big enough for him to fit.

Lucky for her, she was about to find out.

Her thighs trembled in anticipation, her panties already wet with desire. After months of desiring Gunner, he was finally about to make her every fantasy come true and make her his. And Adri sure in the hell hoped she didn't disappoint.

CHAPTER TEN

WHAT THE HELL WAS HE DOING?
He had no business crawling into bed with Adriana, let alone naked. Gunner's self-control normally rivaled that of a monk, and yet his willpower went out the window the minute she'd dropped the towel. Sashaying across the room in her little white-lace ensemble... If he hadn't already been hard, that would've done the trick. He had become accustomed to denying himself as of late. But when Adri blatantly offered herself?

Shit, he was a goner.

He was thankful for the anonymity the darkness afforded him or Adri would see exactly what she was getting. Something straight out of a freak show. His face ached with his transformation; his eyes heated. Fangs filled his mouth, scraping the inside flesh and drawing forth the metallic flavor of his blood. Luckily, the properties in his saliva would quickly heal the scrapes. But he'd still need to be careful kissing her because one drop of his vampire blood and she'd spend the next week on fire with the transformation, not to mention sealing her fate as his mate.

Donors wore necklaces with vials containing vampire blood. It was the Sons of Sangue's way of protecting them, thanking them for the nutrition they offered. Should the donor get in a situation where their death was imminent, they could be given the blood from the vial, gaining them immortality. Their vow to the donor society, though, forbade them from using the blood for any other reason. To betray their pledge would earn them an execution at the hands of the Sons.

Gunner lay stretched out on his back, eyes to the ceiling, trying his damnedest to talk his cock down. At this point, he couldn't dispute that the damn thing had a mind of its own, vetoing every objection he could come up with as to why sleeping with Adri was a bad idea. Gunner could smell her desire, knew what she wanted. It would be easy enough to roll over, part her slender thighs, and give in to the temptation. In the shadows, Adri would never know that a monster, not a man, made love to her.

It wasn't fair of him to disclose his vampirism and betray his oath to the Sons.

But Adri had every right to know who or what she slept with.

According to his motorcycle club, humans were off limits. Only donors should be used for extra-curricular activities. Other humans must not be privy to them. The Sons lives depended on anonymity. Anytime a vampire did not have a donor handy, then they used hypnosis, erasing the human's memory of everything that occurred. He'd do well to keep reminding himself of that.

An MC's rule was as good as law.

A small, cool hand landed on his chest, stilling his rolling thoughts. His skin heated, making his already fast-beating heart race and scramble any further musings. His breaking point had been breached. Turning back was no longer an option. His vampire demanded appeasement. Wanting to be inside Adri in the worst way for months added fuel to the fire raging inside him. Tonight, his fantasy in the flesh was about to become reality.

Damn, but she was gorgeous and seconds away from becoming his.

And he wasn't about to share.

Gunner had best make her well aware of that fact. He rolled over, gripping Adri by the shoulders, spreading her thighs with his knee and settling between them. His cock rested along her lace-covered slit. Nothing short of a hurricane would keep him from possessing her now. He would damn well claim her. Adri's breath hitched as she looked up at him through hooded lids. Gunner quickly dipped his head to the crook of her neck, needing to keep his face hidden lest he be found out. Even in the shadows, he feared her witnessing his unleashed vampire.

He licked a path from her pulse point to ear, eliciting her sexy-as-hell moan, nearly unmanning him. Fuck, he had gone too long without. A slight nip of her lobe drew a bead of blood to the surface. Gunner couldn't help but taste the tiny droplet, causing him to groan from the sweetness. Even though he had recently fed, he ached to sink his fangs into her throat and take what his vampire hungered for.

Adrenaline coursed through him, feeding the junkie in him.

He needed this. *Fuck*! He needed *her*.

Gunner reached down, tearing the thin piece of material separating them, wanting nothing but to feel her flesh against his. Flipping the front closure of her bra, he tossed it just as easily to the side. Gunner leaned back, looking down at her perfection, his heated vampire gaze having no problem seeing her naked, slender body beneath him. Her tiny waist he could easily span with his hands. Her small breasts were perfection, the taut nipples begging for his attention.

Taking one pert nub into his mouth, he suckled it before nipping the flesh of her areola, once again tasting of her life's fluid, teasing his desire for more. His hunger was quickly raging out of his control. Soothing the tender spot with his tongue, Gunner then kissed a trail to her stomach, laving the small button in the center.

Adri arched her back, tilting her head into the pillow, crying out. "Please, Gunner."

"Ask and it's yours."

"I need you … inside me."

"You're aware once I'm inside, I won't allow anyone else to take what's mine."

"I'm yours."

"Jesus, Adri…"

He was more than prepared to oblige…

The cabin door slammed against the inside wall, Tag calling his name. The scent of fresh blood assaulted his senses, stilling him.

"Fuck," Gunner grunted, rolling from Adri, growling in displeasure. "Stay here. I'll see what's going on."

He stood from the bed. Regret rivered down his spine, knowing this night was now lost. He could feel it in his veins as easily as he had Adri's desire moments ago. Something was wrong. Gunner stepped into his shorts and pulled his T-shirt over his head. Waiting a few seconds for the vampire to retreat, he then exited the room and shut the door behind him.

"What's got you hollering…?" Gunner took in the large amount of blood running down Tag's arm. The scent damn near called back the vampire. "What the hell happened?"

Tag pulled out a table chair and sat heavily, his arm dangling at his side. He took in a shaky breath, his skin milky white. He looked moments from passing out. "Bear."

Gunner ripped the sleeve from Tag's shirt and quickly tied it above the large wound. Four large nasty gashes went bone deep into his arm. The bear's claw had easily shredded the muscle. "Jesus. You need medical—"

"No. Fuck," he hissed. "The nearest hospital is miles from here. There's a first aid kit in the bathroom. Just … a few stitches."

Gunner nearly chuckled at the absurdity. Flesh and muscle hung from his arm. He wasn't even sure his saliva could easily heal a wound so deep. He knew they had little choice but to take care of the wound here as Tag was quickly losing large amounts of blood and damn well could be dead before their arrival at the nearest ER.

Adri came out of the bedroom, bra balled in her fist, and wrapped in the towel she had dropped. "What happened... Oh, my God!"

"Ah, damn, I didn't mean to interrupt," Tag grumbled.

Gunner ignored him and said to Adri, "Get the first aid kit from the bathroom."

She quickly did his bidding, coming back fully clothed, aside from the panties he destroyed. Gunner took the kit from her, then placed it on the table, finding nothing with which to stitch the wounds closed.

"Tag, there's nothing but gauze and antibiotics in this kit." Thankfully, the bear had only nicked the artery. Otherwise, Tag would've bled out on his way back to the cabin. "You need to be sewn up, like now."

"There's another kit in the plane ... in the cockpit—" Tag whispered right before he slumped in the chair and blacked out.

Gunner cursed, knowing he had to try and help the wound to begin to heal. He looked to Adri, "Run to the plane. Find the kit to stitch his arm."

Without question, Adri headed for the back door and ran barefoot to the hangar. Gunner took the opportunity to spit into the open wound and use his healing salvia to start the repair of the torn muscles. It would also act as an antibiotic. Holding the shredded pieces together, he then licked the flesh, watching as the muscle and skin began to slowly heal. The bleeding had stopped by the time Adri made her way back.

She stopped just shy of them, her gaze narrowing. "How?"

"The human body can do miraculous things," was all he could think to say. "Hand me the thread and needle."

Gunner knew she questioned what had happened but said nothing as Gunner made quick work of stitching Tag's arm. The wound no longer required the aid of sutures, but Gunner did so for the sake of appearance. Tag had needed a surgeon. No way a wound of that size could be healed without divine intervention or vampire saliva. Cutting the thread with his teeth, he knotted off the last thread then stood back and looked at his handiwork. Messy, but it would do. Had he allowed his vampire salvia to work on its own, Tag might not have sported a single scar. But due to Gunner's sloppy handiwork, he'd no doubt sport several.

Adri went to the sink, opened a drawer, and withdrew a few towels, wetting them. When she returned, she placed a cool one across Tag's forehead, and one over the sutured cut before looking back at Gunner.

Using a forefinger, she swiped something from the corner of Gunner's mouth. "Why do you have blood near your mouth?"

Gunner shrugged. "I suppose it was on my hands when I wiped my face."

Thankfully, Adri seemed to take him at his word. "You should wash up. You have his blood all over your hands and arms, too."

He looked back at Tag. "I'll carry him to the sofa. Will you be okay watching over him while I shower?"

She nodded but said nothing. Gunner placed an arm across Tag's back, and one beneath his knees, then carried him over to the couch and laid him down. The man stirred but did not open his eyes. He'd live.

"What the hell was he doing?" Gunner wondered aloud, knowing Tag had disappeared earlier while he was on the phone with his VP.

"Deer hunting."

Of course, Tag would be concerned with the lack of supplies, not knowing how long they might be hunkered down in the middle of fucking nowhere.

"I think I should sleep out here tonight. I'll grab a pillow and another blanket. I'll watch over him for the night."

He could see the flicker of disappointment of the night lost in her gaze. Hell, he felt much the same way, even if he did feel a bit of relief.

"Get cleaned up, Gunner, I'll make you a place to sleep on the floor."

He walked over to her, not wanting to touch her with his bloody hands, leaned down, and kissed her on her forehead.

"I'll be back in a few minutes."

She smiled sadly. "Take your time."

Gunner turned and headed for the bathroom. Hell, that's exactly what he had wanted to do. Take his time making love to her. Now? He sure hoped his common sense had returned because sleeping with Adri would have been a mistake. Not that he would regret it, but he knew she damn well would.

ADRIANA STOOD ON THE SIDEWALK, humored as she watched Gunner duck, hitting his head in the process, beneath the doorframe of the small blue car. He stood, rubbed the spot on his forehead, then slammed the door, rocking the car on all four tires.

His brown eyes found hers, his grimace changing to a warm smile. "What do you find so humorous, babe? Me hitting my head? Or a car created for circus clowns?"

His comment only intensified her laughter. "What are you? Six-three, six-four?"

"Six-three and way too tall to be trying to fit in that thing. It's got me wishing for the motorcycle I trashed last week."

She drew her brows together, her humor quickly turning to concern even if he didn't have any obvious injuries. "What happened?"

"Driving way too fast on a curve, flipped over a guardrail."

"How did you not hurt yourself?"

"I guess I was just damn lucky," he said with a chuckle.

Placing his overly large hand in the small of her back, he led her in the direction of one of Helena's trendy shops. His touch heated her, making her wish they were back at the cabin, finishing what they had started the evening before. After spending the night on the hard floor in front of the sofa, Gunner awoke, treating her as though nothing had happened between the two of them. Adri, on the other hand, hadn't gotten much sleep because she couldn't stop thinking about it.

Thankfully, Tag seemed miraculously better this morning with nothing more than Gunner's stitches and some puckered skin, luckily showing no signs of infection, as a reminder of the bear he had tousled with. They left him to rest while they ran to town to do a little shopping for clothes.

Stopping just outside the door of a trendy store, she turned and glanced at Gunner. "We can't shop here. I don't have any money, Gunner. And I certainly can't have you paying the prices this store no doubt charges, even if I will pay you back every dime."

Adri supposed Gunner felt she was used to high-end designers, having come from Mateo's stronghold, which wasn't far from the truth. But none of that was important to her. Those were simply material possessions. Being here with Gunner was what mattered. She'd gladly wear previously-owned clothes if it meant staying by his side.

He reached into the pocket of his shorts and withdrew five one-hundred-dollar bills. "Buy yourself a few items to get by on."

"It's too expensive, Gunner. There must be a secondhand store somewhere in Helena."

Gunner rubbed his jaw, looking uncomfortable. It was obvious he wasn't used to worrying about what a woman wore or taking care of their needs.

"You can't wear secondhand panties. I destroyed the one pair you had last night," he said, punctuating it with a smile. It was the first hint Gunner had given that he even remembered what had almost transpired between them. "Buy yourself some nice undergarments. Then if you want to go to some kind of a thrift store, we can go there afterward. I could use a few pairs of jeans and T-shirts to get us by for a few more days. Tag's going to need something as well. His clothes were bloody and torn. You can help me guess his sizing."

"Fine." She took the money from his outstretched hand, hoping that it was for him she'd be buying the sexy garments. That was if she got a chance to finish what they had started. "I'll only be a few moments. Will you wait out here?"

Gunner cleared his throat, once again looking troubled. A quick glance down the street and he said, "Looks like there's a shop down that way tailored to my kind of shopping. I'll be back in about a half hour, so take your time."

Adri nodded, turned, and headed into the shop, the little bell on the door announcing her arrival. A smartly dressed woman near the register greeted her. "May I help you?"

"I'm looking for undergarments. Something ... sexy."

The woman glanced to the front of the store, before looking back at her, a knowing smile on her face. "Something the handsome gentleman you were just speaking with might enjoy?"

Adriana's face heated. She hated being so transparent. "If you could be so kind."

The woman showed her to the back of the store, where she helped measure her for the perfect fitting brassieres and panties. Thirty minutes and four lacy undergarment sets later, she was at the counter paying for her items when she heard the soft rumble of a motorcycle.

The woman finished wrapping the items in tissue paper, then placed the items in a bag, handing them to her. "I do hope you enjoy them," she said with a smile as the man riding the motorcycle stepped over the bike and removed his helmet.

Adri didn't hear anything more as she headed for the door. Gunner had never looked sexier, sporting a pair of leather chaps over an ass-hugging pair of jeans. She had to admit, she approved of the look.

The bell over the door dinged again as she exited the shop and stopped just as Gunner turned around. His black T-shirt read Harley Davidson over what looked to be a motorcycle engine and a pair of wings.

"You find anything?"

Adri nodded. "Looks like you did too. Yours?"

"I would have preferred buying it back home at K&K, but beggars can't be choosers." He laughed. "I wasn't about to crawl back into that car again. You can drive it home. I'll follow. Right after we hit the thrift store I found around the corner."

She handed him back his change from her purchase. "Surely, you didn't get the jeans and chaps from the thrift store."

"Nope. Got them from the motorcycle shop. The chaps were thrown in for free. You like?"

Adri dropped her gaze, unable to help from looking at what the chaps cradled. Her face heated again when she looked back up and Gunner smiled, obviously catching her looking at his crotch. "They look ... um ... nice."

He placed an arm across her shoulders. "Babe, you can look at my package any day. As a matter of fact—"

She chuckled, shaking her head. "Don't even say it unless you plan on delivering."

"Oh, I'll deliver." Gunner winked at her. "We just have a few ... issues to work out first. Now get in the car, head down the street, and take the first right."

Adri couldn't help but wonder what he meant about issues. There was nothing that would stop her from being with Gunner. Maybe he didn't feel the same way? Of course, she was just being paranoid. He had as much said how he felt last night by calling her his before they were interrupted. So what issues could he possibly have?

She planned on finding out, right after they finished their shopping. This was a conversation she didn't plan on saving for later.

CHAPTER ELEVEN

A COUPLE OF DAYS HAD PASSED SINCE GUNNER HAD TAKEN Adriana shopping and all he could think about was that bag full of lingerie she had carried from the trendy shop in Helena. Lord, it was all he could do to keep his hands to himself and not repeat the mistake of a few nights back. Gunner had damn near taken her. He knew once he crossed that line there would be no turning back.

She was it for him.

Letting her go would be near impossible once he slept with her. So, before he totally fucked everything up, he needed to let Adri know what she was signing up for.

Vampire and all.

Gunner had needed to rally his self-control upon their return to the cabin. Sleeping with Adri was out of the question. It was completely unfair and unethical to allow her to go into a sexual relationship with him while being unaware of what he became when his emotions ran high. If Adri decided she couldn't handle the surfacing monster, then he'd hypnotize her and walk away ... for good this time.

There'd be no future for them and no prospective mate for him. The hope for companionship stopped with her. A chill ran through him. Living a life without her wasn't something he wanted to entertain. So, until the current situation was remedied, sleeping with her in the same bed was out of the question.

The nighttime temperatures were still on the cold side, but with a couple of blankets, the hammock had sufficed for a few hours of shuteye. After all, he didn't require much. Adri had questioned him on his complete turnabout from their shopping trip, but so far he had skirted the truth, that he couldn't trust his self-control when he was alone with her. Their friendship had become strained as a result, only engaging in meaningless small talk while in each other's company. And with his brethren from the Sons about to arrive? The situation wasn't about to get better.

Tag stepped onto the back porch. He stuffed his hands into the pockets of his new jeans and rocked back on his heels. One would never know he had been mauled by a bear only days before. Thankfully, he had never questioned his miraculous recovery.

"So what's going on between you two?"

Gunner shrugged but said nothing. With the toe of his boot, he scraped a knot in the wood at his feet. Hell, he wasn't even comfortable sharing his musings with the guy that put his life in danger to rescue the woman Gunner now tried his best to ignore.

"Look," Tag grumbled, "if we're to be stuck here in this cabin together, for God knows how long, then you two need to kiss and make up. The fucking tension around here is thick enough to cut with a damn knife."

Glancing up from the floor, Gunner averted his gaze, peering off to the woods beyond the airplane hangar. "I'd tell you to fly home, but I fear your life is also in danger. I'm sorry I involved you in this. You should've just told me to go to hell."

"Cut the bullshit, Gunner. I may not have signed up to go toe-to-toe with the cartel, but you didn't twist my arm either. I make my own decisions. I'm a big boy. Why don't you try being one and go in there and make up with that pretty little lady? I can make myself scarce for an hour or so."

"You don't understand—"

"What's not to fucking understand? You like her. She likes you." He turned his palms up. "Seems obvious to me. Go fuck her brains out so we can all learn to cohabitate without all this sexual friction going on between the two of you. Hell, at this point, I'd almost rather take my chances with the La Paz soldiers than deal with you two."

Gunner smirked. "That's a hell of a way to talk to the guy who saved your life."

"About that—"

"You're welcome." Gunner slapped him on his good shoulder and meant to walk away, avoiding something else he didn't want to talk about. The last thing he needed was Tag all curious about how easily he had recovered.

Tag grabbed his forearm, stopping him from running away yet again. "Not so fast, big guy. How the hell am I not thrashing about in there full of infection? Or worse yet, dead? I know I lost a lot of blood."

"I stitched you up. Kept it clean."

Tag chuckled. "I saw those stitches. You aren't going to make surgeon any time soon. You don't want to talk about it? Fine. However, I'm damn grateful for whatever you did."

Gunner heard the approaching motorcycles, thankful for the change in subject. He tipped his nose and caught the scent of several of his brethren. They weren't far. Soon, Tag would hear their approach as well.

"Don't mention it. I was glad to help. End of story. There isn't some voodoo shit going on. Call it a miracle. That's all."

Tag looked to the road. "You hear that? Do I need to get my gun?"

Gunner shook his head. "It's my MC brothers paying a visit."

"How can you be so sure?"

He winked at Tag, then stepped from the porch and headed down the long driveway, seeing the five approaching motorcycles.

His VP, Adrian Wellman, rode out front with Dante Santini and Brandon "Neo" McClure close behind. Ryder Kelly and Grigore "Wolf" Lupei, with their respective mates, brought up the tail. Good. The more vampires in residence, the better their chances against Mateo's soldiers. Obviously, Kane Tepes had thought it imperative to have some of his Oakland crew follow along.

The men pulled their motorcycles alongside his newly purchased one. Stepping off their bikes, his brothers took turns giving him a hug.

Tag walked up behind him. "This your crew?"

"My brothers ... every one of them—"

Before he could say another word, a squeal cut him off as Adriana left the cabin and ran for the circle of Sons. Gabriela broke away from Ryder and hugged her best friend.

Giving Gunner a quick glare, because apparently she still had yet to forgive his absence, Adri placed her arm around Gabby's back and motioned to Caitlyn. "Let's go inside the cabin where it's a bit more ... friendly."

He heard Gabby's answered question. "What's going on with you and Gunner?"

Not having time for the women's drama, nor wanting to get involved, Gunner looked at his brothers and growled. "Damn glad to have you here."

"You want to fill us in?" Smoke asked. "I'm not sure Ryder and Wolf know the entire story."

After introducing Tag, Gunner filled them in on their trip to La Paz and their return here. "So, I'm sure Mateo is wasting no time putting together a crew to look for us."

"He have any idea where to look? Follow the radar?" Ryder asked.

"No." Tag rubbed his hands together. "I flew under it. They won't have a clue."

"That yours?" Smoke indicated the new cycle parked next to all of theirs. "When did you acquire that?"

"Couple days ago." Gunner grinned. "Sweet, ain't it? Couldn't ride around in the cage pretending to be a car anymore. Damn thing made me claustrophobic."

Wolf rubbed his long goatee. "You pay cash?"

"Used my card. Who carries that kind of cash?"

"Then those motherfuckers know right where to look," Wolf grunted. "Mateo will be tracing your credit card use. He owns the law in Mexico. They're no doubt monitoring if and when you use credit. It's only a matter of time before they arrive, and we'll be waiting on them."

"Fuck. I hadn't thought about that. Now, what the hell do we do?"

"We wait," Ryder piped in. "The Sons have never been one to back down on a challenge, and we won't now. We bested them once when we took out Raúl, we'll do it again. This time we have the advantage. They're coming to us and not the other way around. Mateo's living on borrowed time. We still haven't paid him back for burning down Gabby's and my house, trying to take my family and friends with it. I think it's about time."

"Viper and Hawk are standing by. They sent Xander and Gypsy north to help Blade and Sting keep an eye on the clubhouse. Should we need more assistance, Viper, Hawk, Preacher, and Rogue are on standby. And … I have Vlad on speed dial." Wolf added the last part with a wicked grin.

"From what I hear about the phantom, he has a wicked sixth sense when it comes to trouble." Gunner was still in awe of the infamous Impaler. "Maybe he'll show up without the invite."

Ryder laughed. "He's never waited for one before. I don't see why he would now. Besides, if we get in trouble, I'm sure his mate, Janelle, will have seen it beforehand in one of her visions. They'll be here."

Either way, Gunner was glad to have the vampires in residence. He wasn't sure where he'd put them all, but they'd make do. The women could have the cabin. The rest of them could set up tents. He had spotted some camping supplies in the hangar while he was avoiding Adri and out snooping around. As for guns, there were a few rifles in the house and lot of ammo, but he was betting each of his brothers came packing. He hadn't missed the AR strapped to the side of Wolf's bike.

They might be vampires, giving them the leg up on strength, but the other team would come packing. As vampires, they could out-muscle Mateo's men any day of the week, but it would be hard to get close enough for hand-to-hand combat when only one side had weapons.

"Where are we sleeping?" Smoke asked, his hand indicating the tiny cabin.

"How long's it been since you went camping, Smoke?" Gunner chuckled at the disgruntled look on his VP's face. "Ain't a hotel within miles. Looks like we'll be setting up some tents out back. Providing we don't get eaten by bears, you'll survive."

"Fuck. Bears?" Neo patted his side holster under his arm. "Damn good thing I brought protection."

"Too soon for jokes, Gunner." Tag laughed. "You might want the guy with the AR to take care of the bear."

"What's he mean, 'too soon'?"

"Tag was attacked by a bear a couple of nights back, Neo." Gunner said as Tag lifted his sleeve and showed the men his stitches. "They don't typically come into our camp, so stay the fuck out of the woods."

"You won't have to tell me twice." Neo laughed. "I didn't get all these tats to have them torn up by a claw. I'll stay here in the open."

"You might have to give Tag a free tattoo when this is over, Neo. He more than earned it. Cover those ugly scars he's bound to have."

"I'd be glad to." Neo reached out and shook Tag's hand. "My honor. You fought with a bear; you deserve to get one on the house."

The men followed Gunner around the back of the cabin and to the hangar where Gunner and Tag started pulling down a couple large tents and several sleeping bags from the rafters. Within a half hour, they had a makeshift camp set up and a roaring fire between the two tents. Tag had gone in to check on the women, coming back with a pot of coffee in one hand and several paper cups in the other.

"It's not whiskey, but it will do. Thought maybe we could use some warming up. Luckily, I found some throw-away cups."

Wolf pulled a bottle of whiskey from his satchel. After adding a couple of fingers to his cup of coffee, he passed the bottle around the circle of men. The Sons sat around the fire, telling tales of the last time they had gone toe-to-toe with the cartel. Gunner couldn't help but laugh about Ryder's tale of burying him alive. He hadn't been under the dirt long, but it sure as fuck felt like an eternity before Wolf dug his sorry ass up.

"Well, one thing I know for sure, I'm not about to volunteer to get buried again. Next time, you can take the honors, Ryder."

He grinned. "No, next time we bury *their* motherfucking asses."

Cheers and raised cups went up when Gunner added, "Just so we are clear, Mateo is mine."

CHAPTER TWELVE

"Are you going to answer my question?" Gabby laughed as she took a seat beside Adri.

It was good to see her again. It felt like being back home in Oregon. Adri hadn't realized how much she had missed her best friend until she saw her coming down the gravel lane on the back of Ryder's bike.

She didn't think she'd ever been happier to see someone … other than when Gunner had stepped foot in her suite back in La Paz. Lord, it had been pure insanity for him to steal her out from underneath Mateo's stronghold. Not only were Gunner and Tag now in danger by her leaving the compound with them, the Sons of Sangue had also become entangled in her mess, Gabby and Caitlyn being there as a testament to their involvement. If she got them killed as a result of her recklessness, she'd never forgive herself.

Hell, she'd be lucky this time to escape with her own life.

Mateo would stop at nothing short of murder for those betraying him. The man who had loaned her his phone at Salazar's came back to mind. Mateo hadn't hesitated to pull the trigger, splattering blood and brains all over the bathroom wall.

Adri shook off the horrific memory as Gabby awaited an answer. She wasn't ready to talk about what hadn't transpired a few nights back or Gunner's lack of attention since. "What question is that?"

"You know damn well what I'm talking about, Adriana Flores. What is going on between you and Gunner? You just glared daggers at him and I'm not supposed to notice? He bravely rescued you from that scumbag you once called fiancé. Seriously. You can't be that ungrateful. You're better than that."

Caitlyn helped herself to a cup of coffee from a newly brewed pot, then took a seat on the chair opposite the sofa. Tucking her foot under one leg, the multi-platinum songstress quietly sipped from the cup. Caitlyn was completely gorgeous with the voice of an angel. And seemingly disinterested in their conversation.

"Can we drop it for now?" Adri asked.

"No, we cannot."

Adri quickly turned her attention to Caitlyn in hopes of getting the conversation off her. She didn't want to talk about Gunner because there was not much to say. "Not on tour?"

"Nice deflect," Caitlyn pointed out, apparently not as indifferent as she appeared. "I'll bite, since Gabby is hell-bent on a topic you aren't comfortable with."

"Well, aren't you just being catty?" Gabby chuckled with a shake of her head. "You know you want the answer as much as I do, Caitlyn."

The songstress smiled, obviously not the least offended. Thankfully, she followed Adri's lead. "We recently ended a European sold-out tour and I'm torn. I'm still trying to decide if I'm ready to retire and walk away from the biz. I think Wolf would be more than happy if I did. He'd get to spend more time with his MC brothers, rather than play personal bodyguard to me. Originally, I thought I'd be done after this tour. Now? I'm not so sure."

"Has Wolf weighed in?" Adri asked.

"He'd never ask me to quit. Hell, we just found each other again after years of being apart. Back when we first met, Wolf thought by walking away from our relationship he was giving me the courage to live out my dreams. He was correct in that aspect. I don't think I would've chased them had he stayed. My head and heart were so wrapped up in him that I didn't give a damn about my career. It nearly killed me when he left."

"He didn't tell you why he was leaving?"

"Nope." Caitlyn took another sip of the coffee. "I'm not about to let him go a second time. My career isn't worth losing him over. And I know he feels the same way, which is why he wants me to make that decision. He doesn't want to be the reason I walked away from it all."

"It's obvious Wolf loves you very much. But" —Gabby turned on the couch and glared at Adriana— "what's it going to take to get you to spill it? Do I need to go out there and kick Gunner's ass? Is he being mean?"

Adri's gaze widened at Gabby's misinterpretation. "You got it wrong. Gunner's been nothing but a gentleman. He's taking care of all my needs since I didn't get a chance to bring anything with me. It's just ... nothing is happening if you get my drift. He's avoiding me and I don't know why."

"So, you haven't slept with him?" The glance Gabby gave Caitlyn had Adri wondering what exactly she was getting at and why it would even matter.

Something wasn't adding up. Gabby had never questioned her relationship with Gunner when she lived in Oregon. They had been friends and nothing more. At the time, Adri was afraid to cross that line with him and possibly put him in danger.

"Is there a reason we shouldn't? I thought you were on my side, Gabs, wanting Gunner and me to be together. You seemed to push me in that direction before I left Oregon. What's going on? Am I no longer good enough?" Adri furrowed her brow. "Is there something I should know, Gabs? Caitlyn? A crook in his penis or some disease he's not telling me about?"

Caitlyn nearly spit the coffee, then coughed into her hand. "I would hardly know what his ... uh ... appendage looks like."

"Then what's with the look you two are giving each other?" She looked back to Gabby. "We aren't supposed to be keeping secrets. What's up with you suddenly wanting to know if I had sex with Gunner?"

"Did you?"

"No. Not that I would have turned him down."

Gabby glanced away. "I was curious is all. I know it's none of my business."

Adri lightly gripped her friend's chin, bringing back her gaze. "There's a reason you wanted to know. You've never once asked me if Mateo and I slept together."

"Ewww…"

"My point exactly. Why Gunner? Does he have a girlfriend I'm not aware of?"

Gabby clasped Adri's hands. "God, no. He hasn't dated since you left. Hell, he moped around like a lovesick fool. We all know you are what's best for Gunner. That's why we're here, Adri. We protect our family. And even if you and I weren't best friends, we'd do so because of how Gunner feels for you."

"How does he feel about me?"

She laughed. "You have to be blind not to see Gunner is head-over-heels in love with you, girlfriend. I felt the unease between the two of you out there. I was hoping by getting you talking we might help you fix it."

Adri placed a finger between her lips and bit lightly on the tip of her nail. Lord, she loved Gunner. Was it possible he loved her as well? "He did come all the way to La Paz to rescue me. That says something. Right?"

"You think anyone other than the Sons would be dumb enough to piss off the cartel? Hell, Adri, he cut the head off one of Mateo's men a couple of months ago and sent it back to him in a potato sack, taunting Mateo. He's been waiting for the son of a bitch to come after him ever since. When Mateo didn't, he hired a pilot to go after you, keeping the Sons in the dark about his whereabouts. This mission was about you. That speaks volumes."

Her anger and annoyance at being so easily dismissed the last few days deflated out of her like a day-old balloon. Maybe, she was being too hard on him. If it were true that Gunner cared for her, then what could his reason be for dodging her at every turn?

"Maybe. But it doesn't explain why he's seemingly avoiding me. We've barely spent any time together the last few nights." Adri signed heavily. "I mean, I've got the bed to myself, Tag sleeps on the sofa, and Gunner has been sleeping outside on the hammock where it's cold enough at night for him to catch his death."

"Did you ask him to share the bed?" Gabby asked.

Adri nodded. "And the one night we did, we almost, maybe would have if we hadn't been interrupted by Tag being mauled by a bear."

"What?" Caitlyn gasped. "But he looks like he's one hundred percent okay."

Adri filled them in on how Gunner miraculously cleaned and stitched his wounds. "Tag healed rather quickly. No infection. Apparently, Gunner missed his calling as a doctor. But since that night, Gunner has conveniently kept himself busy and out of the cabin."

Gabby laid her hand on Adri's knee. "Have you told him how you feel?"

"I told him as much, that I was his."

"But did you tell him you loved him?"

She shook her head. "I've caused him so much trouble anyway. Look at the whole situation. I've put you all in danger. Gunner is better off without me. You all are."

Gabby said, "Tell him how you feel and let him decide what's best for him."

"You ran away from Ryder months ago. I had to come to get you. Remember? You were a sobbing ass."

"How could I forget?" Gabby smiled, her cheeks reddening. "Ryder was a party to the murder of my uncle, but I forgave him long ago. Had it not been by the Sons of Sangue's hands, someone else would have taken his life. My uncle Raúl was a bad man. I wasn't blind."

"Like I was with Mateo?"

"Mateo took over my uncle's business. You had no way of knowing." Gabby squeezed her hand. "You did the right thing once by breaking things off with him and moving to Oregon. Do the right thing again and give Gunner a chance."

Adriana released Gabriela's hand and sat back. Could she tell Gunner how she felt? And if she did, would it make a difference? Adri wasn't sure her heart could stand the rejection. But worse yet, if she didn't try and lost Gunner as a result, then she would live her life fearing she had lost him because she had been a coward.

"If I get the chance later, I will talk to him."

"That's the smartest thing I heard all day." Caitlyn winked. "Don't lose years with him, the way I did with Wolf."

"I'll make sure you get a moment alone with him," Gabby said to Adri. "Gunner will thank me later."

"I sure hope you're right. Otherwise, I don't think I could stand the embarrassment."

Gabby drew Adri into a hug and whispered, "Tell him you love him, Adri. I promise you won't regret it."

Unshed tears stung the back of her eyes. Adri hoped Gabby was correct because spending a life without Gunner in it was no longer an option she wanted to entertain.

CHAPTER THIRTEEN

The Sons of Sangue sat in a circle surrounding a roaring campfire, sharing tales and passing whiskey bottles. Tag was getting an earful of their past shenanigans, minus any vampire happenings. Smoke stood from his folding chair near the fire ring and nodded his head at Gunner, indicating he should join him. Gunner dusted off the front of his jeans as he stood, then followed his VP a good distance away from the others. The Sons would likely pick up on their conversation, but they were far enough from Tag that he wouldn't be able to hear.

"Spike called earlier."

"Something going down at the Washington clubhouse I should know about, Smoke?" Gunner asked.

"He got word from one his brothers in the Devils ... said Mateo was spotted north of the border, just outside of Santa Barbara." Smoke rubbed his hands together. The night was falling with a chill settling in the air. "The rest of the Sons and I think maybe it's best you get Adriana out of here. Let us handle the cartel business."

"You're kidding, right?" Anger quickly simmered beneath his skin, burning hot and bright, threatening to bring out his vampire. Tag sat several feet away; it wouldn't do for him to witness Gunner's transformation. Gunner bit back his rising ire. "Fuck that. I said before Mateo was mine. You sure in the hell aren't taking that away from me, Smoke. You or any of my brothers."

Smoke laid a hand on his shoulder, giving it a light squeeze. "I get it. But think about Adriana for a moment instead of yourself. Dude, she's human. If she gets caught in the crossfire of this, she may get killed. You really want to take a chance on that?"

"What about Tag? He's human."

"If things go south for him, do I have your permission to save him?"

Gunner narrowed his gaze. "You mean turn him?"

Smoke nodded. "We can use another good vampire on the team. And I like him. He's got a big set of balls, flying you down to cartel country with your hare-brained rescue mission."

"If the only other choice is the grave, then turn him. It's my fault he's here in the first place. He doesn't deserve any of this, and yet, here he is. You can talk to the rest of the Sons, but I'm sure they'll agree to you giving him your blood if something should get hairy."

"Then we agree? You and Adriana should get out of Helena? I think you should leave as soon as possible, maybe even tonight."

"Why the fuck so soon? Hell, the party just got started. You know something I don't?"

Smoke laughed. "Dude, I just want to give you a head start. If they travel non-stop, they could arrive in less than twenty hours. Given your impetuous motorcycle purchase on your credit card, it won't be long before they find us. We want to be ready, and we'd best do that without having to worry about you or Adriana."

Gunner rubbed his lightly whiskered chin. Smoke had a solid point. If Gunner was transfixed on keeping Adri safe then he could easily miss any oncoming threat, putting Adri in danger. This time, Mateo might not be so forgiving where she was concerned. Gunner couldn't chance that Mateo might want her dead. But, fuck, it damn near killed him to leave Mateo to his brothers. That motherfucker should be his. His ego, though, needed to take a backseat to keeping Adri alive. Draining Mateo of his life's blood was one temptation he might have to miss out on.

"Can't you chain the son of a bitch up, then let me have him?" Gunner hated the idea of leaving the honors to one of his brethren.

"What purpose would that serve? Let us take care of it, dude. You don't want Adri looking back on this knowing it was you who took him out."

Gunner hated to admit it, but his VP had a point. Adri had at one time been in love with Mateo. If he delivered the killing blow, would she one day resent him for it? Gunner didn't think so, but he couldn't take the chance. Ryder and Gabby's relationship had barely stood his betrayal of taking down her uncle Raúl, even though it hadn't been Ryder who delivered the killing blow. Viper had gotten the honors since Raúl had been the one to kill his son Ion.

"I can't argue with your logic, even if I want to. Every part of my being wants to be the one to kill the motherfucker." Gunner looked up at the cabin. Warm lights glowed in the windows. Adri was likely in there catching up with Gabby. Telling her they had to leave wasn't going to sit well with her. "We'll leave at daybreak."

"Why wait?"

Gunner used his thumb to indicate the way leading to the cabin. "Because she needs time with Gabby. I'm not about to interrupt their little reunion."

"You got a point," Smoke laughed. "I think we're best to stay out here and away from their gossip. Let's get back to the whiskey; the hell with the coffee Tag brought out."

"You won't get any argument from me. I'm just glad you guys thought to bring some with you." Gunner slapped Smoke on the back. "Let's rejoin them. If I'm to leave at daybreak, I'll at least get some camaraderie tonight."

Gunner sat back on his empty chair flanked by Smoke and Tag. Diablo, Ryder, Wolf, and Neo sat across the fire. "Where's Angel, Diablo? She wasn't up for the long ride?"

Diablo took a sip of the whiskey, then used his shirt sleeve to wipe the top of the bottle. "She stayed back at the shelter. A few residents checked in last week. Angel didn't want to drop everything into Lisa's hands. That, and she's keeping an eye on my son Tyler. I wasn't about to drag him out here. He's too young to get involved in my affairs."

"Can't say I blame you."

"Speaking of," Diablo rose. "I should call her and let her know we arrived. She's bound to be worried."

Gunner watched his Sergeant at Arms walk off in the direction of the back porch as he pulled a phone from his jean pocket. Gunner couldn't help but envy him. Although Angel had found out accidentally about Diablo's vampire side, she hadn't freaked the fuck out. Now, they were a mated pair, something Gunner wished for with Adri.

Maybe once this was over, he'd approach her with the idea of becoming his ... permanently. He wouldn't mind the idea of sharing his life with her for eternity. Gunner just hoped she felt the same way. Otherwise, he'd have no choice but to cut her loose again. Adri hadn't been allowed to make her own decisions where Mateo was concerned, right down to their upcoming nuptials. She deserved to have a voice, and if that was for her to walk away and live her own life without entanglements, then Gunner meant to let her go.

Grabbing the bottle of whiskey Diablo set in the dirt at the foot of his chair, Gunner took a long pull and welcomed the burn that followed. Hopefully, when this mess was behind them, Adri would choose him, vampire and all.

"You can't be serious?" Adriana glared at Gunner.

Just when she thought she couldn't get more frustrated with him. First his inattention and now he wanted her to pack up and leave. Gabby and Caitlyn had just arrived less than twenty-four hours ago. She wasn't about to go anywhere.

"I'm not going to run from Mateo if that's what your plan is. If he shows up, and we don't know for sure that he will, then I'll face the threat even if it means leaving with him to protect all of you. Running won't stop him from looking for me."

Gunner gripped her shoulders lightly. "Babe, think about it. Mateo is coming and he won't be coming by himself. I can't chance you might get killed in the crossfire."

"You don't seem too worried about the others. Anyone could be caught in the gunfire. It's me he's after. If I'm here, then I have a better chance of stopping him. Maybe I can reason with him."

"Reason with him?" Gunner laughed incredulously.

He stepped back and paced the small area between the kitchen and the living area. His boots thudded heavily off the scarred wood, attesting to his agitation. Was she scared of Mateo? Hell, yes. But what Adriana feared more was, if she left them to stand against Mateo and his army, someone else would lose their life, and that she couldn't live with.

When Gunner had come to the cabin before sunup, he'd asked Gabby and Caitlyn to give them a little privacy. Adri wouldn't have cared if they'd stayed. As far as she was concerned, Gunner could damn well say what he had to say in front of them. But his asking her to pack her belongings had taken her by surprise. Gunner was delusional, though, if he thought for a moment Mateo would not continue to look for them. He'd likely have his soldiers slaughter everyone left behind while he continued his hunt.

Gunner stopped his pacing, his warm eyes holding hers hostage. If she didn't know better, she'd swear he felt much the same way about her that she did him. "Mateo isn't after them. It's you he wants, babe, and I'm not about to allow him to take you, not again. Or worse, kill you for disobeying. Have you thought of that? Don't underestimate him."

He had a point. Adri couldn't help but remember the young man who'd lent her his cell. The bloody image was forever burned in her brain. Gunner was correct, she couldn't rule out Mateo doing the same thing to her. Maybe the best thing she could do for everyone would be to disappear in the hope he'd leave everyone else alone in his quest to find her.

And that meant Gunner as well.

If he got caught in Mateo's crossfire, she might as well step in front of one of Mateo's bullets because Adri no longer wanted to live without the man standing before her. She loved him with her whole being, even if she'd yet to utter the words.

Gunner had bravely come to her rescue when she'd thought all was lost. If she had told him no instead of making a hasty decision to follow her heart all of this could've been avoided. Maybe had she stayed in Mexico, Adri might have even convinced Mateo to leave the Sons of Sangue alone and not follow through with his need for vengeance.

Adri held out her hand. "Give me the keys to the car. I'll pack my belongings and say my goodbyes everyone."

"We aren't taking that claustrophobic cage. We'll take my bike and leave the car for Tag, should he need it."

"I am agreeing to leave, Gunner, but you're staying here with your MC brothers. I'm not putting anyone else in danger. And that includes you. This is on me and the choices I made. Tell Mateo if he comes here that I left and he can damn well find me. That you have nothing more to do with me. You have to convince him, Gunner, or he will kill you." Adri gripped Gunner's hand and entwined her fingers with his. "Assure him you don't know where I am."

"I'm no coward, Adri. I told you before that Mateo should worry about me, not the other way around. If I get a hold of that motherfucker, he will die. Besides, Mateo won't believe me, not for a second, if I even thought to go with your cockamamie idea. The La Paz airport has a record of our being there. He knows who took you." He brought her hand up to his lips and kissed the back of it. "There is no way in hell I'm turning you loose. What I said the other night, I meant. I will damn well protect my own."

Adriana sucked in a shallow breath. He really considered her his? "If that's true, then why have you been ignoring me?"

Gunner dropped her hand and looked away. He was hiding something; she could feel it in her bones. "It's complicated."

"There isn't anything you can tell me that we can't work out." She placed her palm over his heavily beating heart, gaining back his dark gaze. "Unless you have a girlfriend or…"

"Fuck." His large hands palmed her cheeks, his nearly black gaze holding her captive. "There is no one else, Adri. I swear to all that's holy, if you walk away from me again I'll go to my grave lonely."

"I can't let anything happen to you. If I go…" she whispered.

"I'll go with you. Understood?"

She nodded, not really wanting to go without him. Adri had put on a brave face, but in all honesty, she'd wanted Gunner by her side.

Always.

Dropping her gaze to his lips, Adri wanted him to kiss her. His full lips were meant for kissing, and yet, even in the darkness of the room, he hadn't kissed her on the mouth. She hadn't argued as his lips had been almost everywhere else. But now? She wanted them on her lips, to taste him, savor him, drink him in.

"Ah, hell," was all he said before he lowered his head and slanted his lips over hers.

Gunner pulled her flush against him, his groin growing hard between them. There was no mistaking he wanted the same thing, but for now, there wasn't time. Fisting his shirt, she anchored herself, licking the seam of his mouth and gaining access. Gunner groaned, his tongue sweeping hers before entering her mouth as she wished for another part of his anatomy to fulfill her. If they only had more time…

Something sharp scraped the pad of her tongue; the metallic flavor of her blood tickled her senses.

Gunner quickly released her, stepping back. "I'm sorry, I should've been more careful."

Did he have a jagged tooth? "It's okay, Gunner. Really. I'm sure it's just a scratch and I think it's already begun to heal."

He ran a hand through his hair, looking as though he wanted to say something, but then he turned and walked to the bedroom. Adri quickly followed. By the time she got there, he was jamming some of their clothes into a backpack.

"Grab whatever else you need to take; I can put your things in the sidesaddles. We really should get on the road."

Gunner wouldn't even look at her. Was he fretting about cutting her tongue? She walked over to the bed and placed her hand on his forearm, stopping him. "Gunner, I'm alright. Hell, I wish you wouldn't have stopped kissing me."

A lopsided grin grew on his face. "Good. Because when we get where we're heading, I plan to do a lot more of that."

Adri smiled. "Promise?"

"Babe, I plan to do a hell of a lot more than kiss you." His tongue darted out, swiping his lower lip as though still savoring her taste. "Get your things so we can get on the road."

Adri ran and grabbed a small grocery sack from the kitchen and, upon her return, started putting the rest of her things into it. The sweet spot between her thighs thrummed in anticipation of his promises. She planned to hold him to them as soon as they stopped for the day. No more distractions.

Just the two of them.

He handed her a helmet. "Ready?"

"I feel like I've been waiting a lifetime already."

Gunner chuckled. "Your wait is about over, babe. Fuck, all I can think about is getting inside you."

"Then why are we standing here talking?"

"Damned if I know."

Adri followed him through the cabin, carrying her helmet and small bag. Truth be told, she wasn't even nervous about giving herself to him. All she could think was *it's about time*.

Reaching the Sons crew and Gabby and Caitlyn, they quickly said their goodbyes. Adri gave them both a hug and promised to catch up with them once the Sons of Sangue stopped Mateo and his men.

"Stay safe," Gabby said. "I know Gunner will protect you, but don't do anything stupid like thinking you can handle this shit on your own."

"What about you and Caitlyn?" Adri couldn't help but fear for them. The cartel soldiers were ruthless. Hard telling how many men Mateo would have with him.

"I know you don't understand. But, Adri, just know it's Mateo who should be worried. Not the other way around. Caitlyn and I will be fine."

Gabby was correct. Adri didn't understand at all, but she didn't have the time to question her friend, not with Gunner already heading for his motorcycle. She gave each girl another quick hug and jogged in Gunner's direction. Her stomach clenched at the sight of him waiting for her. Whether it was from nerves or anticipation she wasn't sure. Next stop, Adri wasn't going to let Gunner off the hook. He had made promises that she meant for him to keep.

CHAPTER FOURTEEN

EIGHT HOURS ON THE BACK OF GUNNER'S MOTORCYCLE AND they were finally nearing their destination. Adri wasn't one to complain, but her backside felt every one of those two-hundred-plus miles. She was feeling like the Runaway Bride and the Road to Hell. Had it not been for stopping for food and restroom breaks along the way so she could stretch her tired and sore muscles, Adri feared not being able to lift her leg high enough to get off the back of his bike. Her ass felt permanently fused to the leather seat. Long hours in the comfort of an automobile she could handle. Straddling a much smaller seat was an entirely different story.

Too bad Gunner had felt it necessary to leave Tag the car or she might've offered to follow. It wasn't like Tag didn't have transportation. He had the plane.

Okay, so maybe it wasn't practical, but still.

When Gunner had stopped to gas up a few hours ago, he had called Smoke with their whereabouts and to check on the Sons' current situation. Thankfully, Mateo had yet to show his face. Half an hour later, Gunner had received a text telling him that Sawyer "Sting" Barnett had booked them a cabin near Saint Mary's Lake in northern Montana. Gunner's VP had felt it best to register the cabin with Sting's alias, since he had yet to patch over to the Sons, hoping to throw Mateo and his soldiers off their trail. They had stopped long enough to enter the address into the map on his cell. After memorizing the directions, he removed the battery and continued on their way toward Glacier National Park in northern Montana.

The remote location would provide them cover until Mateo and his men were taken out. Or at least that had been Gunner's hope. Adri prayed he was correct because she sure in the hell didn't want to be responsible for even one more death, not when it came to her friends and his MC. Going back to Mateo was no longer an option. Either it would seal her fate at becoming his wife or he'd kill her outright for daring to disobey. Not to mention that Mateo wouldn't stop until he got his revenge on the Sons of Sangue.

It was simple.

Mateo needed to be taken down.

Passing through a fenced-in property, Gunner stopped long enough to close and secure the gate before continuing down the stone driveway. He pulled up to a small cedar-sided cabin. It looked to be well-kept and slightly larger than the one they had come from in Helena. Gunner cut the engine, stepped over his seat on the bike, then helped her alight.

Adri removed her helmet, placing it on the seat before taking a gander at their surroundings. The cabin squatted down the long lane at the rear of the property while fencing encompassed what looked to be at least three acres of ground. Woods surrounded the outside perimeter but left the fenced-in area clear of brush, giving them a clear view should anyone approach from the front and sides. The back was an entirely different matter. Mateo and his men could easily sneak up on them via the woods behind.

Gunner hung his helmet from the handlebar grip, then took her hand and led her up the two steps to the small porch. He punched the six numbers Smoke had texted him into the keypad and opened the door, allowing Adri to walk ahead of him. The interior walls were painted a warm tan with a few rustic decorations and nature-themed pictures hanging on the wall. A pair of bull horns hung over the entrance. A cream-colored throw rug adorned the center of the room adding a bit of warmth to the hardwood floors.

A leather loveseat and end table sat against one wall with a small table and two chairs flanking the opposite side. The kitchen wasn't much bigger but had the cutest red retro appliances. A wood-burning stove no doubt would heat the entire cabin, being centrally located between the kitchen and the seating area. Adri was pleasantly surprised to find a stackable washer and dryer in an alcove just off the kitchen. The cabin wasn't large by any means but was well-equipped to provide shelter and comfort.

While Adri finished looking around, Gunner left to scout the grounds before moving his motorcycle to the back of the property. Following his outdoor inspection, he returned, closed the door, and locked it. Gunner tossed their bags onto the loveseat, then walked to each window, drawing the curtains. The living area bore no drapes, but the added natural light would help the cabin from appearing too claustrophobic.

"I found a small shed out back where I was able to store my bike, keep it out of sight." Gunner opened the fridge to find it empty. "Nice place to hunker down for a bit but I'll need to go to the store we passed several miles back. We're going to need to stock up. Will you be all right staying here a few days?"

Adri's face and neck heated, knowing how Gunner must feel with her having come from such extravagance. "It's perfect."

"You're used to better."

"I'd rather be here any day over Mateo's fortress. I spent most of the time in my bedroom … alone. If I left the room, it was with an escort."

"You weren't allowed to roam free even in your own home?"

"It was Mateo's, not mine. I was merely a guest … or dare I say his captive." Gunner glanced away. Adri wished she knew what was going on in his head. "Honest, Gunner, this place is quite cozy."

"Cozy?" He chuckled drearily then grabbed his bag and pulled out a bottle of whiskey. Uncapping it, he took a long pull, then said, "This entire cabin could probably fit in your suite back in La Paz. Christ, I can't begin to give you what Mateo did."

"You're under the impression those things matter to me."

His gaze came back to her as he set down the bottle on the stand next to the loveseat. "What does matter to you, Adri?"

She took a couple of steps, stopping just shy of him. "Certainly not where I lay my head. Your impression of me is off the mark. My friends matter. You matter, Gunner. If you're okay, then that's what I care about. I could live in a tent if it meant getting away from Mateo. I thought I was stuck in La Paz, stuck marrying a man I abhorred. But then you came along, saving me from a life not worth living."

His darkened gaze was his only response.

"I don't think I could ever thank you enough for coming for me. I didn't deserve your heroism."

At first, she didn't think he'd yet respond. But then he licked his lips and said, "You being here is all the thanks I need but I'm no hero, Adri."

"You put yourself in danger—"

He placed a palm on her cheek, stopping her from saying anything further. "And I'd do it all over again. A hundred times if that's what it would take."

"Why?" She had to know his true reason for flying to La Paz, putting not only himself at risk but Tag as well.

"Isn't it obvious?" He moved his hand to her shoulder, drawing her closer. "Because I fucking ... care about you. I have since the first day I saw you in that cantina in Mexico, even knowing you belonged to someone else. Part of me didn't care that you were engaged. I wanted you for myself, but the timing wasn't right. When you showed up in Oregon, I thought maybe I had a chance. I think I spent more time in Oregon while you were there than I did in Washington, just wanting to be in your company. Hoping you might notice me."

Gunner had paused before telling her that he cared. Was it possible she meant more to him than just a friend? Adri loved Gunner, heart and soul. She could only hope that one day he'd feel the same. "You never told me how you felt, Gunner."

"You had just broken up with your fiancé. I didn't want to be a burden. I thought I had time. That you would be around for a while so we could get to know each other better but then you left. You got on his yacht and never looked back."

"Is that what you think? I left to protect you. All of you. Mateo destroyed Ryder and Gabby's beach house, almost taking several of us with it. I wish I could've seen Mateo's true nature when I first met him, but it took him taking over Gabby's uncle's business for me to see the level of evil he was … is capable of. I'm so sorry, Gunner. I should've stayed in Oregon with Gabby … with you."

He leaned closer, his lips scant inches away, and whispered, "And if you had?"

"I would've had months to show you how I felt. I wasn't going anywhere, or so I thought at the time."

"What am I to you then, babe? A friend?"

Adri dropped her gaze to his mouth, hoping for his kiss. "I think you know better."

His breath fanned her lips, causing them to tingle in anticipation. "Do I?"

She lost the ability to speak, drawn in by his dark gaze, and only nodded. Lord, she loved this man. She wanted to grab on and never let go. If she only had the guts to tell him.

"You have my promise, babe, I won't allow Mateo to take you from me ever again, nor anyone for that matter. You're mine," he said, then slanted his lips over hers.

He slid his hand from her shoulder to her nape, anchoring her as he deepened the kiss. His free hand snaked around her back, pulling her flush. Gunner used his tongue to gain entrance to her mouth. His kiss felt like a possession, like he was sealing a promise never to be broken. Adri savored his taste of man and whiskey, her tongue whispering over his. Lord, she wanted more … more than she'd ever wanted from another. Moving her hands up his chest, she flattened them over his sternum. His heart beat incredibly fast against her palms. She wanted his mouth over hers, his cock inside her. Her knees weakened at the idea of having him take her body and soul. Gunner must have known what she wanted, what she desired. His hard length lay trapped between them as testament.

Slipping a hand down his steely abdomen to his rigid groin, she pressed her palm against him, drawing a moan from him. He deepened his kiss and tightened his hold. Her body aligned with every hard inch of his. She had waited long enough. When Mateo had arrived months ago and she had willingly boarded his yacht, Adri thought she had destroyed any chance she might've had with Gunner. But she'd been given another shot.

The heady thought that Gunner might love her warmed her heart and gave her hope for her future, a future with Gunner.

Dare she hope for a life with him though while Mateo still drew breath? Adri feared the worst, that the Sons might fail and Mateo would yet threaten Gunner's life. Should anything happen to him she'd never forgive herself. As much as she hated Mateo, she would do anything, sacrifice anything to spare Gunner's life. Her heart ached, fearing the very real possibility.

Life was so full of uncertainties and what-ifs that she felt the need to seize the given opportunity to be with her true love. Adri would be damned before turning down this blessed second chance. She'd make it a memory to last a lifetime. Or better yet, hopefully, this would be the start of their life together, for she'd never stop loving the man before her. Adri silently prayed the Sons would be successful in taking down Mateo. Never had she wished the death of another, but today she longed for it.

CHAPTER FIFTEEN

GUNNER BROKE THE KISS AND STEPPED BACK, TURNING HIS face away, knowing his eyes were unnaturally black. He rubbed the short hair at the base of his skull and avoided looking at her. Lord, they hungered for the same release. The scent of her desire tickled his nose and brought out the monster in him.

Only once before had Adri seen his vampire unleashed, right before he'd erased her memory of it. He was only a fraction away from fucking things up again, maybe for good this time. His gums ached with the oncoming emergence of his fangs. If he took things any further, there would be no holding the beast back.

"I'm sorry. That shouldn't have happened."

Adri took a step forward. "Gunner—"

He put out his hand, stopping her. "Give me a moment."

"What's wrong?"

Gunner meant to walk away but Adri gripped his chin, forcing him to look at her. He stared down at her with his ink-filled gaze, waiting for her to acknowledge the anomaly.

She dropped her hold and stepped back. "What in the world?"

Gunner reached out to stop her but she continued to stagger until her legs met with the loveseat and she dropped onto it. He could hypnotize her, make the deviation slip from her memory. But that no longer seemed like a viable option. Gunner wanted her to see the real him, vampire and all. If she could handle the truth, that he wasn't completely human, then maybe he could one day ask her to be his mate.

Lord, he wanted nothing more than to have her for all of eternity.

He wasn't about to allow her to retreat. Not this time. Gunner approached the loveseat and knelt before her. Grasping her trembling fingers, he brought her hands to his face, laying her palms against his flesh so she could feel the change in him. Muscles stretched, and bones popped, causing her eyes to widen.

Her breath stuttered out of her. "I don't understand."

"You will." Gunner pulled back his lips on his emerging fangs. "What you see is real, babe."

"Vampire?" Adri pulled back her hands, tucking them under her legs. "Oh, my God."

Gunner reached out to touch her, but she jerked away. "I won't hurt you, Adri. Never that."

"But will you … bite me?"

He smiled sadly. "Only if you ask me to."

Her brow furrowed as she placed her hand over her neck, no doubt fearing he might attack. "And why the hell would I ask you to do that?"

"Because it can be pleasurable when done right."

Adri's shoulders shuddered in what Gunner could only surmise was distaste. "I'll have to take your word on that."

"You have to know I would never take anything not freely given from you."

"Does anyone else know what you are?"

"The Sons of Sangue do."

"And they're okay with it?"

"Of course. They're also vampires."

Her brow crinkled again. "All of them?"

Gunner nodded, reaching for her hand. This time she allowed his touch.

"And Gabby knows this? Wait…" Her mind seemed to drift off as she glanced over his shoulder before looking back at him, her eyes widening. "I remember. She never reacted to Ryder looking like a vampire … looking like you do now."

"You remember seeing Ryder?" he whispered, barely audible.

She shook her head, looking away again. "I'm not sure. It seems like I dreamt it and somehow I'd forgotten about it … until now."

"You believe that you saw Ryder … as a vampire?"

"I saw you as well. Not that long ago." Adri looked back at him. "How could I have forgotten?"

"You recall everything?"

"It seems foggy, but yeah, I sort of remember. You kissed me right before… I don't know. It's like my memory is playing tricks. Kind of like I dreamt what happened. Was the kiss real, Gunner? Did I see you as I do now? Or was it all just a dream?"

Gunner placed his palm on her cheek, running his thumb over her bottom lip. "It was real, babe. I hypnotized you. I needed to make you forget."

"I faintly remember you telling me that. So you hypnotized me?"

He nodded his head.

"Why would you do that to me?"

"Because no one is supposed to know about us."

"Vampires?"

"Correct." He dropped his touch. "The world is not ready for our secret. They wouldn't understand."

"I'm still processing it and I know you. You're a vampire? Ryder, Smoke, Wolf, they are all... Vampires exist?"

"I'm still the same person I was five minutes ago. Ryder, Smoke, and Wolf are the same. Being a vampire doesn't change who we are."

Her lips turned down in distaste. "Only that you drink blood."

He nodded again. "To survive. But we don't need to kill humans. We only take what we need. There are women, called donors, who know what they are offering us. They are sworn to secrecy in order to feed us safely. If we can't get a donor, then we need to hypnotize the human into forgetting the process of communion."

"But I now remember. What if the person you hypnotize remembers as well?"

"You also said your recollection was like a dream. I imagine if anyone's memory returns, they will assume the same because to believe vampires are real would go against the lie they've been taught all their lives."

Adri reached out and used her fingers to push up his upper lip, exposing his fangs again. "But here you are. Real as any predator."

"I'm not a monster, babe, but yes, vampires are real. Will that change anything? How you feel about me?" Lord, he wasn't sure he wanted the answer, but he had to ask anyway.

"I'm not sure—"

"Please don't walk away, not that. I can make you forget again if it's too much to handle."

She pointed a finger against his sternum. "Don't you dare use your mind tricks against me again, Gunner, or I'll…"

"You'll what?" He grinned, feeling a little more secure. She hadn't run out of the room screaming, nor did she appear abhorred as she had moments ago. "You won't let me touch you?"

Gunner ran a hand up the inside of her calf, stopping at her knee. Fuck, he could scent her desire kick up just from his mere touch. He couldn't help pushing her a bit further. He moved his hand up her thigh, stopping just shy of her V. Her breath caught; her eyes fixated on his.

Gunner licked his lips, his gaze now staring at the juncture of her thighs. "Do you know how bad I want to taste you?"

"I believe you already have," she whispered. "We kissed just moments ago."

He chuckled at her naivety. "Not there, here," he said as he ran a finger slowly down her center, covered by her jeans.

Adri sucked in a breath. Gunner detected a rise in her desire. Hell, he wanted to run his tongue along the same path, taste her. Fuck, he wanted far more than that. He wanted to possess her heart and soul.

"I should probably stop."

"Why?"

"Because if I don't, babe, I'll carry through. I'll fuck you and I won't stop until I make you mine. And I won't share. Not now ... not ever. You best know what you are signing up for before you say yes."

"Yes," her whispered reply carried to his ears.

As if the pressure in his jeans a moment ago wasn't bad enough.

Gunner stood and headed for the front door, locking the deadbolt. He sure in the hell didn't want any interruptions for the next several hours. His trip to the store could wait. When he turned, the sight before him damn near stole his breath. Adri stood, pulling her shirt over her head, leaving her top half covered only by a deep purple lace bra that she must have purchased back in Helena with his money.

Damn, he certainly approved.

She wiggled out of her jeans, producing a matching thong that barely covered her. His nostrils flared. Even standing across the room from her he could scent her desire which was like a match to kindling. Just seeing her in that coordinating ensemble set him afire. Lord, he feared he wouldn't last long. It had been far too long since he last fucked a woman. But this wasn't that ... never with Adri. He wanted to take his time. Hell, he wanted to make love to her. If he couldn't tell her how he felt, then he'd damn well show her.

Adri looked at him with apprehension, obviously uneasy with what she had just agreed to. Fuck, he couldn't blame her. Gunner stood before her as a monster, a fully turned vampire. There was nothing normal about what she now beheld.

Closing the distance, he gripped her hands and brought them to his chest. "Are you sure, babe?"

She nodded but said nothing.

"I won't hurt you." Gunner dropped her hands and framed her face, grinning slyly. "And I promise not to bite."

"You said it could be pleasurable."

Her sudden acceptance brought out his chuckle. "That it is but I'd never do so without your permission."

"Would you feed from me?"

"Not unless you asked me to."

Adri licked her lips. "Are you hungry?"

"Lord, for more than your blood." He groaned. "You have no idea."

"Then take my blood, Gunner. I want to know what it feels like."

"I—" *Shit*. He stepped back and ran a hand down his face. He couldn't even put into words what her admission did to him. His heart swelled. If he took her blood, there would be no turning back for him. He'd want her as his mate and he'd do everything in his power to make it so.

"Please."

Gunner tilted his head to the ceiling, needing a prayer … anything to keep him from doing as she asked. "You have no idea what you—"

Her hand on his chest had him looking back at her. Just her touch restarted the fire in him. He no longer wanted to deny her … him. His gaze held hers as he ran his knuckles along the side of her neck. He could hear her pulse pounding through her veins. There was no doubt fear still entered the equation and yet she asked it of him anyway.

"Why?"

"Because if I know how it feels then maybe I won't fear you."

"You fear me now?"

"A little, and I hate that I do. You said you don't take more than you need. You said you don't harm humans. Prove it to me. I want to know everything, Gunner. Please."

His willpower broke with her last whispered plea. Gently cupping the back of her skull, he tilted her head to the side and licked a patch from her collarbone to her ear, earning him a moan. The sound was all the encouragement he needed. Drawing his fangs from behind his lips, he sank them into the side of her neck, tasting her sweet nectar. Never had he tasted anything so fucking sweet. Adri sucked in a breath as her blood began to flow over his tongue. Her hands fisted his shirt as her desire rose. He could scent it, feel it in the way she clung to him, aligning her body fully against his.

He knew she sought release, that the drawing of her blood had driven her toward a climax just out of her reach. Gunner smoothed his free hand down her abdomen to the juncture of her thighs, sliding a finger beneath the purple lace. He dragged it along her already slick folds before sinking it inside her. Fuck, she was wet. Her muscles gripped his finger as she began rocking against his hand. Her breath became shallow.

Gunner suckled her flesh, hard, drawing from her, knowing it would drive her over the edge. Adri cried his name as her muscles convulsed against his fingers, damn near causing him to come. He needed to be inside her ... now. Withdrawing his fangs, he licked the twin holes, sealing them. Gunner picked her up and cradled her against his chest, carrying her to the queen-sized bed in the next room. It wasn't large by any means, but he'd make do. His cock wanted appeasement and Gunner wasn't about to deny it—or Adriana—a second longer.

CHAPTER SIXTEEN

ANTICIPATION HAD ADRI'S BREATH CATCHING IN HER throat. Gunner had just given her an incredible orgasm. Ready to surrender her mind, body, and soul to a man she had secretly loved for months, one she feared never to see again, she couldn't wait to find what making love with him might be like. She shivered at the thought of riding out an even more intense climax. Adri already felt as if her chest might split open due to the fierce drumming of her heart.

Gunner gently laid her atop the queen-sized comforter and stepped back, his ink-filled gaze holding her hostage. Even as a vampire, Adri found Gunner impossibly hot. The worry she spotted in his eyes was unfounded. She wasn't about to go anywhere, not after waiting what seemed like a lifetime. The unleashed vampire didn't scare her. No, Adri found him just as tempting as the apple was to Eve. Maybe, she'd even bite him in return. The thought had her licking her lips, wondering if it might be just as pleasurable.

Without drinking his blood, of course.

Grabbing the shirt collar at his nape, Gunner slowly pulled his T-shirt over his head and tossed it to the side. The thick muscles at his hips looked like handlebars flanking his rock-hard abs. A light dusting of hair traveled down his chest like an arrow, disappearing into the top of the low-riding waistband at his hips.

Adri drew her lower lip between her teeth, getting a peek at the impressive bulge tenting his jeans. She wanted to feel him sliding inside her, every steel inch, and wasn't beneath begging for it. Vampire or not, she wanted to be his now and forever. If he chose to leave once his mission was over, she knew she'd never love another.

Of course, she was setting herself up for heartbreak, but loving him hadn't been an option. It was as necessary to her as drawing her next breath. If there was such a thing as a soul mate, he was it for her. Never had she felt more complete than she did in the past few days. If she had it her way, she'd never leave his side again. She just needed him to admit he wanted the same.

When Gunner had informed her that biting could be pleasurable, it had been an understatement, to say the least. His fangs had triggered a climax like no other and already she was hopeful for him to do it again. There was nothing quite like the feeling of his fangs deep inside her neck, drawing her blood, and giving him complete control over her life ... or death for that matter.

Flipping the button through the hole of his jeans, Gunner stopped her musings cold as he carefully lowered the zipper and pushed his pants from his hips to the floor, revealing again that he preferred going commando as his cock jutted out. She fisted the comforter to keep from reaching for it and appearing too needy. But, boy, was she. He stepped forward and knelt beside her, the mattress dipping beneath his weight.

"Are you sure this is what you want?" Gunner asked, his voice thick from the large fangs filling his mouth.

Adri shivered, thinking of moments ago when those sharp points were gum-deep into her throat, damn near bringing forth another orgasm.

"Will you bite me again?"

His deep chuckle inflamed her. "Only if you'd like."

"Is it safe?"

"If you mean for me to drink more of your blood, then no, it's not without the possibility of you becoming anemic. But to bite you for play? Absolutely. I take it you enjoyed it."

"Very much."

Adri thought of all of the women who came before her and frowned. How many women had he fed from? Given orgasms to? He wasn't even hers and yet she never wanted him to feed from another. The green-eyed monster ran thick through her veins.

Gunner ran his thumb across her lower lip. "A change of mind?"

"The women you spoke of earlier, the society that you feed from?"

The corners of his eyes turned up with his grin. "Jealous?"

"No … maybe." Adri rolled her eyes. "Surely—"

He stopped her next words with a kiss, one so deep it damn near stole her breath. Who cared about anyone before her? She would be his future. Gunner crawled over her, spread her thighs with his knee, and laid between them. Hand at her nape, he used his tongue to mate with hers, leaving the juncture between her thighs throbbing with hunger. His cock nudged against her purple lace thong, keeping him from entering her as she desired.

Pulling back, he looked down on her in primal need. "I'm here with you. You have my promise those other women don't matter, babe. They never did."

"When you feed, do you give them orgasms as well?"

Gunner lifted, bracing his hands on either side of her head. "I'm not saying I haven't fucked some of them. But if they have an orgasm when my only intention is sustenance, that's on them."

"What do you mean?"

"If they have an orgasm, and some do, it's the nature of my kind. It's a sexual act to feed. It's why we have so many willing to give us their blood."

"Then promise me you will only feed from me from now on."

"You have nothing to worry about, babe."

"Why?"

"Because you're all I want. Right now, my cock is aching to get inside you. I've fucking waited months for this."

She bit her lower lip. The idea he had wanted her as she had him was enough to make her drop her worries for the moment. "You have?"

"Damn straight. Now, unless you tell me no, I intend on doing just that."

"Condom?"

He shook his head. "I can't get you pregnant and my vampire DNA keeps me from carrying or contracting diseases."

"How is that even possible?"

Gunner chuckled again. "You sure are full of questions."

She shrugged. "I—"

He kissed her briefly, stilling her words again. "We're done talking. Are you telling me yes or no?"

Adri grinned and nodded her head.

"Thank the fucking saints..."

Gunner wasted little time, sliding down her body, kissing a path to her stomach, and caressing her navel with his tongue before dipping lower to her thong. Adri squirmed beneath him, wanting, needing his tongue between her legs, driving her toward another climax.

"I'll buy you another pair of these." He gripped the purple string at her hip between his fangs and easily ripped the flimsy material from her.

Using his hands, he spread her thighs wider, his black gaze now looking down upon her in hunger, making her every muscle tense with desire. Licking a path up her thighs, he stopped just shy of her already slick folds. He looked at her briefly before dipping his head and dragging his tongue along her slit, causing her to moan.

"Fuck, you taste better than the finest bourbon."

Adri tilted her head into the pillow, her hands still fisting the comforter. Her thighs trembled as his tongue expertly worked her. Using two fingers, he slid slowly in and out of her, adding the friction needed to accomplish her goal. She needed more, just a bit... But before she reached the precipice, he withdrew, earning him damn near a sob.

"Not yet, babe. I want you to come while I'm inside you. I want to feel your orgasm."

Aiming his cock, he slid into her ever so slowly, stretching her fully until he was seated. Drawing in a breath, she relaxed her muscles, allowing him to slide in even further. Adri had never felt more complete, as if she had found her other half. Her heart swelled with the belief there was only one person for her and, thankfully, she had found him.

His warm gaze held hers. "We good?"

Adri nodded, wrapping her legs around his waist and framing his face with her hands. Never had she looked upon anyone more handsome, even in his unnatural state.

"Thank fuck," he muttered, just before he began to move in and out, each powerful stroke shoving her further up the mattress.

Her breath labored; every muscle strained for the pinnacle that seemed just beyond her reach. She moved her hands to the back of his skull, watching him in fascination as his lips peeled back and revealed his long, razor-sharp fangs. She gasped, not out of fright but in anticipation. Gunner dipped his head, moved aside one cup on her bra, and drew the nipple into his mouth, suckling it right before sinking his fangs deep. The quick pinch of pain was quickly soothed by the flood of pleasure, tipping her over the edge. Adri closed her eyes and moaned as she came.

White hot lights exploded like a kaleidoscope behind her eyelids. "Gunner…"

He withdrew his fangs and quickened his pace; his ass muscles tightened beneath her heels. Sliding deeply a final time, he groaned, spilling his seed inside her. He'd said she couldn't get pregnant, but there was a part of her that wished she could carry his child. Gunner rolled to his side and tucked her tightly against him. His heart beat rapidly against her cheek. He lay quiet for so long Adri thought he might've fallen asleep.

"Everything okay?" Adri whispered, not to awaken him if he had.

"Are you kidding me?" His chuckle resonated against her cheek. "I'll never be okay again."

Adri waited for him to elaborate further.

"That was fucking stellar, babe." He kissed the top of her head. "I'm never letting you go."

To death do them part. Nothing felt more right than lying nearly naked in his arms. She still wore the purple lace bra that he had purchased for her. No longer a matching set, she thought with a smile. He was correct about one thing; Adri wasn't about to leave his side again. Mateo be damned.

"Round two?"

Adri looked up at the smile that stretched across his handsome face. "I think I might need a moment of recovery first."

His answering chuckle was the last thing she heard before snuggling into the heat of his hard body and drifting off to sleep.

THE BRISK WIND KICKED UP dust from the dirt road outside the SUV, clouding the view from where he had been sitting the past ten minutes. How the hell had he wound up in the middle of Montana?

Adriana Flores.

He should've listened to his second-in-charge long ago and put a bullet in her insolent fucking skull. Lord, he wasn't sure she was even worth the trouble anymore. Instead of using his instinct, he'd allowed his ego to get in the way. Adriana belonged to him, always had, and it was about damn time she learned that even if he had to kill every one of her friends to prove it.

Mateo Rodriguez buttoned his long double-breasted Saint Laurent wool coat as he stepped from the rented black Mercedes Benz. He grumbled as the dirt dusted his polished shoes and pressed pants. He couldn't get out of here fast enough. This grunt work was for his men, not him, for fuck's sake. A few members of his crew had driven ahead, verifying some of the Sons of Sangue had squatted here. Once they had located and what was thought to be Adriana's last known whereabouts, they had given Mateo the coordinates. Taking a private jet, he flew into a nearby airport, hoping to quickly put this unfortunate situation behind him. The problem was Adriana wasn't anywhere to be found.

So, where was she?

He looked around, the wind tousling his hair. They were in the middle of fucking nowhere. Why anyone would want to live in this wasteland was beyond him. The little cabin he'd spotted down the long lane on his drive-by appeared to be smaller than the bedroom suite she occupied in La Paz.

The ungrateful little bitch.

Oh, he intended on apprehending her and taking her back to Mexico posthaste. She'd be his bride by month's end if he had to duct tape her to do it. Mateo had lost his patience with her and wasn't about to wait a moment longer. He'd planned to fuck Adriana nightly until he got the heirs he needed to one day take over his business. No one outside of his ancestry would do.

As for Adriana's friends? He planned to destroy them. Their blood would be on her hands. This was her fault for defying him. Leave no survivors and he'd be assured this little inconvenience wouldn't happen again.

Two of his men stepped from the dense cover of the forest and jogged over to the SUV. Alejandro stopped short of him. "There are eight of them that I counted, sir, two of which are women."

Mateo rubbed his clean-shaven jaw. This might be easier than he had originally thought. Fifteen of his soldiers, armed to the teeth, stood at the ready to do his bidding. "You get eyes on Adriana?"

"No, sir."

"How long have you been watching their camp?"

"Five hours. We stayed out of sight and far enough back not to alert them that they had company. Using the binoculars, we were able to count eight. I'm sorry, though, we never spotted Adriana among them."

"Damn it. I need to know where she went. Gunner Anderson, the man in the picture I had shown you, was he among them?"

"No, sir. But the pilot who flew them from Mexico, he's here."

"You saw him?"

Alejandro nodded. "Yes. The one that was in the airport security photo."

Mateo's jaw hardened. If the pilot was here, then that meant so were Gunner and Adriana at one time. How far had they gotten while his men stood there with their dicks in their hands wasting more fucking time? Mateo still had the cell number Adriana had used to contact Gunner from his soldier's phone.

"Let me make a call. If he left with her, then no doubt he used his cell at some point."

His driver opened the back door to the SUV and Mateo slipped into the dark interior, quickly dialing his FBI connection. His informant should easily be able to trace the number and maybe even get them a location.

The line picked up. "This is Mateo."

"What can I do for you?"

"I need you to trace this number." Mateo rattled off the digits.

The line went quiet except for the tapping of keys. "Cell is registered to a Gunner Anderson."

"I don't need his fucking name. I need a location."

More tapping keys were heard before the man said, "It appears to have been last used yesterday in Montana."

"I already know that, asswipe. Tell me something I don't know." Mateo was quickly losing what little patience he had.

"Looks like he stopped along Highway 89. He may have removed the battery after that because the trail goes dead."

"Coordinates?"

"I'll text you the exact location," the informant said. Mateo ended the call and stepped from the vehicle, approaching his second in charge.

"Joseph, you, Enrico, and Tobias, you're coming with me." He pointed a finger at the others. "Alejandro and the rest of you? Stay here. Make sure all eight in the camp are dead. No loose ends or I'll have your fucking heads. When it's finished, return to La Paz and wait for me there. We'll take care of Gunner Anderson. When we're done, there will be nothing but pieces. There won't be anything left of these *parásitos*. Adriana will have no choice but to come home with me and be my dutiful *esposa para ser*."

CHAPTER SEVENTEEN

Gunner towel-dried his hair, then wrapped his waist in the terrycloth. Upon exiting the bathroom, he found Adri still sound asleep, her dark hair tousled and hiding part of her face. Lord, she was beautiful. Just seeing her there warmed his heart and brought a smile to his face. He certainly liked being the reason she couldn't get her cute little ass out of bed this morning. Fuck, he simply couldn't get enough of her. But Adri was human after all. He'd need to allow her time to rest.

Vampires were insatiable and it didn't help that Adriana made him even more so.

Around five, Adri had fallen fast asleep again, her slight snore an indicator that he had exhausted her. He may not need much shuteye, but she did. After holding her snug the last few hours before dawn, Gunner rose at five past seven, tucking the blankets around her, and proceeded to the shower. They didn't have much in the way of supplies in the cabin. He'd need to get groceries. He'd spotted a can of coffee the night before, but that wasn't going to sustain her hunger. Gunner, on the other hand, wouldn't need to worry about his for a few days, thanks to Adri taking care of his nourishment.

Heading for the kitchen, his heart warmed as he recalled her insistence that he only feed from her in the future. Adri had been jealous of the donors Draven Smith provided for nutrition. Not that Gunner would miss any of the donors who had accommodated him in the past, but he wasn't sure Adriana would be able, or even want to, keep up with his appetite. If she were the one feeding him, he'd damn well desire sex … multiple times if last night was an indicator. Gunner wasn't sure he'd ever tire of her and yet he feared he had worn her out in less than twenty-four hours.

Dumping some grounds into the filter, Gunner then poured water into the pot. It wasn't long before the pleasant smell of coffee filled the air. Had he stopped for food, he'd also be making her a breakfast of eggs, bacon, and toast. She'd no doubt be famished when she woke.

If he took her to town, Gunner feared it might be more dangerous for her should she be spotted by allies of Mateo. Or he could head out while she snoozed and take a chance she'd be okay until his return. The cabin was out of the way and they were now a couple hundred miles from where Tag's plane had landed. The only ones who knew their whereabouts were the Sons. After Gunner had removed the battery from his cell, making them untraceable, no way Mateo and his men could possibly find them so quickly. Besides, if they had made it as far as Montana, the Sons would take care of them. Mateo and his men didn't stand a chance against a den of vampires. Once Mateo and his crew were out of the picture, then and only then, could they head home.

Home.

Gunner wanted to take Adri to Washington. Her residing in Oregon was not about to happen, not with him much farther north. The problem was he still lived at the clubhouse with a few of his brothers. Granted, he had the bedroom with the en suite, but it wouldn't do if he meant to bring Adri back with him. If she agreed, then finding them a house would be second on his agenda. The first would be getting her to agree to be his mate. He wanted what most of the Oregon Sons had, strong women vampires at their side … and maybe a baby or two if Adri was of the same mind.

He swiped a hand down his face. How the hell had he gone from chasing adrenaline to pursuing a family? The right woman had a way of settling a man down, he supposed. That woman for him was Adriana. With her, he wanted it all, which wasn't about to happen unless he changed his lifestyle.

The soft pad of feet caught his attention as she made her way to the kitchen.

"You didn't sleep long."

Adri shrugged, covering a yawn with the back of her hand. "I smelled coffee."

She wore his T-shirt from the night before, the hem riding just below mid-thigh. And if he guessed correctly, there was nothing beneath it. Damn, it wouldn't do well to get a hard-on with only the towel covering him.

He bit back his sudden rising desire. "Women and their coffee. Unfortunately, there isn't anything to eat in this place. I'll need to go to the store."

"I can go with you."

"I worry about you being seen in town."

"We are miles away, Gunner. I'll be fine."

Adri grabbed a mug from the cupboard and poured herself some coffee. She leaned back against the counter across from him. Taking the mug to her lips and sipping, she moaned.

"You keep that up and we won't be going grocery shopping at all." Her answering smile further warmed his heart. He'd never get tired of seeing her happy. "Finish your coffee, babe, then we can go get you some food."

"I'm pretty sure we covered our trail. But I can stay here and enjoy my coffee while you go if you think that's better. I promise to stay indoors. No one will even know the cabin is inhabited. I'll keep all the lights off and the doors locked."

Gunner doubted that Mateo would've been able to find them so quickly, but he still worried about leaving her side. He couldn't protect her if he wasn't there. Once they got to town, he'd put the battery back into his phone and call his VP to see if they had eyes on Mateo and his soldiers yet.

"How are you feeling, babe?"

"Glorious." Adri smiled again, this one sexy enough to burn the towel from his hips. "A bit sore, but I'm not about to complain."

Gunner laughed. "Then I should give you a few hours of rest."

"Groceries first, big guy. Because now that you mention it, I am getting hungry."

"If you go with me, we can stop at that little diner we passed next to the grocery store a few miles down the road."

"A few? That was at least fifteen minutes from here."

"We could sit here arguing the distance or we could get on the road. Your choice."

"Good point. But shower first and" —Adri stood and stripped the towel from his waist— "I might be needing this. Get dressed, big guy."

Gunner chuckled again, unconcerned about his state of undress as he watched her walk away. He grabbed a cup and poured himself some coffee, taking a few sips of the hot liquid before setting the cup on the countertop. Gunner scratched his whiskered chin. Maybe Adri might need help lathering her back. Approaching the open door, he could hear the water running and imagined it sluicing down her naked form. His cock quickly stood at attention.

Breakfast was going to have to wait.

"Any news?" Gunner asked his VP as he kept sight of Adriana through the window of the fifties-style diner.

He had excused himself from their shared booth a moment ago to make his phone call while she finished her breakfast of bacon, eggs, and hash browns. He could consume human food, though it held no nutritional value, therefore it didn't hold much appeal. Adri, on the other hand, needed to refuel. It had been a good twelve hours since she had consumed much of anything. Following their romp in the shower, they'd quickly dressed and headed for the small town they had passed on their way to the cabin.

"They're here," Smoke informed him.

"You get eyes on them, Smoke? See Mateo?"

"Nope. They haven't come close enough to camp. We could scent them, though. I'm betting they don't realize we know they're out there."

"I need you guys to be careful. Don't underestimate these fucks. I want you all back on the West Coast when this is said and done. No man left behind."

"These fuckers don't stand a chance with us and you know it."

Gunner blew out a small breath. He sure hoped Smoke was correct. But without spotting them, they had no way of knowing how many Mateo brought with him. "Tag? Is he still at camp?"

"He refuses to leave. We tried talking him into flying the fuck out of here."

"He's human."

"You don't think I realize that? One bullet hole and he could be done."

"That happens, you take care of him."

"Of course."

Gunner paced the small sidewalk. He brought Tag into this mess; he wasn't about to let him die. "As we discussed before, you do what you have to in order to keep him alive even if that means giving him vampire blood."

"Kind of unfair if he doesn't know we exist, though. What if he doesn't want to become one of us?"

"What's even more unfair is letting him die."

"Your call, P. Anything happens, I'll give him my blood."

"Good. As I said, no man left behind. Sons and Tag survive at all costs. You want me to leave my battery in my phone so you can get a hold of me? Let me know how things go?"

"Hell, no," Smoke all but growled. "These fucks may have a way of tracing you via the GPS in your cell. The cartel have their fingers everywhere. Call in a day or so. I'm sure it will be over by then. They aren't about to waste their time hanging around Montana. They've already been laying low a few hours."

"Stay safe but give 'em hell, Storm."

He chuckled. "I don't plan on dying in Montana. You keep Adri out of sight and lay low. Let us take care of these fucks."

Gunner bit down on his molars, angry that he wasn't going to be the one to drain the motherfucker. He hated like hell that his men were the ones taking out Mateo and his crew. Fuck, he wanted … needed to be the one to end Mateo's life. But his VP was correct, Adriana's safety came first.

"As much as I hate not being a part of their takedown, you're right. What's important is Adriana." Gunner watched as she finished her breakfast and blotted her mouth with the napkin. He had already paid the bill so she'd likely be heading his way in a few short minutes. "Look, Adri's on her way out of the diner. She doesn't need to hear this shit. You cut that motherfucker's head off for me, Smoke."

"I'll consider it an honor." Gunner heard the smile in Smoke's voice. "You take that battery out of the phone, head North, and I'll talk to you in a day or so."

"Stay safe."

"You too, brother."

And the phone went dead. Gunner powered off the cell, flipped it over in his palm, then took the back off, and popped out the battery. Adriana pushed through the glass and steel doors of the diner, the smile on her face making him feel better about not joining his brethren in fighting the cartel. He'd do just about anything for this woman to protect her, even if his adrenaline-addicted self wanted to head back to Helena and help his brothers drain every one of the sons of a bitches.

"Enjoy your breakfast?"

"Almost as much as my shower."

"Keep that talk up and we won't be getting groceries."

Adri linked an arm through the bend of his. "Who were you talking to?"

"Smoke. I needed to know if they had spotted your ex in Helena."

The smile quickly fled her face. Gunner hated to be the reason. "He's going to kill Mateo?"

"It's the plan, Adri. Him and his men. Are you okay with that?"

She nodded, averting her gaze. "This will never end if he lives. I realize that. But there's a small part of me that remembers the boy I used to know. Maybe hoping he could be redeemed, move on, and find a new love."

He creased his brow. Hearing her speak of Mateo in such a manner started the anger simmering in his gut again. "You still care for him?"

"I shouldn't." She squeezed his forearm from where her hand lay. "Hell, I should detest everything he is. And most of me does. It's just that a small part of me feels like I'm the reason he has to die, you know?"

Gunner unlinked his arm and brought her around to face him, grasping her biceps. "You are not the reason, babe. That man brought this on himself. He burned down Ryder's house, trying to take you with it. Never forget what he's capable of."

"I know." She meant to look away again, but he brought her gaze back to his. "You have a big heart, Adri. You love with the whole of it, but you owe Mateo nothing. And if we don't deal with him now, he'll come back for you time and again. Make no mistake, I'll kill him the moment he comes anywhere near you. I won't even hesitate. But what I don't want is you looking at me, knowing I took his life, and turning this thing between us into something ugly."

Tears gathered in her eyes, but she blinked them away. "I could never hate or despise you. Can't you see, Gunner, that I love you?"

His heart beat against his sternum, filling with the three words she had just spoken aloud. He was afraid to question her, that maybe he had heard incorrectly. Her *Mi amor* came back to mind. "Say that again."

"That I love you?" Her smile returned, filling her gaze ... gone were the unshed tears. "I was afraid to say it aloud in case you didn't feel the same. Or that maybe I was a burden to you."

"God—never that." His vampire simmered just beneath the surface. Gunner couldn't be happier that she felt for him the same. Biting back his fangs emergence, he said, "Adri, I love you. Christ, I always will."

Gunner framed her face, leaned down, and slanted his lips tenderly over hers. It wasn't a deep kiss, one meant to convey the love he had held inside for so long. Lord, he cherished her since the day he laid eyes on her. Her spoken, *"I love you."* Never had anything touched him so deeply. Gunner was halfway to convincing her to be his mate. It wasn't a pledge to be taken lightly. Adri would have to go through the painful change, something he wouldn't wish on his deepest enemy ... well, maybe Mateo deserved the fiery hell. But Adriana did not. He'd hold her through it, channel away as much of the pain as he could. If she said yes, Gunner meant to stay by her side the entire time.

"Let's get this grocery shopping done so we can back to the cabin. I plan to show you just how much I love you."

"Promise?"

"With every beat of my heart, babe. I'm all yours."

Adri drew her lower lip between her teeth. Gunner was almost afraid to ask what now worried her. Finally, she said, "Does that mean no more donors for you?"

Gunner laughed. "I could easily feast on only your blood, babe. But—"

"No buts. Only me."

Gunner dropped his hold and shook his head. He loved that she was jealous. "Let's get this shopping done. You're going to need your strength for later, babe."

"You think?"

"I know," he said with a wink.

He'd leave the conversation that her blood would no longer nourish him once they became mated for later. Like *after* she became his mate. He quite liked her possessive side.

CHAPTER EIGHTEEN

ADRIAN "SMOKE" WELLMAN POCKETED HIS CELL FOLLOWING his conversation with Gunner. Peering out of the hangar door, he noted the deathly quiet in the yard. Mateo's soldiers continued to hide out in the woods but he knew they were still there; he scented the son of a bitches. For now, he'd rather they weren't aware Smoke knew of their presence. His plan was to do a little recon, see if he could detect how many of them there were, and report back to his brethren in the cabin.

It was a bit of a jog to the back porch, long enough it would be easy for one of the chickenshit soldiers hiding from sight to fire off a few rounds. Unless he was struck in the heart, he'd survive being shot, but that didn't mean it wouldn't hurt like a son of a bitch.

Detecting no movement beyond the line of trees, Smoke strode across the yard. Even though he wasn't about to tempt fate by being out in the open for overlong as one lucky shot could end his immortality, he didn't want to draw attention to the fact the Sons knew they hunkered down amongst the foliage. These fuckers had no idea that Gunner and Adriana were miles away. He'd rather have the element of surprise on their side.

They needed a solid game plan.

Drawing the soldiers out of the woods could be key to their survival. They needed to get vampire eyes on their guns, making it possible to dodge some of the oncoming bullets. Their speed alone would keep the soldiers from firing off too many rounds. Once the vampires got close enough, there would be massive carnage. No human could win a hand-to-hand battle with a vampire. They'd be no match for their bestial strength. Mateo no doubt wanted his mission to be quick and easy. Take out Gunner and his brethren, capture Adriana and head back south of the border. By sending Gunner and Adri away, they had already thwarted the biggest part of Mateo's plan.

Smoke couldn't detect the exact number of soldiers waiting for them. At best guess, he noted seven to eight unique scents, though there could easily be more. He sure as fuck hoped Mateo was hiding among them and had underestimated the Sons. Smoke wanted this shit over with, here and now, so he could head back to the coast. Hiding out in the middle of nowhere wasn't high on his list of things to do.

Partying at the Blood 'n' Rave was.

Gunner was putting a serious damper on his sex life, Smoke thought with a chuckle.

Reaching the backdoor, he stepped into the small, darkened interior of the cabin. The place was far too enclosed for his liking. Add in his brethren and their mates waiting inside for Smoke's plan of action and the space was damn near claustrophobic. As an ex-fireman, he wasn't a fan of tight spaces.

Smoke wanted to complete the mission, not only for Gunner but for the entire crew, so they could get back to life on the coast. Mateo was quickly getting under his skin with his bullshit possessiveness over Adri. She chose Gunner. Mateo needed to get the fuck over it. Not to mention it was time to teach the bastard a lesson. No one messed with the Sons of Sangue, though Smoke didn't plan on allowing Mateo to live long enough to learn from the schooling. It would be game over for him, leaving the La Paz cartel to find a new future, hopefully, one that didn't involve the Sons.

This shit was getting old.

Smoke planned to get back on his bike before Mateo's body was even cold and hightail it for Washington. Not that he had someone special to get back to. Hell, no. Smoke kept his options open, unlike Wolf and Ryder, whose beautiful mates, Caitlyn and Gabby, sat on the sofa chatting as if there wasn't a present danger waiting outside. He definitely liked these two. They were badass.

But even so, there would be no mate in his future.

When it came to women, Smoke preferred variety.

An image of Rocky Barta came to mind as if calling him a liar. Gorgeous as she was, though, even she couldn't tempt him to settle. Settling was for quitters. And he was anything but. After meeting Rocky, a friend of Vlad Tepes' mate, Janelle, Smoke thought she might be someone cool to hang with for a short period of time. Short being the operative word. But being a high-priced model on just about every fashion magazine cover? Smoke highly doubted he had been a blip on her radar. Hell, they had barely met before Ryder interrupted and took him and Gunner from the club. Sons of Sangue business trumped everything ... including partying with gorgeous women. He certainly wouldn't mind running across her again, maybe even spending some time in her company.

"Gunner and Adri are safe?" Ryder asked, drawing his attention. Adrenaline ran thick in the small cabin.

"They're secure." Smoke cleared his dry throat, the hoarse sound a bit more pronounced from his brisk walk to the cabin. His signature rasp came from his stint as a fireman, a job he'd left long before becoming a Son. Toxic fumes had almost cost him his life when his mask and regulator had been knocked from his head by a falling beam. He might have died had it not been for his team's quick action and rescue. Grabbing a bottle of water, he took a pull before continuing, "Let's hope Mateo's out there so we can finish this once and for all. Not only has he pissed off Gunner, but I think it's safe to say we all want a piece of the bastard."

"Gabby and I certainly have a score to settle with him. Fucker torched our house, that's not to forget the people inside at the time. I'll gladly be the one to end the son of a bitch's life. I'm not too forgiving when it comes to my family and friends."

"It doesn't appear he brought an army, Ryder. I scented maybe seven or eight of them, possibly more. The wind's kicking up out there. Even with my keen sense of smell, I had trouble detecting anything. What's our game plan? Anyone got an idea of our best plan of action?"

"We split up," Tag said. "Some of us can go to the hangar. The rest stay here. Probably sooner rather than later. Otherwise, we're just sitting ducks in this cabin. According to Ryder, they've used fire before, so I wouldn't put it past them to try and light this place up with us in it. That would surely get us running, and with them waiting for our exit."

"Good thinking, Tag. That would split their numbers as well. You, Wolf, Caitlyn, and Neo head to the hangar. Ryder, Gabby, Diablo, and I will stay here."

"Is there a path to the hangar that would camouflage our movement?" Caitlyn asked.

Smoke shook his head. "It's better if they see you. We want some of their focus off the cabin. Let's not make it obvious, though. We don't want them to know we're aware they're out there. You guys will need to keep Tag safe."

"What the fuck?" Tag all but growled. "I can damn well take care of myself. Protect the women. Maybe we should get them out of here before all hell breaks loose."

Neo chuckled. "I'm pretty sure these two can take care of themselves, Tag. You won't need to be worrying about them. Besides, we could use them. We still have no clue how many men Mateo brought with him."

"If he's even out there." Smoke took another pull from the water bottle. "We can hope."

"He's known to let others do his dirty work." Wolf looked at Caitlyn. "You sitting this one out, sunshine?"

A smile crossed her face. "Not on your life."

Tag said, "At least take one of the shotguns. They're in the cabinet by the back door. There are two with plenty of ammo. I'll take the rifle unless one of you want it. I'm a pretty good marksman. I'll get up high, get them as they come out of the trees."

"Good plan, Tag." Smoke nodded. "From what I could tell, they're in the woods to the east of the property. So far, they haven't tried to surround the place or the wind would have given away their location. Still, don't let your guard down for a minute."

Gabby grabbed the shotguns from the cabinet and handed one to Caitlyn, before giving her some of the ammo. "Not sure you'll need this, but it couldn't hurt."

"We could sit on the back porch and shoot those bastards as they come out of the woods, Gabs. But what fun would that be," Caitlyn said with a wink.

"That's my girl." Wolf placed a kiss on the top of her blonde head., then slung his AR across his back. Smoke knew he likely wouldn't need it. "They get close enough, drain those motherfuckers dry."

Ryder lifted his chin, his nostrils flaring. "Well, I'll be damned."

"Mateo's men heading our way?" Diablo asked.

"Nope. This one's friendly." The door to the cabin swung inward. Ryder smiled. "Well if you both aren't a sight for sore eyes."

A large vampire with long black hair stepped over the threshold. His lips were a thin line and his eyes were already black as midnight. Vlad Tepes was one scary as fuck vampire. His mate, Janelle Ferrari, followed him through the door, looking pretty intimidating herself. Thank fuck they were on their side. Even though Smoke was pretty sure they had the cartel soldiers handled, the odds just went up exponentially.

Vlad draped an arm over his mate's shoulders as he glanced around the already too-small interior of the cabin. "Someone call for backup? The cavalry has arrived. Who's ready to get this party started?"

Ryder apparently had no problem scenting the couple just before their arrival. Smoke blamed the wind for his inattention. Thankfully, Vlad had an uncanny way of showing up when he was most needed.

Tag stepped around Ryder. "Who the hell is this?"

Wolf chuckled. "Tag, meet Vlad Tepes and his significant other, Janelle. I believe they've come to help."

Tag's brow creased. "Like the Impaler?"

"Like him?" Vlad's deep voice damn near shook the rafters of the small cabin. "I beg your pardon."

"Your momma must have hated you," Tag said with a shake of his head. "But if these guys say you're all right, then that's good enough for me."

"Who is this—"

"How did you know to look for us?" Ryder thankfully interrupted. Vlad wasn't known for his humor. But Smoke had to hand it to Tag. He had a huge set of balls on him. This was one scary as fuck vampire that dwarfed the others in the room.

"Janelle saw a lot of blood being spilled. One of you wasn't going to make it."

"Who?" Diablo asked.

Vlad's dark gaze landed on Tag. Smoke made a mental note to tell Wolf and Neo before heading for the hangar that if anything happened to Tag, to make sure he was given vampire blood per Gunner's request. Janelle's visions were never wrong.

"She's a psychic?" Tag asked.

"Something like that." Vlad easily dismissed the human and turned to Wolf and Ryder. "I figured you could use our help."

"Damn, straight." Wolf rubbed his hands together. "The more the merrier. We got us a mother-fucking-party! These shits-for-brains won't know what hit them."

CHAPTER NINETEEN

"Where're you taking me?"

Adri's smile, one he could easily see waking up to every morning for eternity, warmed him. She had the face of an angel. What she saw in him he wasn't about to question, lest she realized he wasn't the catch she initially thought. Gunner was certainly no one's hero.

She wore a pair of black leggings that hugged her backside like a glove. Damn, but she had a delectable ass. Gunner had a hell of a time removing his gaze from where his hands itched to be. He wouldn't mind pulling her into his embrace and taking what he was yearning for again, though they needed to talk first. Gunner wanted her as a mate, no question about it. But he needed to see where she stood on the idea of a long-term relationship. And by long-term, he meant a life sentence. Vampires didn't get divorced. Adri needed to be well aware of that.

Soon enough, they'd have that conversation.

"I thought we'd take a walk around the lake," Gunner said. "The cabin is too cramped. One could easily go stir-crazy cooped up in there and I'm pretty sure I was damn close to it. I thought we could use some fresh air. Not to mention a distraction."

The white-hooded, cropped sweatshirt she wore ended at the waistband of her leggings, giving him tiny peeks at her smooth flesh as she moved. Adri put the sexy in comfortable. It was all he could do to keep a lid on his libido, and his hands, to himself. Gunner bet she could make a pair of overalls look erotic. Her sleek, shorter black hair swung slightly as she headed down the trail ahead of him. The new hairdo sophisticated her and made her more provocative. Hell, Gunner hadn't thought that was even possible. He had been pining away for her for so long and now she walked in front of him, more alluring than ever. Letting her go wasn't going to happen. He'd beg her to be his mate if he had to.

Spending time by the water might help get their minds off the mess they left behind in Helena, even if for just a brief bit. Gunner would've preferred to be in on the action with his vampire brothers, to take Mateo's life himself, but his need to protect Adriana trumped his desire for revenge. Having her to himself would go a long way in placating the adrenaline junkie in him.

Viewing St. Mary's Lake from the cabin windows didn't do this place justice. Taking a little time outdoors to curb his cabin fever was exactly what he needed. Mateo likely had his hands full with the Sons and wasn't anywhere in the vicinity. Gunner doubted the bastard would survive the war he'd started with him and his brethren.

Had he stayed in the cabin, Gunner would've paced a worn path in the floors, not knowing how things were going in Helena. Later, he'd chance putting his battery into his phone to check in with his VP and make sure Adri's nightmare was put to rest. Gunner prayed every single one of his brothers survived. If any of them fell to the cartel, their blood would be on his hands because he had started this battle by sending Juan's head to Mateo, followed by having the balls to land in La Paz and take what the kingpin thought was his. Adri didn't belong to Mateo. She had a will of her own and had the right to choose who she wanted. Gunner hoped that person was him.

"You think it's safe to be out here? We don't know if Mateo has been captured yet."

Gunner didn't miss the fact she hadn't said killed. "I think we're perfectly safe, babe. Your ex and his men are nowhere near St. Mary's. How about we drop the topic for now? Enjoy this time together. Once we get back, we'll be surrounded by my MC brothers; we'll be lucky if we get any time to ourselves."

"I'm sorry."

"No need to apologize. I know you're worried."

"Of course, let's change the subject." Adri smiled, turning her face upward to a break in the trees. Sunlight poured down on her face, highlighting her beauty. A few seconds later, she looked back at him. "Can I ask you a question?"

"Anything."

The sun peeking through the clouds warmed them. She pushed her sweatshirt sleeves up to her elbows. "Sunlight doesn't bother you?"

Gunner chuckled. Most people thought of the fictional nosferatu who were sun-ashed and cross-fearing. Real vampires were far from what people saw in the movies. He lifted his sunglasses from the bridge of his nose and looked down at her, before letting them fall back into place. "My eyes are light sensitive, the reason I mostly wear shades when the sun is bright and I'm outside. I'll also sunburn before most humans, but I won't turn to ash."

Adri nodded, no doubt pondering what made him a vampire, other than the obvious of him consuming human blood. She moved ahead, continuing her stroll along the edge of the lake. A red-winged blackbird stirred in a tree above them before taking flight with a dozen of his friends. The heavy scent of pine tickled his senses. Gunner loved the outdoors, which was his reason for taking his motorcycle from Helena and not the car.

"Fictional vampires from books are quite different."

"So, crosses, holy water, and garlic don't bother you?"

"Not at all. As a matter of fact, one of the Sons is an ex-preacher. Bobby Bourassa. He's a believer in God and the afterlife. He and Xander both sport tattoos of crosses."

"What about you?"

"I'd like to believe there's a higher power looking out for us. With so much evil in the world, I have to believe Satan is actively at work. If there's an evil force, then I can't help but believe there is a good force to balance it out."

"I grew up Catholic." She shrugged. "I believe there's a God."

Gunner tucked her beneath his arm and pulled her into his side, kissing the top of her head. "I hope you're correct. Lord knows there's a lot I need to be forgiven for."

She placed her arm around his back, tucking her hand into the back pocket of his jeans. The simple gesture tightened his groin. No way in hell they'd make it back to the cabin before he fucked her again. "What have you done?"

"A lot." He licked his dry lips. No reason for him to be nervous. Adri already knew what he was capable of, but it mattered how she viewed him. The last thing he wanted was for her to tack on the word "monster" to his vampire. "Ripping the head off one of Mateo's men and sending it back to him in a potato sack wasn't one of my finer moments."

"He provoked you."

"He had it coming."

They continued in silence for a bit before Adri asked, "What about superpowers?"

She truly amused him. "Like Batman?"

Adri stopped walking, untangled herself, and looked up at him, her gaze wide. "Please tell me this isn't where you confess to turning into a bat? That might just be a deal breaker."

"Nope. A deal breaker, huh?"

She smiled. "Yep."

Gunner ran a knuckle down her downy cheek. "I'm nearly as human as you, babe. Except, in order to kill me, you must instantly stop my heart. Taking my head will also accomplish that."

"Then will you live for eternity? Or will you grow old and die?"

He grabbed her hand, entwined their fingers, and started along the path they'd been following. "Eternity is possible. Human blood is our fountain of youth. As long as we have it, we won't get older or die. My heart beats more rapidly than yours. Any cuts or wounds will heal themselves."

"Then your superpower is that you can regenerate?"

"Something like that. And I'm much stronger than any human. I can run faster and jump higher. I can sense when someone is nearby. My hearing, sense of smell, and eyesight are much keener than a human's. We learn to adapt and use the entirety of our brains."

"Which allows you to hypnotize humans."

"Sort of. It's a trick we learn."

Adri continued along her way down the path in silence. Gunner could tell something bothered her. He had given her a lot to process. Maybe Adri felt it was more than she could handle. Worse, maybe she felt she could no longer love him.

Stopping near an opening in the trees, Adri peered out across the clear lake. The breeze had kicked up and caused whitecaps to appear across the water. The trees sheltered them from the worst of it. An oncoming storm threatened to end their hike. While he didn't care if they got wet, Adri was human and if lightning spread out across the area it could get dangerous for her.

"Maybe we should head back to the cabin."

She looked at him. "I'd like to stay for a bit longer. It's so beautiful here."

Gunner dropped his hold on her hand and framed her face between his palms. "You're beautiful."

Leaning down, he slanted his lips over hers, hoping to find Adri hadn't had a change of heart. He'd be able to feel it in her response. The last thing he wanted was to scare her. Hell, he desired her by his side the rest of his days, eternity if he were so blessed. Teasing the seam of her lips with his tongue she opened for him and he deepened the kiss. He pulled her flush against his abdomen. Lord, he wanted back inside her, to show her the depth of his love. Adri had spoken the words, but could she love a vampire?

She threaded her fingers through his hair, moaning against his lips. Gunner moved his hands, one to her nape and one to her lower back, pulling her against his thickening cock. He'd need to stop or chance the emergence of his vampire. Now wasn't the time to go full-blown monster on her.

Gunner broke the kiss, releasing her. Lord, she was beautiful with kiss-swollen lips and lids heavy with desire. "Are we okay?"

She drew her brows together, frowning. "Why would you think otherwise?"

"I'm a vampire, Adri. Even now I'm only a breath away from turning. You bring out the monster in me. Hell, I want to take you right here in the woods. That's not what you deserve."

"And what do you think I deserve?"

"Decadence. Luxury."

She smirked. "You recall I already had that. It wasn't what I wanted."

"Thank fuck."

"Gunner, I want *you*. It's why I'm here, running away from the bastard in a thousand-dollar suit. Any day with you in a small cabin is a better day than what I was living in La Paz. Never doubt that."

"Then what were you thinking about moments ago? You grew quiet. I thought maybe you might be freaking out, thinking you made a mistake."

"I happened to think the vampire in you is kind of sexy. I think you should keep him."

Damn, but she'd be his undoing. "Good thing, because I can't get rid of the bastard. Then what had you worried? I could see it in the face."

"Are all the Sons of Sangue members vampires?"

He rubbed the back of his skull, knowing they treaded on a topic he'd rather wait for another day. She had processed so much already, the last thing he wanted was to scare her with the fiery pain of a mate's turning.

"Yes. All the Sons are vampires."

"What happens when I grow old and you don't?"

"There is much to learn." Gunner pulled her back into him, wrapping her in a hug and kissing her forehead. "Let's forget the future for now and finish our hike."

"It looks like it might storm."

"We're surrounded by mountains. It may pass over us. You want to chance it or head back to the cabin?"

She turned her head as though she had heard something. "Do I hear a waterfall ahead?"

Gunner nodded. "It sounds like it's not that far from here."

"Can we go see it before we return?"

"Whatever you desire, babe. Maybe we can even test the water, take a little swim."

"We don't have swimsuits."

Gunner grabbed her hand and tugged, leading her toward the sound of rushing water. His erection thickened with each step at the thought of making love to her under the falls. He prayed the oncoming storm would hold off.

"Babe, you aren't going to need a swimsuit."

CHAPTER TWENTY

THE SOUND OF THE FIRST BULLET CARRIED TO SMOKE'S ears just before it whizzed past his hair, narrowly missing his skull. The flash could easily be seen within the darkness of the forest. He had dodged the fucker's first shot. He'd been ready. Now that they had made themselves known, it was game on. Moments ago, Vlad and Janelle had slipped into the forest behind the soldiers, waiting for them to make a move. The plan was to drive Mateo's men from their deep cover and into the open.

Smoke spotted Tag lying atop the hangar with his rifle at the ready to pick the motherfuckers off as they exited the woods. Caitlyn and Gabby were positioned with shotguns at their sides. Not that they'd necessarily need them, but as a backup. They would dodge bullets like the rest of the Sons until the soldiers came close enough to be drained.

If Vlad and Janelle left them any to toy with.

Smoke rolled his neck and welcomed the emergence of his vampire. Fangs punched through his gums, allowing his thirst for blood to take over. In the end, nothing would be left of these assholes to find. All remains would be torched.

The first soldier popped from the cover of trees. His ashen face was contorted with fear, looking back to where he'd come from, as if he had seen a monster. Smoke bet he had.

Seconds later, the man dropped, a red hole blossoming in the center of his chest. Tag's hit had been dead nut.

Remember never to piss him off.

Diablo and Ryder sprinted in the direction of the woods, Caitlyn and Gabby close at their heels. Smoke headed for the far side, Neo and Wolf right behind him. One dead soldier, and if Smoke guessed correctly, at least two more at the hands of Vlad and Janelle, which had started the oncoming stampede. There would be no mercy this day; only death sentences would be handed out. His crew, Vlad, and Janelle had the motherfuckers surrounded.

Bullets rained down on them, fast and furious. Smoke cursed as two tore through his thigh and forearm. The pain was but an afterthought to the hunger for blood running through him. He meant to take their life's blood and leave nothing but empty shells.

Screams of terror came from the woods as more men fled Vlad's vision of hell. Neo close-lined one of them, before landing on him, and tearing a softball-sized hole in the man's neck. Caitlyn grabbed another by the throat, sinking her fangs deep. His scream was short-lived.

Smoke heard, "That's my girl," right before Wolf flipped the third onto his back and tore a massive hole in his throat.

Four, possibly seven down, if not more. No doubt Vlad was introducing some of them to hell in the woods. Another man hit the daylight but before Smoke could get to him, Tag dropped him; a red hole oozed blood between his eyes. Two more soldiers shot out of the woods. Smoke grabbed the first, just as the man fired the Glock he carried, unloading a few rounds into Smoke's abdomen. Son of a bitch. He grabbed the man by the head and twisted, feeling bones break beneath his hands. He sank his fangs gum-deep into the dead man in order to satisfy his desire for blood. The warm fluid flowed down his throat, quenching his hunger.

Diablo grabbed another man before he got any shots off and bit down on his neck. Smoke watched the man's limbs tremble in Diablo's hold. It wasn't but seconds before he ceased to move at all. Two more were taken down by Ryder and Gabby to his right. The sound of the guns being fired ceased. The woods and surrounding area grew silent. The stench of death surrounded them.

Smoke counted nine corpses lying at their feet when Vlad and Janelle strolled from the cover of the trees. The scent of blood filled the air, making it hard to detect if any humans remained.

"How many did you take out?" Smoke asked Vlad, his radar still up in case any humans remained. The last thing he wanted now was an ambush.

Vlad shrugged, blood rimming his mouth and staining his fingers. "Janelle and I each took out one. We didn't want to have all the fun."

Janelle wiped the blood from her mouth. "Where is the human?"

"Tag?" Smoke asked, his gaze going to the top of the hangar. "He's a sharpshooter. Took out two with deadly accuracy."

"He's still in danger." Janelle placed a bloody hand on her temple. "We must—"

Her words cut short as a shot rang out. Smoke's gaze went to the metal building, watching as one lone soldier holding an AR aimed at the pilot, standing just feet from Tag. Another shot sounded just before Tag flipped over the edge. Smoke, closest to the building, ran with inhuman-like speed for the falling man. He caught Tag just before he hit the ground, which would have no doubt ended his life on impact.

Vlad easily scaled the building, catching the soldier before he had time to escape. Even from his position on the ground, Smoke could hear the man's screams cut short as he heard tendons and bones snap, just before the man's head hit the ground.

Smoke looked down at Tag, his breath garbled with blood. Two bullet wounds had entered his chest. He had but seconds to live. Gunner had told him to save Tag at all costs. Like it or not, the pilot was about to become a vampire. Vlad landed next to Smoke, having jumped from the roof, the soldier's headless body still in his lethal grasp.

"Save him," Vlad all but growled. "Janelle witnessed his near-death for a reason. Tag isn't yet meant for death."

Taking his wrist to his mouth, Smoke ripped a hole with his fangs. Blood quickly pooled to the surface and began flowing from the wound.

Smoke had but seconds before Tag's life ended. He held his wrist over Tag's mouth and said, "Drink."

Tag's gaze widened slightly before going closed. The man was quickly slipping away. Smoke pried open his mouth and laid his bleeding wrist against his lips. Tag coughed up more blood, mixing his with Smoke's. He prayed it was enough. Smoke licked the wound on his wrist closed, then laid Tag on the ground.

Janelle approached and placed her hand over his heart. "Don't worry, Smoke. Tag will live to see another day."

Smoke glanced at the lifeless body between them. Lord, but Tag already looked dead. He couldn't even detect the rise and fall of his chest. "How can you be so sure?"

Janelle smiled. "Just know that I am."

Tag groaned before coughing up a fair amount of more blood. His hands fisted on his bloody shirt and he groaned, causing a cheer from the surrounding vampires. Caitlyn and Gabby picked him up and carried him to the cabin where they laid him on the hammock. The next week would be pure torture for Tag as he went through his turning, but he'd survive it.

"What about Gunner, Janelle? Can you see if he and Adri are okay?" Diablo asked.

She shook her head. "I can't call up my visions on will. If I see him in any kind of danger, I'll contact one of you."

Wolf and Ryder walked up with four dead bodies between them. They tossed them on top of the headless corpse Vlad had dropped at his feet.

"If I counted right, that makes twelve." Smoke's gaze took in the other bodies scattered about the yard. "With luck on our side, the gunshots won't bring the locals."

"This far out, they're likely to think someone is hunting. We can only hope," Neo said.

"Mateo isn't among them," Ryder growled. "I would have preferred to end this here, but it looks like we aren't yet done."

Wolf rubbed his goatee. "Let's hope his cowardly ass is still in Mexico."

"The woods are clean," Vlad said. "While you guys were taking care of the rest of the cartel soldiers, Janelle and I combed the area. There are no humans for miles."

"Then let's hope the chickenshit bastard sent his men to do the dirty work," Diablo said.

"Something tells me this isn't over." Smoke had a bad feeling Mateo had somehow escaped the carnage but was still in the area. "Let's hope I'm fucking wrong, as we have no way to get a hold of Gunner."

ADRIANA STEPPED THROUGH THE clearing in front of Gunner, guiding him from the trail to the water's edge. The beauty of the falls gave her pause. St. Mary's was truly stunning. Water rushed over the rocks, the sound nearly deafening. Dropping Gunner's hand, she put her arms out and spun in a circle, basking in the warmth of the sun peeking through the clouds. Gentle winds rustled her hair. She could stay here for eternity and not get tired of the surrounding land. There didn't seem to be anyone around, as if they were the only two for miles. With the life she left behind in Mexico total chaos, the peace and solitude called to her.

"What do you think?"

She turned to Gunner and smiled. "Can we stay here forever?"

His chuckle warmed her. "I would give you anything, babe. If staying in this area is what you really want, I'll make it happen."

"You'd leave Washington and move here?"

"If that's what you want, then yes."

Never had anyone put her desires before theirs. "What about the Sons of Sangue? Your friends?"

Gunner gripped her hand, guiding her along the bank, and heading in the direction of the falls. "If it meant never losing that smile on your face, then I'd pack up and move tomorrow. I can always start a Sons chapter here with Kane and Kaleb's blessings."

"Thank you, Gunner, but I don't really want to move here." This man had forever captured her heart. No other could fill the space he had taken residence in. Knowing him as she did, though, he'd never be happy away from the action. "This place wouldn't keep you interested for long. You'd be bored before we ever laid down roots."

"You do make a good point. How about you run naked through the woods daily? It might go a long way in capturing my interest here."

Adri rolled her gaze and laughed. "It's always about sex with you men."

"Vampires," he corrected. Gunner pulled her closer and tucked her beneath his arm, kissing her temple.

"A very sexy one at that."

"You find that side of me hot, do you?"

"Turn into a vampire and I might just show you how much so."

He gave her a wink that looked like it might have a promise attached to it. Adri wasn't opposed to ending the hike and showing him just how alluring she found him. That might need to wait for a bit more privacy, though. It may appear that they were alone, but with her luck, about the time she got naked, they'd discover other hikers among them.

Adri looked up at him, catching a faraway look in his gaze. "Something bothering you?"

"I was just thinking about my brethren, wondering if things have escalated yet in Helena." Gunner looked down on her. "While we're here enjoying ourselves, they're likely doing what I should be."

"We can go back—"

"Fuck! No. I can't chance you getting hurt or Mateo getting his hands on you."

"You care very deeply for them."

"My friends? They're my family, babe. They're all I have."

"All the more reason to return to the coast when this is over, to be closer to your … our friends. But that doesn't mean we can't come back here for vacations."

"If you ever want to come back all you need to do is ask. I'll fly you around the world if that's your heart's desire."

Nibbling her lower lip, Adri stopped and looked up at Gunner. Her knight in shining armor didn't ride a horse; he came in on a motorcycle. "What did I do to deserve you?"

"Months ago in Mexico, you took pity on me and asked me to dance."

"Best decision of my life."

Gunner raised a brow. "I can make that the second-best decision. We're all alone out here."

Adri giggled. "And we're also out in the open."

Untangling herself from him, she jogged off in the direction of the falls. It had been a long time since she had felt this free. A quick look at the skies established their bit of sunshine would be short-lived as clouds started to move in. Adri wanted to reach the falls before the storm hit. After seeing it close up, then they could head back to the cabin. The magical beauty of this place needed to be seen ... even if meant getting caught in a little rain. Besides, in a day or so when they returned to the coast, they might never make it back here despite her desire to.

Gunner's chuckles followed her as he strolled lazily behind her in no apparent hurry. It was as if they were the only two people in Montana. Lord, the man turned her insides to a mass of quivers. If she were to spend an eternity with anyone, it would be Gunner. She'd never tire of looking at him. He put the S in sexy. Adri hoped he felt the same way. He loved her, and had even said as much, but was it enough? What if, after his mission, the adrenaline rush diminished and he tired of her?

Adri mentally slapped herself.

She wasn't about to let her insecurities ruin the beauty of the day.

Reaching the edge of the falls, she looked back at Gunner only to find him directly behind her, causing her to falter. He had closed the twenty-five yards faster than humanly possible, attesting to his vampire skills.

He gripped her waist to keep her from sliding on the wet rocks and whispered into her ear, "You didn't think I'd let you get away from me, did you?"

"I hope not."

The way he breathed the word, "Never," against her ear sent shivers vibrating along her spine.

"The falls are stunning."

"Ready for a swim?"

"If it storms it won't be safe."

"I have a better idea. Follow me."

He grabbed her by the hand, carefully stepped across the slippery rocks, and led them behind the wall of water. Their clothes quickly became soaked, chilling her to the bone. Goose flesh popped out along her skin and her limbs began to tremble. The water was colder than the day was warm. Now that they were out of the sunlight it was downright icy.

"A swim is definitely out of the question. I'm already cold," Adri said, her teeth chattering.

"I have no intention of allowing you to freeze, babe. Once we're in the grotto behind the falls, the water will no longer reach you and you'll have me to keep you warm."

She slipped on one of the stones but Gunner quickly steadied her. Soon enough they were safely tucked into the cave behind the rush of water. Her damp clothing wasn't helping her case of shivers. Without the benefit of the sun, her whole body began to shake.

"Mmm…mm-maybe we should head back."

Gunner pulled her back against his chest, wrapping his arms around her. The chill seemed to quickly abate as his heat seeped into her. It wasn't long before her tremors ceased and a new warmth built deep within her abdomen. The water free-fell like a wall in front of them, completely encasing them in privacy. Now that Gunner used his heat to warm her, there was nowhere else in the world she'd rather be … not now and not with any other person. His constant care and consideration made her love him even more. Unlike her ex who was too consumed with money and power to ever love anyone but himself.

Adri turned in Gunner's embrace, aligning their bodies. Tilting her face, she reached for him, bringing his lips to hers. Gunner anchored her against his hard body and returned her kiss with fervor. Gone was his gentleness, replaced by a man with fierce desires. He teased her tongue with his, deepening the kiss with the promise of what was to come. At this moment, she'd deny him nothing. Adri wanted Gunner, vampire and all.

His hands moved down her back to cup her ass, where he easily lifted her into his arms. Adri wrapped her leggings-clad legs around his waist, crossing her ankles at his lower back. He carried them deeper into the alcove and farther away from the rushing water. Gunner stopped, releasing his hold. Adri slid down his front, feeling his hardness now resting between them. It was a heady thought that a man such as he would want her so resolutely. Once she got her footing, he stepped back. She hadn't missed the way his face had morphed into his vampire form. His razor-sharp fangs protruded just past his upper lip, causing her to shiver, but not from the chill.

"Still cold?"

She shook her head.

Gunner pulled his shirt over his head and tossed it to the rocks. He sat crossed-legged on the hard surface, then guided her toward his lap. Adri stepped over his legs and straddled him. His erection nestled at the juncture of her legs, her leggings and thong doing little to separate them. The coarseness of his jeans far more hindered them.

Gunner leaned forward, his fangs scraping the flesh of her neck. His breath feathered over her ear. "You're killing me, babe. I need you."

Those three words went straight to her heart. She could not deny him, nor did she want to. Adri stood, stripped off her leggings and thongs, and dropped them. Gunner placed his hands on her hips, guiding her back to his lap. The heat of his touch thoroughly warmed her. Adri couldn't help but move along his thickness, still covered by his jeans. It wouldn't take much for her to orgasm, the friction of the material adding to her arousal. Being in this man's arms was euphoric.

"Babe." Gunner smiled, his black gaze damn near hypnotic. "A little help here…"

Her cheeks warmed, more than ready to do as he asked … but not in the way he intended. It was her turn to taste him. Adri grabbed his shirt and placed it upon the rocks before she moved back and kneeled before him. She flipped the button of his jeans and then carefully lowered his zipper. Gunner had thankfully gone commando. She wrapped her hand around his thickness and released him, her gaze taking in his sheer size. His eyes widened as she licked her lips.

"Babe." He sucked in a breath as she lowered her head, her lips surrounding the head of his erection. "Fuuu … ck."

Adri wrapped her fingers around the steel base, tightening her grip as she took more of him into her mouth. She slid her tongue along the thick vein at the front and slowly withdrew. His hand rested against the top of her head. Adri continued to work him slowly, the saltiness of his precum seasoning her tongue.

He leaned back, bracing himself on his splayed hands and groaned. Adri circled the velvety tip with her tongue before taking his fullness into her mouth once again. She could tell by the rigidness of his thighs and his hissed curse that he held back.

Gunner placed his hands at the side of her head, causing her to release him. "Damn, not this way. I need to be inside you when I come."

Adri drew her bottom lip between her teeth again. This vampire undid her. Love. Desire. Hunger. Straddling his lap, the tip of his cock nudged her opening just before she sank fully onto him. Tilting her head to the ceiling of the cave, she moaned. Gunner filled her and not just physically. More so than any other man ever could. He was the sunlight to her darkness. Never would she have to suffer at the hands of another. He was her protector, her lover ... her vampire.

She moved slowly, rocking against him before withdrawing and reseating herself. It wasn't going to take long for her to go over the precipice; not with her on top, moving against him. Shivers of delight traveled through her, causing her breath to quicken. Gunner's fingers imprinted her hips as he guided her movements.

Tiny white lights exploded behind her closed eyelids, leaving her gasping his name. The sound was lost among the crashing of the water behind them. Her climax washed over her at the same time Gunner stiffened, reaching his own orgasm. He leaned forward, wrapping her in his embrace and kissing the crook of her shoulder. His breath feathered over her flesh. They stayed connected for long moments, neither in a hurry to move.

Gunner had forever changed her life.

No other man could ever take his place.

Gunner had become as important to her as her next breath, as the next beat of her heart. She belonged to this vampire, this man. And she could only hope for the day he would give himself fully to her. She wanted what Gabby and Ryder had, what Caitlyn and Grigore had. Adriana wanted

Gunner for all eternity, even if that meant becoming a vampire herself.

CHAPTER TWENTY-ONE

GUNNER WEAVED HIS WAY DOWN THE MUDDY PATH BEHIND Adriana, heading back to the cabin. Her ass displayed nicely in her damp, clinging leggings. He had spent the past hour making love to the stunning woman in front of him but he was far from sated. Truth be told, his vampire still hungered deeply for her. He'd need to be mindful that she was merely human. Although he had yet to hear any complaints from her, he thought with a smile.

The storm had let loose about thirty minutes ago but had thankfully moved through the area quickly. The grotto had kept them from the worst of it as the rain came down in buckets. Water ran down the path in rivulets, making the trek back slick. Gunner followed closely behind Adri, ready to catch her should she slip or fall. The fresh scent of rain filled his senses, veiling the many other scents of the forest. Sniffing the air, Gunner didn't think any other beings were near but he wasn't about to take chances. He'd be sticking by her side like glue. Mateo was still out there somewhere, whether in Mexico or somewhere in Montana.

Coming up beside Adri, Gunner looked down at her and gripped her hand. "You doing okay? Or do you need to rest? I could carry you the rest of the way."

"I'm a big girl, Gunner." She smiled, squeezing his hand. "Although I appreciate your care, I can walk ... much slower than you, of course. But when we get back to the cabin and get into some dry clothes, we need to talk."

"Something I need to be worried about?"

Gunner hated the fact he didn't have a clue what her plans were once they returned to the coast. Did she want to stay in Oregon with her friends? He hoped with all that had transpired between them she'd want to relocate to Washington. Even if that meant moving her into the Sons of Sangue clubhouse with him for a short period of time. His number one priority would be to get them a place of their own. Having the guys underfoot would be a huge pain in the ass, but having Adri with him would be worth the temporary inconvenience.

"No." There was a slight catch in her voice. "Just something we need to talk about. I'd rather we get back to the cabin and warm up first."

"I could carry you. We'd get there much quicker."

Adri laughed, easing his anxiety. "And miss this gorgeous scenery? I'm enjoying our stroll, Gunner. No need to take it at the speed of light."

Gunner stepped over a fallen tree in the path and helped Adri over it, easily lifting her. Whatever she had to say, he didn't plan on letting her go without telling her his true feelings. He'd never hold her against her wishes or force her into something she didn't want. She'd already had that with Mateo. The bottom line was, Adri could make her own decisions. Even if he didn't like them, he'd respect them.

The rest of the journey they walked side-by-side in companionable silence. Adriana was it for him. No one in the world he'd rather be with. If she decided against moving to Washington to be with him, then he'd consider moving to Oregon.

After making love to her a second time behind the falls while they waited out the storm, Gunner had placed the battery back into his cell and called Smoke. Frustration damn near ate him alive at leaving his brethren to handle his fucking mess. It should have been him draining the bastards. But thankfully, Storm had informed him that the soldiers had been taken care of, and none made it out alive. Unfortunately, Mateo wasn't among them. Gunner figured the coward could have sent his men to do the dirty work, staying in Mexico. Maybe he hadn't even planned to take Adriana back at all, thinking she was no longer worth his trouble.

Lord, Gunner could only hope.

He hadn't bothered removing the battery again, knowing Mateo's men had been dealt swift justice. Even Vlad Tepes and his mate had arrived just before the battle. Smoke spoke of Janelle's vision concerning Tag, which had brought the pair to Helena to offer their assistance. Tag had been mortally wounded.

Jesus! This was all his fault.

He should've been there, maybe even somehow stop the bullet that ended Tag's mortality. Gunner had dragged Tag into his mess. Smoke had assured Gunner that he had been given vampire blood and had already begun his change.

Even in that he had failed his friend. Gunner should have been there to help him through his change. Smoke, Diablo, and Neo were going to stay with him through the week until he was able to fly back to Washington. The rest of the Sons were heading back to Oregon come daybreak.

When Gunner told Adri about his phone call to Smoke and that the soldiers had been dealt with, he had hoped to be able to tell Adri that Mateo had been taken care of as well. Instead, they'd likely have to deal with him again sometime in the future. Mateo wasn't going to be thrilled that his men had been taken out by the Sons of Sangue. He'd want retribution. When Gunner and Adri arrived back at the cabin and they had the conversation she seemed intent on, then he'd tell Adri about her ex.

As they approached the end of the heavily wooded area at the backside of the cabin, Gunner sniffed the surrounding area, unable to detect any humans in the vicinity. The rain continued to dilute his sense of smell. The brush to his right rustled. Gunner pulled on Adri's hand, stopping her. When she looked back at him, he placed a finger to his lips. A swift fox darted across the path in front of them, causing Adri to jump.

"I'm sorry." Gunner grimaced. He hadn't meant to scare her. "I heard a noise. I wasn't sure what it was and we still need to be careful."

"I thought you said the soldiers had been dealt with."

"They were, but we can't be too careful in case some of them weren't with the others."

"Is that a possibility?"

"Anything is." Gunner started Adri down the path again. Another few minutes and they'd be safely tucked back into the cabin. "We'll need to be careful until we can get back to Helena and my MC brothers."

"Are we leaving here today?"

"We can stay a few more nights. I told Smoke we'd be back before they headed for Washington. You can fly back with Tag. I'll take the bike with Smoke, Diablo, and Neo. Disappointed that we will be leaving here?"

"No. I want to go home."

"Then I'll see that you get there."

Her gaze left his. Something made her weary. "I'm not sure where home is anymore."

The last thing Gunner wanted to do was push her. She needed to come to her own conclusion about where she wanted to land.

"Home is where you make it. No one can tell you where that is."

"Where is home for you? Washington?"

He nodded. His home had always been with the Sons of Sangue, had been for some time. Damn, he wished he knew what she was thinking. Home for him now would be wherever Adri was. And he'd tell her that soon enough. Gunner tugged on her hand and they headed back down the path, coming to the clearing behind the cabin. He took great care to sniff the air and listen to their surroundings, still finding themselves completely alone.

"Let's go." he said, and they left the cover of the woods. "Let's get you into the cabin and some dry clothes."

"I can't say I'll argue with you. My leggings are nearly dry but my sweatshirt is doing little to keep me warm."

"Why didn't you tell me?" he asked. "I would've carried you and ran the rest of the way. We would have been here long ago."

"I was enjoying our walk." Adri smiled up at him, warming his heart. Mateo, wherever the fuck he was, better never try to lay one hand on her again. To do so would be to sign his death certificate. "I wasn't in a hurry to return to the cabin. I'm sure it's just as chilly inside due to the passing storm."

Gunner punched the code on the keypad and entered the cabin ahead of her. "Wait here while I take a quick look around."

"You think someone is inside?"

"We can't be too safe." After doing a sweep of the cabin finding it empty, he returned to Adri. "Go take a shower and put on something to keep warm."

"Aren't you coming?"

"I need to gather some kindling for the wood-burning stove. It'll be dark before long and we're going to need some heat."

Adri stepped into the cabin. Gunner closed the door behind her, relocking it. He stood silently canvassing the area. Other than the sounds of scurrying animals and the scent of rain-soaked vegetation, he didn't detect anything amiss. He'd gather the wood, use the ax by the shed, then stack the chopped pieces by the back door, enough to get them through a couple of nights. Spending any more time here without the aid of his brethren would be foolhardy. He was only one man, one vampire. Should Mateo be in Montana, Gunner doubted he'd be alone. As much as he thought he could protect Adri, he wasn't about to risk her life on his ego.

Finished stacking a fair amount of firewood, he grabbed several pieces before letting himself into the cabin. The sound of the shower carried to him through the opened door of the bathroom. Lord, the thought of joining her started a small flame in his belly. His hunger for her was never far from the surface. Adri's comfort, though, trumped his need. And damn if he wasn't feeling needy. Gunner shook off the fire building in his abdomen and walked over to the stove and dropped the wood to the floor with a thump. Opening the cast iron door, he tossed in several pieces before lighting it. It wasn't long before the flames licked the wood and heat began to fill the small area.

Adri's scent reached him long before he felt her presence behind him. He stood, turned, and enveloped her in his arms, kissing her on the forehead. She wore a pair of tight jeans and a fuzzy sweater that ended just beneath her breasts. *That was going to be a serious diversion to his attention*. He thought about getting her a blanket to hide her skin, at least until they were done talking. Stepping back, he placed his hands above the waistband of her jeans, enjoying the soft feel of her flesh beneath the pink Angora.

Not helping.

Talk first, get her horizontal second.

"So what did you want to talk about, babe?"

Adri stepped away, gripped his hand, and pulled him to the couch. Gunner sat beside her, their thighs aligning. Damn, but she was one huge distraction.

"Are you hungry? Thirsty?"

She tucked her sleek black hair behind her ear. Her clean scent carried to his nose, tickling his libido. Adri was the crack to his addiction.

"I'm fine. I can make myself something to eat later from the groceries you bought. Are you … um … are you hungry?"

"I can go a few days without eating."

"You'll let me know if you need to feed?"

Gunner smiled, leaned down, and briefly covered her lips with his. "I'll let you know. Now, what has you so worried we need to have this chat?"

"Not exactly worried."

"What is it?"

"Not what but who. Gabby and Caitlyn."

He knitted his brows. "What about them?"

"Are they vampires?"

Gunner nodded.

"Were they born vampires?"

"Only men are born vampires. Those that are not turned into vampires, but born into the life, are called true bloods."

"So, how did Gabby and Caitlyn become vampires?"

"They were turned."

"By whom? Did they ask for it?"

"Full of questions." He smiled. "Gabby and Caitlyn had both wanted to become vampires. Ryder turned Gabby and Wolf turned Caitlyn."

Adri looked down at their entwined hands. She seemed to contemplate Gunner's words for a long moment before glancing back up. "What if I wanted to be? Would you turn me?"

Gunner ran his free hand down his chin. "You don't know what you're asking for."

"I want to be like them. Like you. I want to be with you, Gunner."

"You don't have to become a vampire to be with me."

"I'll grow old and die."

"You will," he said, not wanting to entertain the idea. But did she really want the life of a vampire? There would be no turning back, stuck with him for eternity. A blood drinker, for crying out loud. Adri needed to know that. Being mated shouldn't be entered into lightly.

"Then make me a vampire."

"First, I'd need the Sons of Sangue's approval for that."

"Why?"

"It's MC law. I need them to authorize our union."

"Sounds a bit archaic."

He chuckled. On the outside, he supposed it would appear so.

"You don't think they would approve of me?"

"Lord, no. I know they'd approve, babe. They didn't come this far out here to help slay the cartel for the fun of it. They came to help free you."

Her lips turned down. "Then it's you who doesn't approve."

Gunner took in a deep breath before slowly releasing it. "I one hundred percent approve."

"Then I don't see the problem."

There was no getting around the truth. Adri needed to hear that she would be tying herself to him for all eternity. "If I were to do as you ask, then you would be mated to me."

"Mated?"

"Like a marriage but more permanent."

"How can that be?"

"Because there is no divorce for vampires. Mating is for life ... eternity. You couldn't walk away from that. We would be partners for life. Are you ready to enter into that kind of commitment with me?"

"I—" she stopped, her gaze leaving him and going to the wood-burning stove. When she looked back, he saw the resolution there. "I think so."

"You have to know so. There is no second guessing this."

"Do you not want me for life ... as your mate, as you called it?"

"Fuck, babe, I couldn't want anything more." His breath was held in his chest. Gunner needed her answer to one question before he'd even think of bounding her to life with him. He dropped his hold on her hand and framed her face, forcing her gaze to stay on his. He'd see the hesitation should it be there. "Do you truly love me?"

"How can you even question that?"

The weight on Gunner's chest lifted. "If it's true then I need you to tell me. I need to hear it from your lips again."

"Gunner, I am so in love with you it hurts here." Her hand splayed over her sternum. Moisture gathered in her eyes.

"I love you, too. But you need to think about your decision to become a vampire. There is no turning back," he said, leaning down to capture her lips.

He put everything into the kiss. Love; heart and soul. Possession; for all eternity. Adriana was to be his and soon he'd pledge his life to her for infinity. There would be no turning back. Mateo be damned. Adriana was his ... to be his mate. If the motherfucker ever showed his face near her again, Gunner would drain him of every last drop of his evil blood.

TAKING THE STEPS AT THE back of the cabin, Gunner stepped into the cover of night. It was just past midnight. Though the storm had long passed through the area, the clouds remained. Not a single star could be seen in the heavens, leaving the area pitch black. The sounds of chirping bugs and animals scurrying just beyond the trees easily carried to his ears, while the heavy scent of rain continued to cling to the forest. It was on nights such as this that Gunner loved to leave the confines of the Washington clubhouse and run through the trees beyond the ditch. The vampire in him felt more at peace deep in the woods than he ever felt in the hustle and bustle of a city.

The interior of the cabin had begun to chill. Wanting to tend to Adri's comfort, Gunner had stepped out to get a few more logs to throw on the fire. He couldn't help but take a few minutes to breathe in the nighttime fresh air. Adri had been fast asleep following another round of making love. This time, he hadn't taken her with abandon. No, he had taken his time, memorizing every curve, every freckle, every nuance. Later, she had fallen asleep in his arms, cuddled to his side, her hand covering his heart.

Adriana Flores belonged to him. Soon, he'd ask her to be his mate.

Gunner smiled with a shake of his head. The truth of it was, he had belonged to her from the moment she asked him to dance back in Mexico.

When Adri had expressed her desire to become a vampire, to be his mate, his breath held tight for fear he had misheard. For so long he had believed she was lost to him. But no more. He would move all of the earth to keep her from harm or from ever being at the hands of Mateo again. Just the man's name brought a scowl to his face. Lord, he didn't even want to think of what she had endured at the hands of the La Paz kingpin. Gunner would make sure that one day her ex paid for his crimes against her. Mateo might not have come personally this time to collect her, but that didn't mean Gunner was finished with him.

Far from it.

The rustling of vegetation from deep in the trees caught his attention. Either a bear bumbled nearby, or something far bigger than a small woodland animal did. The hair on the back of Gunner's neck rose. Tipping his nose skyward, he tried to detect what was within the cover of trees, but the scent of rain and mud covered whatever ambled there.

Something felt off.

Gunner turned to pick up some logs and return to the cabin to make sure Adri was safe where he left her, snuggled beneath the comforter on the bed.

The first shot rang out, clipping him in the shoulder and spinning him back toward the dark forest. He growled, dropping the logs, as a second bullet entered his biceps. More shots rang out, making the dark woods lighting fire from the muzzles. Bullets rained down, hitting his abdomen, his arms, his thighs, all narrowly missing his heart. Gunner needed to move, to protect his heart from a kill shot. He backed up, stumbling back against the steps.

The bullets were coming too quickly.

Too much blood loss.

Gunner couldn't even reach his vampire. *Fuck!* Adriana came to mind. He had failed her. Slipping down the steps, Gunner heard her scream from inside the cabin, wounding him much deeper.

"Not enough ... blood," he whispered just before his world went black.

CHAPTER TWENTY-TWO

ADRIANA THREW OPEN THE REAR DOOR OF THE CABIN. WHAT she saw had her knees nearly giving out as she stumbled back. Gunner stretched across the steps, lying in a pool of his blood. *So much blood.* Several bullet wounds pierced his body. Placing a hand over her lips, she stifled the scream bubbling up from her stomach. For a second, with his eyes rolled back into his skull, his body unmoving, she thought him dead. But then she caught the slight rise and fall of his chest. A quick look around the area gave no clue as to where the shots had originated; the threat was still out there.

No matter.

She needed to get Gunner away from further danger, even if she got caught in the fray. Adri sprang into action, grasped him by the wrists, and began pulling him toward the door. He was deadweight and so heavy she'd barely moved him. Crying out, she put her entire body into the effort, dragging him farther onto the small deck.

Just a few more feet.

"Lord, God … please."

Tears streamed down her cheeks. She tugged again with all her might, just as four men appeared through the cover of the woods, one of them Mateo. Yanking with all she had, Adri managed to get Gunner halfway through the door before

Mateo and his men stepped onto the blood-smeared porch. Adri let go of Gunner's wrists as Mateo skirted his body and advanced on her, backing her into the cabin.

Pummeling her enemy's chest with her fists, she cried out, "You son of a bitch."

Mateo's menacing chuckle enraged her. He gripped her wrists in one of his large hands and yanked them behind her back, pulling her flush against him. "My dear *esposa para ser*."

Adri spat in his face. "I will never be your bride."

Rage lit his gaze as he wiped the spittle from his cheek. "You would rather wind up like *tu noviecito*? I can see that you both end up in shallow graves."

A sob clogged her throat as she watched two men carry Gunner into the room and drop him to the area rug. Adri would have run to his side had Mateo still not held her hostage. She struggled in his grasp, kicked his shin, then narrowly missed his groin with her knee.

"You best watch where you kick, *mi pequeña reina*," Mateo whispered into her ear. His putrid breath caused her to shiver in disgust. "Or I'll clear the room and fuck you right here in front of your dying boyfriend."

Adri stilled her effort to break loose, lest Mateo carry through with his threat.

His jaw tightened. Turning to his men, he said, "Take him to the bedroom and close the fucking door. I don't need my *esposa para ser* further traumatized."

Adri's gaze went to Gunner's prone form. "Please, don't hurt him anymore. I'll do whatever you say."

"I'm surprised the *bendejo* isn't already dead. He won't live much longer, and neither will you unless you hold true to what you say."

Adri's gaze followed Gunner, where the men thankfully laid him on the bed. She offered up a silent prayer to let him survive. The best she could do for Gunner now would be to go with Mateo and his men. Give him the chance to heal himself. The men closed the door upon their exit from the bedroom, shutting her out.

"Go back outside," Mateo ordered. "Keep the parameter secure. You see anything out of the ordinary, you let me know."

The three quickly did as they were told, leaving Adriana alone with Mateo. She was glad for the closed door so that Mateo wouldn't be privy to Gunner either. There was still hope that Gunner's vampire blood might yet heal him. She couldn't overpower Mateo and his men, nor would the Sons of Sangue likely come looking for them. According to what Gunner had told her of his call to his VP, his MC brothers had wrongly assumed Mateo wasn't in the country.

Mateo finally released her. Adri stumbled back, putting space between them. When her legs contacted the loveseat, she sat heavily on its surface. Her gaze dropped to the rug marred from Gunner's blood. She sucked back another sob, placing a trembling hand to her mouth.

"I'm nearly as human as you, babe. Except, in order to kill me, you must instantly stop my heart. Taking my head will also accomplish that."

There had been no blood spatter directly over his heart. Adri could only hope that his DNA was already at work healing him behind the closed door, though, she had no clue how long that might take. Adri needed to buy Gunner some time. Even if that meant leaving with Mateo.

"How did you find us?"

"I tracked the GPS on *tu novio's* phone."

Adri gasped, recalling Gunner replacing the battery back into his phone. Following his call to Smoke, Gunner hadn't taken it back out.

"What do you want?" Adri wiped away her tears. She wouldn't give Mateo the satisfaction of seeing her fear.

He smirked. "*Tu novio* took something from me and I want it back."

"Why, Mateo? You own everyone and damn near everything in La Paz."

"I want you."

Nausea threatened to consume her. There would be no reasoning with him. Even though everything inside her warred against it, she said, "Then take me with you and leave Gunner alone."

"I can't do that, *mi pequeña reina*."

"Why? You're getting what you want."

"I have yet to hear from my men back in Helena. Once I know they've taken care of the situation there, then we'll all head back to La Paz. Make no mistake, you will be going with me."

"I won't marry you."

He grinned sardonically. "I already tried to do this the right way. Marry you. Share everything I have. Now, you leave me no choice. I don't need a marriage certificate to fuck you."

"You would rape me?"

"You call it rape." He shrugged. "It makes no difference to me."

"You're insane."

Mateo crossed the floor in two strides, gripped her wrist painfully, and yanked her to her feet. "Be careful how you speak to me, *mi pequeña reina*. Or I'll do as I said and fuck you here, right in front of *tu novio*."

"My *boyfriend*" —she emphasized the English word— "would kill you if you tried."

"*Yu eres una puta*. The man is in no shape to fight me, let alone my men. If he isn't already dead, he's in there now coughing up blood. How would he stop me?"

Adriana wanted to put a knife straight through Mateo's black heart. If she got anywhere near the knife block in the kitchen, she'd do just that.

"Why, Mateo? Why do you want someone who abhors you?"

"No one defies me, *mi pequeña reina*. Not even you."

"You still call me your little queen, even after all I've done."

"I once loved you. You were my world. But make no mistake, I now say it with sarcasm. You will be treated no better than a prisoner once we return to Mexico. I will fuck you when I see fit. And when I tire of you, I'll leave you to my men. They will use you until you beg me for death. Even then I may not show you mercy."

The man was far more evil than she had ever thought. There no longer was a plan to save Gunner, let alone her. They were screwed. And once Mateo found out he wasn't going to hear from his crew in Helena, all hell would break loose.

"I DON'T NEED A BABYSITTER," Adri groused.

Sitting cross-legged on the loveseat, she was glad Mateo had left the cabin, giving her a couple of hours reprieve. She watched the young soldier stride across the floor, keeping a vigil at each window. At best, he looked to be just out of his teens. He held an AR tight against his chest, trigger finger stretched along the side of the gun, readying himself for what? War? Adri wasn't about to tell him there weren't any neighbors or likely anyone for miles. And since the Sons of Sangue had no idea Gunner laid damn near dying in the next room, or the fact Mateo was in the United States, that wasn't about to change. Let Enrico stay on full alert and keep his attention off her.

Would the Sons come looking for her and Gunner if they didn't show up in Helena?

They weren't expected for another few days.

A lot could happen in that amount of time, starting with Gunner being buried for real this time. Adri shook her head at the notion, not wanting to entertain the possibility. Not after she and Gunner had reunited. Not after she had found her true love. She could only hope Gunner was in the bedroom healing himself and would be able to get them out of this mess … her mess.

Mateo had left Enrico to guard her while he patrolled the grounds surrounding the cabin with Joseph and Tobias. Mateo'd had enough of her "smart-ass mouth," as he had said, and left her care with the youngest and smallest of the four. Apparently, he didn't think Adriana or Gunner was much of a threat. The young soldier, however, would no doubt turn the gun on her if needed.

Enrico continued his patrol, not responding to her babysitter comment. Attempting to pay her little mind, he continued his pacing from window to window, peering out over the grassy area to the front of the cabin while Mateo and the other two men likely canvassed the woods behind. *Did he even know English?* Adri caught a few compassionate glances her way, or at least that's what she hoped it to be. Maybe he wasn't truly aligned with Mateo. She'd play on his sympathies, use them to her advantage. If she could get out of his sight for a short time, she could check in on Gunner. There had been two doors leading into the bathroom. One from the living room and one from the bedroom. If she could get into the bathroom…

"Excuse me," she said.

"*Sí, señorita.*"

"I have to pee."

"I would have to ask Mateo," he said, his English fairly good.

"Really? You want to interrupt him because you can't handle watching over me as I go to the bathroom. Is that the message you want to give your boss?"

He seemed to ponder her response, then thankfully replied, "Then go. Leave the door open."

"So, you can watch?"

His dark eyes narrowed. "I would not touch what belongs to Mateo."

"Then you're in luck," Adri winked, trying a bit of flirtation to get him to bend to her will. "I don't belong to him."

"According to Mateo, you do. My orders come from him. Go to the bathroom but leave the door open."

Well, hell, that didn't work. Adri huffed, stood, then headed for the restroom. Leaving the door to the living area open wouldn't allow her to sneak into the bedroom to see how Gunner was holding up. Anxiety clenched her stomach like a vise. This was her one chance; she had to make it work.

Once inside, she peeked her head around the door. "I'll leave it ajar. I really have to go … um…"

Enrico chuckled. The young man at least had a sense of humor. Good. Maybe he'd trust her just enough to continue his lookout while she did her business, paying her no mind.

"Just be quick about it."

Adri flipped on the ceiling fan to create a sound buffer. It rattled, moaned, then came to life thankfully loud. Quietly lowering the lid on the toilet, Adri sat on it. She slipped out of her shoes, then positioned them so the toes could be seen through the open door. Unable to see Enrico from her position, she hoped he had decided to give her a bit of privacy. Being careful not to be seen, she slid behind the door, opened the one to the bedroom, and slipped inside.

Her heart sank and her stomach roiled.

Gunner didn't appear to have healed at all. As a matter of fact, he looked worse. Tears clogged her throat. The rise of his chest was the only indication he hadn't already passed. Adri approached the bed, gripping his cold hand, his fingers limp and non-responsive. His translucent skin was cold to her touch, the veins and arteries standing out in contrast.

Adri leaned close to his ear and whispered his name. Gunner's eyelids fluttered open. He turned his head to look at her. There was warmth in them. His tongue darted out and wet his dry lips. Lord, he looked but a hairbreadth away from death.

"What can I do?" she asked.

"Bloo ... blood."

Adri took her wrist to his lips, but he shook his head.

"Take my blood, Gunner. You need it."

"Ca ... n't."

"Why?"

"Fangs." He wet his lips again. "Lost too much. I ... I can't ... turn."

"Just a sec." Adri quickly returned to the restroom, time being of the essence. After all, how long could she use the bathroom as her excuse to be gone?

After peeking into the living room and still not seeing Enrico, she opened the medicine cabinet behind the sink, finding a pair of scissors. Not perfect, but it would do. This was going to hurt, jagged cut and all. Returning to the bedroom, she bit into her lower lip, then used the sharp point of the shears to make a small slit higher up her forearm, hoping she hadn't gone too deep but yet enough to help Gunner. Holding her forearm to his mouth, he latched onto the wound and sucked. Adri could feel the pull from his lips, telling her he was getting something. His skin color slightly deepened, even from the small amount of blood he had ingested.

After a few shallow sips, he released her and licked the wound. "Go ... before they catch you."

"Did you get enough?"

Gunner shook his head. Damn, but she wanted to crawl onto the bed and hold him until his strength returned. What more could she do?

"I'm ... I'm still weak. I need more. But my fangs..." He pulled his upper lip back, showing they had punched through his gums.

"What can I do?"

"Get one..." —he took in a shallow breath— "one of the soldiers ... near."

She understood what Gunner needed. If she lured Enrico next to the bed, Gunner might have enough strength to hold the young man and drain him of his blood, helping his body to quickly heal. His complexion was already looking much better than when she entered the room, just from the small amount he had consumed. Adri left his room, quietly closing the door. She slid back to the stool and slipped back into her shoes.

"What is taking so long?" Enrico asked, using the barrel of the gun to push the door open, just as she stood.

Adri pretended to adjust her leggings, then turned, and flushed the lever. Reaching for the switch to the fan, she silenced the noisy motor and shouldered past Enrico. "Sorry. Those things take time."

He inspected the room, then followed her back to the living area. Adri covered her forearm with her hand, not wanting to draw attention to the already healing wound. Reclaiming her seat across the room, she watched the soldier once again attempt to ignore her. Adri couldn't help but feel sorry for what Gunner was about to do. But given the order, she had no doubt Enrico would shoot her. Plus, Mateo and his men had tried to kill Gunner. And would have, had it not been for his vampire DNA. Enrico, along with the others, deserved what was about to befall them.

A vampire's rage.

Rubbing the tender spot on her arm, she hoped Gunner had gotten enough blood to act. Moments ago, he hadn't the energy to speak, let alone move from the bed. Taking a deep breath, she knew she'd need to have blind faith in him, that he'd be strong enough to do whatever was necessary to get them safely back to Helena where his brethren waited for them. Adri was so ready to put this nightmare behind them and get on that damn plane.

"Why are we still here?" Adri needed to get Enrico talking.

He turned from the window and placed the butt of the AR on the floor in front of him, wrapping his fingers around the barrel. His gaze darkened in something sinister, causing Adri to shiver. Mateo had threatened to turn her over to his men when he was done with her; this one looked all too agreeable to that.

"You're very pretty. I can see why Mateo would come to retrieve you. But are you worth his aggravation?"

"I asked you a question, not your opinion."

"Smart-mouthed. I'm sure Mateo will enjoy breaking you of that. My orders are to stay here until he hears from the others. Once we know they have accomplished their mission, we'll head back to Mexico."

"And what about me?"

"You're to be Mateo's bride. You'll return with us."

Adri knew they meant for Gunner to die but she needed to hear his confession to make herself feel better about sending Enrico to his death. "And what about Gunner? Will you allow me to get him to a hospital?"

He chuckled. "I'd be surprised if he's even alive."

"Let me check on him."

"I was given explicit instructions that you weren't to go in there for any reason. The last man who helped you had his brains blown out against a bathroom wall."

Of course, he'd know that. And Adri still felt bad about the mishap. "Can you at least check on him?"

"No."

Adri stood and sauntered closer. "Please."

He moved the gun from her reach. "No."

She licked her lips, drawing his gaze to them. "I have to know he's no longer suffering."

"Mateo said—"

"If you're quick about it, he won't even know. What would it hurt to check to see if he has a pulse? I'd feel better knowing he's at rest." Adri nibbled the fingernail on her pointer, then ran it seductively across her lower lip. "I'd consider it a personal favor, one I'd be willing to repay ... when Mateo's not watching, of course."

Enrico watched her; something much like interest flared in his gaze. Seconds ticked by, enough so she thought he'd deny her. Finally, he snatched up his gun, then used the barrel to indicate she should return to her seat. Adri backed up, her gaze holding his as she sat back down. Folding her hands in her lap, she hoped he'd do as asked, if for nothing else than a loosely made promise of something he might ask of her in return someday.

It worked like a charm.

"Fine," he grumbled, then headed for the closed door of the bedroom.

CHAPTER TWENTY-THREE

Pain rivered through Gunner's torso and limbs. Christ, how the rain of bullets had missed his heart, he didn't know but was thankful, nonetheless. Extreme trauma had caused his vampire to stay dormant. But no more. Adriana's blood now coursed through him, giving him the vigor and added kick he needed. His strength increased with each passing second from the small amount he had been able to ingest, but he needed more.

Adri had risked her life to save him.

Damn, but he didn't deserve her.

Gunner was to be her protector, her rescuer, not the other way around. By letting his guard down while gathering wood to see to her comfort, he had missed the fact they were no longer alone. Adri now paid the price for his negligence. Mateo and his goons had gotten too close, and she had once again become his captive, precisely what he had promised wouldn't happen.

The tables were about to turn.

Once Adri lured one of them into his room it would be game over. He'd sink his fangs deep into the fucker's throat. The more blood he consumed, the faster he'd regain full strength. Gunner would take them down one by one, ending with Mateo. The motherfuckers were about to get a one-way ticket to Hell.

The doorknob twisted and the hinges on the door squeaked. What looked to be the youngest and greenest of the three soldiers entered the room. *Good.* He'd be the likeliest to make a grave mistake. The man tucked his AR beneath his arm, the barrel pointing in Gunner's direction. He used the end of it to poke Gunner in the leg. Holding his breath, Gunner didn't move a muscle. Let the man think him dead.

"Is he…" Adriana's voice trailed off.

Through cracked eyelids, Gunner could see she stood just inside the doorway, yet out of harm's way. He didn't want her to witness the brutality he was about to deliver.

"Enrico?"

"He's not moving." Enrico poked Gunner a second time with the barrel.

"Is … is he … dead?" Adri's voice trembled as she tripped over the words.

"I do not know, *señorita*."

"Please check… Is he breathing?"

Good girl, get him to move closer.

Enrico grumbled something about *stupido señoritas* but did as asked. He leaned down, his face now inches from Gunner's. "I don't think he's—"

"Adri, leave," Gunner growled, just as he grabbed the soldier by the head and twisted his neck, giving him access to his throat.

Enrico's limbs flailed. He lost his grip on the gun, sending it clattering to the floor. He released no more than a squeal before Gunner wrapped his arms tightly around Enrico's torso and sank his fangs deep into his throat. Enrico's struggles slowed before going limp in Gunner's iron embrace. Hot blood surged into Gunner's mouth and continued to flow down his throat until there was none left.

Gunner released his grip, dropping the man. Enrico slid to the floor like an under-stuffed ragdoll. Strength and vitality hastened through Gunner, his wounds now rapidly healing. Standing, he picked up the man's discarded AR and headed for Adri. She hadn't followed his directive. But to her credit, she hadn't shrunk from the horror either.

He handed her the rifle. "Anyone who comes through that door, use it."

"I've never shot a gun."

"Just pull the trigger, babe."

"What if it's you?"

"Then fucking aim low until you know who it is. I'll heal."

Gunner headed for the back door, damn near yanking it from its hinges. Rage traveled through his veins, spurring him into the unknown. He had no idea where the other three men had gone, but this time the motherfuckers were the ones going down. Gunner would show them no mercy.

One soldier stood several yards away to the left of the cabin, leaning against a fence post, smoking a cigarillo, oblivious to the nightmare about to unfold. He barely had time to react before Gunner leaped from his position and landed on him like a cat to prey. Gunner ripped a large, gaping hole in the man's throat, spitting the torn flesh to the ground. The soldier hadn't had time to utter a peep, let alone use his gun that leaned against the wire fencing. Gunner dropped him, wiping the back of his hand across his mouth. He craved blood but lusted for vengeance more. His heated gaze swept the area behind the cabin, narrowing on the woods just yards away.

Two soldiers down. Two to go.

Gunner tilted his nose, scenting another human in his vicinity. Catching movement to his right, he ducked behind a row of hedges and crept in the direction of the trees. The oblivious man walked from beneath the dark cover of the forest, AR close to his chest, his finger held at the ready along the length of the metal. Gunner scented the panic in the soldier as he came upon his fallen comrade.

"What the fuck? Tobias?" The man jogged over to the dead man and knelt down to check for a pulse. His gaze widened, seeing the large hole in Tobias's throat.

"Jesus." He quickly crossed himself, as if that would help him see another day. He stood, his gaze darting across the yard. "Mateo?"

No answer came.

Gunner sprinted from his cover and tackled the third soldier to the ground before he had a chance to level his rifle. The gun left his grip, tumbling feet away. Pinning him down, Gunner sank his fangs deep into the man's throat, ingesting more blood until the man's eyes glazed over and his dark soul left his body, no doubt fast-tracking to Hell. Gunner stood, his bloodied hands fisted at his sides as he looked for the coward who had yet to show himself. There was no movement near, but he could scent Mateo, smell the fear in his perspiration.

He wasn't far off.

Gunner kept his back to the cabin and shouted, "Mateo."

The coward wouldn't likely give up his position, not if he had witnessed what had befallen his men. No matter. Gunner wasn't about to give up until Mateo was just as dead as the others.

"I'm coming for you," Gunner growled.

A gunshot sounded from inside the cabin.

Jesus. Adri!

Gunner sprinted for the back door, hearing a second shot, then narrowly missed being hit by a third bullet. Inside the cabin, he saw Adri with her back pinned to Mateo's front. His arm was banded in front of her, her AR now laying on the floor several feet away. The front door was open, the lock missing, having been obliterated by of the first fired shot.

Gunner spotted blood running down Mateo's thigh. Adri had fired low, as she was told, and only wounded the son of a bitch. The third shot had been from Mateo's gun aimed at Gunner and missing him. What caused Gunner to slide to a stop, though, was the pistol Mateo now held against Adri's temple. Her complexion had paled; her gaze gone terrified.

"Drop the weapon, Mateo."

"And let you kill me the way you did my men?" He chuckled hysterically, no doubt having seen what Gunner had done. "What the fuck are you?"

"Your worst nightmare."

"So many bullet holes. How the fuck did you survive? You should be dead."

Gunner had never known fear as he did now. One wrong move and Mateo could easily pull the trigger. "I'm not, motherfucker. Now release Adriana."

"I'm leaving here … with her."

"You might want to think that through."

"If I let her go, you'll kill me."

"I'm going to kill you either way." Gunner raised a brow. "Your choice is on how merciful you want me to be."

"You'll never get away with it. I have more men—"

"Already dead."

Rage contorted his features. "I will kill you and all of the Sons of Sangue, *bendejo*."

"You had your chance," Gunner growled, and as he said it, Adri threw an elbow into Mateo's groin, then quickly spun from his loosened grip. Gunner smiled, baring his bloodied fangs. "Now, I have mine."

Adri dove out of the way just as Gunner leaped, but not before Mateo turned the gun on him, getting a shot off. The bullet ripped through Gunner's gut, knocking him back a few feet, but did little to stop him. His strength was tenfold from the amount of blood he had ingested. He could easily rip the motherfucker's head from his shoulders.

Gunner roared, then rushed Mateo, his shoulder hitting him at the waist and knocking him against the kitchen counters. Glassware fell from the open shelves, hitting the countertops, and sending broken shards across the floor. Gunner picked Mateo up and body-slammed him to the floor, Mateo's head bouncing off the wood, shards of glass biting into his flesh.

Gunner gripped Mateo's head and twisted hard. Bones cracked and flesh tore. The insanity in his gaze dulled as Gunner held the man's head between his soiled hands, Mateo's body lifeless at his feet. Gunner stood, dropped Mateo's head to the floor with a thud, then turned, bloodied and battle-worn.

He turned, his heated gaze landing on Adri. "You okay?"

Adri ran into his arms, where he enveloped her in his embrace, hoping to block her from the view of the carnage at his back. Adri had witnessed such horror and yet she wrapped her arms about his waist as if offering him comfort. After what they had been through, there was no doubt she could handle the change. She was one tough babe and he had almost lost her. Had that happened, life for him would cease. Gunner didn't want a world where she no longer existed.

His Adri, now and forever.

If she'd have him, he planned to ask her to be his mate.

SMOKE KICKED DOWN THE STAND to his motorcycle, cut the twin engines, then stepped over the leather seat. Hanging his skull cap from the handle grip, he then pulled off his gloves, placing them inside the cap. Diablo and Neo stopped alongside him, killing their engines.

"Looks like we got company," Smoke said, pushing his overlong bangs from his face. He used his thumb to indicate the side lot to the Washington clubhouse. Two motorcycles were parked next to an Aston Martin with its top down.

Sawyer "Sting" Martin and Cy "Blade" Moon from the Devils had been watching over their clubhouse in their absence. They had both expressed interest in patching over to the Sons of Sangue. But it wasn't the pair he had been referring to; it was the sports car that didn't belong.

"Looks like Vlad and Janelle decided to grace us with their presence again," Diablo said. He laid his helmet on the seat of his bike, then patted Neo on the shoulder on his way to the door. "Let's go see what they have in store for us this time. Shooting the shit out here ain't about to accomplish a thing."

Smoke entered the clubhouse first. Sting and Blade were in the middle of a game of pool while Vlad and Janelle lounged at the back of the room near the large picture window, overlooking Coal Creek and the woods out back. Two glasses of a deep red wine sat on the table between them.

"About time you three made it back." Vlad picked up his glass, held it up to the three in a salute, then took it to his lips for a sip. He placed it back on the table and leveled his glare. "You take your fucking time or what?"

Diablo chuckled. "While I have no idea the mode of transportation you both took, we rode our bikes ... all the way back. That's almost a 600-mile trip. Wasn't going to do it in a couple of hours."

"I tried telling you a car is the way to go. But you boys don't listen." Vlad gave Diablo a wink, then reached out and entwined his fingers with Janelle's. "I'll keep my Aston Martin."

"You here for a chat?" Smoke asked. Not that it wouldn't be okay for Vlad to stop by at any given time, but the big vampire didn't usually make social calls.

Neo abandoned the small talk, and walked over to the pool table, leaving the VP and Sergeant at Arms, Diablo, to talk business. "I got next game," he said to Sting and Blade.

"We'll get to my reason for being here in a moment. How's Tag?" Vlad asked.

Smoke grinned. "You likely already know with Janelle and her visions, but he was coming along fine last I saw him. A few more days and he'll be good as new."

"My visions don't work that way. I usually see when someone is in trouble. You left him on his own?" Janelle asked.

"No. With Gunner and Adri. After cleaning up the mess in St. Mary's, they returned to hunting cabin in Helena." Smoke walked over to the wet bar and grabbed a bottle of Gentleman Jack. He poured a couple of tumblers full and handed one to Diablo. "They'll fly back with Tag when he's ready. Caitlyn drove Gunner's motorcycle back with the Oregon crew. We'll pick it up from them later. Gunner insisted on seeing Tag through to the end."

"As well he should. He brought the man into the mess. That makes Tag Gunner's responsibility." Vlad's dark gaze narrowed. "I take it the rest of the mayhem has been taken care of then."

"Mateo and his crew will no longer be bothering anyone. We made sure there wasn't anything left to be found in Helena. And Gunner cleaned up the mess at the cabin where he and Adri stayed, leaving a sizable donation for repairs. I doubt we will hear from the owner." Diablo tossed back his two fingers of whiskey and set the glass down on the bar top. "I hate to be the first to leave the party, but I have someone waiting on me."

"Please give Angelica our best," Janelle said.

"I'll do that." Diablo said his goodbyes to the rest of the men, then left the clubhouse.

Vlad ran a hand down his whiskered chin. "Now that I see the situation is handled, I'll get to the reason for our trip. The cartel won't let this go if they believe the Sons took out their kingpin and several others. Don't let your guard down, Smoke. Not even for a minute."

"That goes without saying."

"I see trouble brewing with the Devils," Janelle told him. "Visions that seem to be cartel related. This isn't something that should be taken lightly."

"We heard they were running drugs again for the cartel." Smoke took a sip from his glass, mulling over her latest premonition. "I'll make sure Viper and Hawk are aware of the situation. Blade and Sting, they're willing to patch over."

Janelle lowered her voice to nearly a whisper. "My visions show me that Sting is still wearing a Devil's patch. It appears, though, he's working for our side, that he's not being honest with them. If I'm envisioning something from the future, it usually means the person is in danger."

"You see Sting as an infiltrator?"

"Yes."

Smoke downed the rest of his whiskey, then poured himself another. "Then we need to hold off on patching him over."

"I believe it's wise to have someone on the inside. But due to Janelle's vision, he'll need to be cautious," Vlad said. "Talk with my grandsons, because I think it best that you turn him first. Don't leave him defenseless against the Devils."

"I'll talk with Gunner, Viper, and Hawk. We will do what's best."

Sting handed his cue stick to Neo and approached the three of them. "I can't help but overhear. I'm not sure what you mean by turn, but I'm in. I'll head back to Santa Barbara and lay low within the Devils organization, report back to you. I've never been agreeable to them working with the cartel."

Smoke nodded. "Then it's settled. As soon as Gunner and Adri return, we'll put the plan into action."

"We don't need any of you dying at the hands of the cartel, let alone the Devils. You'll need to be careful, Sting. Keep two steps ahead…" Janelle put her fingers against her temples and grimaced.

"What's wrong?" Vlad visibly tightened his grip on her hand, concern crossing his features.

Janelle sucked in a deep breath, letting out a small cry. "It's Roxanne."

"Rocky? Rocky Barta?" Smoke's heart clenched at the mention of Janelle's best friend.

She sat back, took a deep breath, and opened her eyes, her gaze now laced with worry. "I see a bloodied split lip … and lots of bruising. Dear, Lord, Vlad. We need to get to her. Rocky's in danger."

Vlad stood, then held out his hand to Janelle and helped her to her feet. Pulling her into his embrace, he kissed her temple. "Then we go to New York City."

A tear slipped down Janelle's cheek. "I see a hospital bed, with lots of monitors, wires, and tubes…"

"I hope we aren't too late to stop your vision, *iubi*. We need to be there for her before it happens." He released his hold on his mate, his hand still entwined with hers. "We'll be heading out. Keep me informed on this mess with the Devils. If you need me, call and I'll head back."

"You stay with Janelle," Smoke said. "We'll handle things here. I'll get a hold of Viper as soon as Gunner and Adri make it back." Smoke couldn't help the sick feeling creeping into his gut at the mention of Rocky. He had only met her once, but his attraction went deep. "Keep me posted as soon as you know anything about your friend."

"I will." Janelle dropped Vlad's hand and gave Smoke a brief hug, before following Vlad to the door. Seconds later, the four men were alone.

"You want to fill me in, man?" Sting asked.

Smoke smirked. "Other than you're going to spy on your old crew?"

"Not that. What the fuck did Vlad mean by turn me?"

Grabbing another tumbler, Smoke filled it nearly to the rim with the amber-colored whiskey. "You might want to drink this first. You're going to need it."

CHAPTER TWENTY-FOUR

After spending the week in Helena, it was good to be back on the coast. The scent of the ocean carried to her nose, reminding her of the beach house in Oregon where she had stayed what seemed like years ago. But this, this felt more like home. Not that Adriana had much to compare it to. Her parents were both gone and being an only child, she had lived alone in Mexico. Once Gabriela had left the country and traveled north with Ryder, there had been no reason for her to stay. Moving to Oregon had been a given, just as moving to Washington was. Now that they were back at the clubhouse, though, everything was about to change. Adri hoped that didn't mean things would between her and Gunner.

They had flown back to Washington with Tag, where they had left him at his aviation field to get a little rest before meeting everyone at the clubhouse. Watching Tag fight through the agony of turning into a vampire had put Adri on edge. Could she suffer through the same? Although Gunner hadn't yet asked her to be his mate, she knew what her answer would be. Any amount of suffering and pain would be worth an eternity with him.

Tag had seemed to take the news on his vampirism well, had even learned from Gunner to feed from an unsuspecting waitress at closing time in a small diner in Helena. Adri had watched with interest as Tag sank his fangs into the woman's throat, completing his change. The woman, having been hypnotized by Gunner, was none the wiser as she straightened her work smock, then headed for her car. Tag hadn't once complained. But considering the situation, he had been given the gift of immortality, a better alternative to death. The Washington Sons of Sangue had agreed Tag would be a welcome addition to their MC. He'd keep his business at the Training Wing. The Sons would benefit from having an airplane pilot and an aviation field at their disposal.

"Ready, babe?" Gunner asked, most likely feeling her anxiety.

"Will they hold the mess I made against me?"

"It was a mess of my making." He leaned down and kissed her on the forehead. "I came to you, not the other way around. And I'd do it all over again. The Sons won't fault you for my actions."

Gunner placed his large hand at the center of her back and led her toward the front door, following her inside. Smoke, Blade, and Neo stood around the pool table, playing a game and throwing back whiskeys. Diablo and Angel, the woman Adri believed to be his mate, sat on the overstuffed chairs at the back of the room facing a large picture window that overlooked the woods out back. A young boy about the age of eight sat in a high-backed kitchen chair playing a video game.

Angel swept her feet to the floor, stood, and walked in Gunner and Adri's direction. Her warm smile welcomed them.

"We've been waiting for you. Will Tag be joining us? I'm looking forward to meeting him."

"He'll be along shortly." Gunner leaned down and kissed Adri atop the head. "This is Angel, Diablo's old lady. Why don't you get to know her while I have a chat with the guys?"

Angel gave Adri a brief hug, then led her to the chairs that had been occupied by her and Diablo. Adri took the seat he had occupied as Diablo now stood with the men gathering at the island bar.

"I've been hearing a lot about you. You already know the guys. The one doing his best to ignore us is Tyler. He's Diablo's son."

"Nice to meet you, Tyler."

The boy looked briefly up from his game. "You, too."

Angel chuckled, love for the boy evident in her dark blue eyes. "Sorry about his manners."

"He's perfectly fine. I was young once too. How old is he?"

"Eight going on eighteen."

Adri lowered her voice. "Is he…? I mean a … uh?"

"Vampire? No. Diablo had Tyler before his turning. Tyler's mom died and he was left with her sister. Lisa raised him as her own, along with her son, Billy. She helps me run the safe house. And Tyler knows what we are. When he becomes an adult, he'll be given the choice to turn or stay human. Either way will be fine with us."

Adri glanced around the room, taking in the clubhouse. She couldn't help but wonder if Gunner planned to move her in here with him or help her find a place of her own. Although they had talked in Helena and on the plane ride back, they seemed to avoid the topic of what the future held for either of them.

"It really is good to be back, even if Washington isn't where I lived before."

"Oregon, right? Diablo told me about the house being burned down where you had lived in the guesthouse. That must have been traumatic."

"It was. But thank the good Lord, no one was hurt. It was what made me decide to go back to Mexico, though. I couldn't have Mateo hurting my friends."

Angel swept her long hair off her shoulder. Not only was she beautiful on the outside, but she also seemed to be on the inside. With Gabby and Caitlyn in Oregon, Adri was going to need a friend here.

"Are you staying in Washington or were you planning to go back to Oregon?" Angel asked.

"She's not going anywhere," Gunner answered for her, proving he had been eavesdropping from over by the bar. He walked over to their chairs and looked down at Adri. "That is if she agrees."

The heat of his gaze warmed her. "I was hoping to stay in Washington ... if I can find a place."

"There's no need to look, babe. You'll be staying with me."

"Here?"

Gunner shrugged. "Until we can find another place."

Angel reached over and placed her hand atop Adri's. "You both can always stay at the safe house. It would save you from the testosterone levels around here. We don't have any residents at the moment and we'd love the company."

"Lisa doesn't live there with Billy?"

Angel shook her head. "Diablo fixed up the old Devil clubhouse they used during their last mission for her and Billy to use. It would be my pleasure to help you and Gunner."

Adri looked at Gunner. Staying at the clubhouse would mean sharing the place with the Sons in tight quarters, but ultimately it was his decision. She would be happy wherever Gunner elected to stay as long as she was by his side.

Gunner pulled Adri from her seat and wrapped her in his embrace. "Tonight, we'll stay here in my room. It has an en suite, so you won't have to share with the guys. Tomorrow, we can make plans for the future … *our* future."

Our future. Adri liked the sound of that.

"The invite is always open," Angel said.

"Thank you. I appreciate it," Adri said. "I'm too tired to move much tonight anyway, even if all I own is in a small bag. I swear I'll be asleep the minute my head hits the pillow."

"We'll need to get you a new wardrobe."

"You don't need to buy me things, Gunner. I can get a job and earn my keep. Buy my own things."

Gunner leaned down and whispered next to her ear. His breath feathered delightfully across her flesh. "I have a better way for you to earn your keep. Just say the word and I'll clear this welcoming party."

Adri drew her lower lip between her teeth. His offer was tempting but she didn't want to be rude to his friends, not after just arriving. "Diablo, Angel, and Tyler came here to welcome you back. I'd like to get to know her a bit better... If that's okay?"

"Fine," Gunner growled, giving her backside a pat. "But later, I'm clearing this fucking place."

"Smoke, Neo, and Blade ... don't they live here?"

"Yes. Tonight, though, they'll be heading for the Blood 'n' Rave, on the president's order, so I can get some alone time with you. Besides, there's something I need to ask you."

"Can't you ask me now?"

Gunner chuckled. "In due time."

"Give me a hint?"

"Nope." Tilting his nose up, Gunner no doubt purposely changed the subject on her. "Tag's here."

"How do you know?"

"Part of my vampire traits. We always know when another one of us is close by."

Seconds later the door opened and Tag entered the clubhouse. The Sons greeted him with enthusiasm, passing out tumblers of whiskey, in salute to the newest member of the Washington crew. Adri sat back down next to Angel.

"Are they always like this?"

Angel grasped the bottle of wine from the table between them and poured them each a glass, handing one to Adri. "As I said earlier, we have room at the safe house."

Adri grinned, taking a sip of the wine. She was going to enjoy being a part of the family. "Gunner said we'll stay here tonight. He said he has something to ask me."

"Any idea what that might be?"

"No." Adri took another sip. Dare she voice her desire aloud? "But I can hope."

"What are you hoping for, Adri?"

"To be his mate."

"Maybe you'll get your wish."

"You know something I don't?"

"I see the way he looks at you. That man is in love."

Adri smiled, looking back at Gunner. His dark gaze strayed to hers and all Adri could think about was clearing out the clubhouse.

"I think Gunner knew you were right for him long before he flew to Mexico."

She sure hoped Angel was correct, because nothing was more important to her than becoming his, now and forever.

DAMN, GUNNER COULDN'T REMEMBER ever being this nervous. Not even when Ryder had told him they planned to bury his ass alive in the backwoods of Mexico. It was a simple question he needed to ask Adri, one that had a yes or no answer. He already knew Adriana loved him; she had confessed as much. So, why asking her to be his mate had him tied up in knots, he didn't know.

What was the worst possible outcome?

That she wouldn't be willing to give up her humanity.

After her witnessing the brutal reality of his life back at St. Mary's, he wouldn't be surprised if she had changed her mind. Becoming a mate to a vampire meant leaving behind your mortal life. Once she ingested his blood, the time for second-guessing would be over. Pledging her life to him meant for all eternity. Add in the fact that being turned felt like being lit on fire from the inside, which Adri knew, having witnessed Tag's fiery change, she'd likely think twice about wanting to say yes. And well she should.

Moments ago, Gunner had ushered everyone from the clubhouse, wanting to be alone with Adri when he asked her the most important question he had ever asked … of anyone. Diablo, Angelica, and Tyler had headed to their home, while the rest of the crew took Tag to the Blood 'n' Rave for an introduction to the donors. They'd make sure he got the VIP treatment.

Adriana was still in the en suite, washing up while Gunner paced the area rug. Was it possible she had a case of nerves as well? Surely, she wouldn't be afraid to be alone with him, not after all they had been through, which left the possibility of her changing her mind about him.

For Gunner, there would be no other.

Adri was his true love.

The sound of running water in the bathroom stopped and the door opened. Adri stepped into the bedroom wearing one of his T-shirts again. Gunner's breath stuck in his throat. Adri had never looked sexier. Her black hair brushed the collar on the white cotton, her complexion standing out in contrast, her face free of makeup. Her long, slim legs seemed to go on forever, which were perfect for wrapping his waist. All he wanted to do was remove his shirt and bury himself inside her and to hell with his inquiry.

It was the apprehension he saw on her face, though, that nearly gutted him.

"Come here, babe." Gunner opened his arms and she rushed into them.

Enfolding her in his embrace, he kissed the top of her head. His heart damn near leaped from his chest, hammering against his sternum where she lay her cheek. Lord, he loved this woman. He needed her to know that, to know regardless of her decision to become his mate, he wasn't going anywhere.

"You know I love you, right?" He felt her smile against his chest. "I always will, no matter what happens."

Adri pulled back enough to look up at him. Her tongue darted out, wetting her lips, tempting him to kiss away the worry in her gaze. Now was not the time to carry her to bed, to show her how much she truly meant to him.

No. This was about so much more than sex.

"I love you, too." She flattened her palm over his beating heart. "So, why do you look at me in fear? I'm not going anywhere. My home may have been in Oregon before with Ryder and Gabby. But not now. Now it's with you … in Washington. Unless you no longer want me here."

"You're my home, Adri. I'd follow you anywhere." He released his arms and framed her face between his hands. "You won't be able to return to Mexico if you agree to be with me."

Adri's smile reached her warm brown eyes. "I don't care if I ever step foot there again."

"Good."

"So, is this about moving in together? Or in here?"

Gunner dropped his hold and led her to the king-sized bed. He sat against the headboard and pulled her onto the bed so that her back aligned with his front. He wrapped his arms around her waist and kissed her hair, still wet from the shower. The scent of vanilla carried to his nose.

"I don't care where I live, babe, as long as it's with you."

"So, what has you worried? I'm not going anywhere."

Worried? Hell, he was petrified. Gunner already knew what it felt like to live without her, and he'd move Heaven and Earth to never allow that to happen again.

"I know moving in here isn't ideal, so if taking Angelica up on moving into the safe house for the time being is what you want, then we'll do that. Living here wouldn't give us a lot of privacy anyway. But this is about more than just moving in together."

Adri laid her hands over his forearms, the heat of her touch carrying to his groin. "We wouldn't have privacy at the safe house either, Gunner. Staying here is fine until we find something else."

He chuckled. "You might not say that after a few days of putting up with the guys."

"Is that what you wanted to ask me, then? To move in with you?"

Gunner leaned forward, resting his chin on her shoulder. "It's a bit more complicated than that. You know vampires don't marry."

She nodded, her fingers wrapping his forearms.

"We take mates."

Again, she said nothing, shifting a bit so she could look at him. He could see the worry in her gaze, feel the tremble in her touch.

"Earlier, when I spoke to the guys, I asked them a question. It was an informal vote, but they all agreed that you're perfect for me. You've won over my brethren."

"What if they hadn't liked me?"

"There was no chance in hell that they wouldn't. But I needed it to be okay with them as well. As I told you before, it's part of our code. We don't take creating another vampire lightly." Gunner took a deep breath. "Adri, I want you to be my forever. I'm trying to ask you to be my mate. Would you at least think about it?"

Adri turned in his embrace. Framing his face with her hands, she kissed him hard, giving him a sense of relief. He had been worried about nothing. Lord, her ferocity was a turn on. Holding onto her tightly, he returned the kiss with fervor.

"I wasn't sure you'd ask … that you'd want me forever. Yes, Gunner. A thousand times yes."

His heart swelled. Adri hadn't denied him, even after all she had witnessed at his side. He worried she'd view him as no better than her ex. Gunner drew her back for a kiss, deep, hard, and full of promise.

Adriana Flores would be his for eternity.

Running his hands through her hair, he looked into her dark eyes. "You know what that entails?"

"That I become ... a vampire."

"Like Angel, Gabby, and Caitlyn. It won't be an easy transformation, Adri."

Worry laced her gaze again. "I watched Tag go through his. There were times when you sat behind him and gripped his shoulders. His pain seemed to alleviate. Did that hurt you when you touched him?"

Gunner nodded. "I absorbed some of his agony into me."

"You felt his pain."

"Yes, but by doing so it made it more bearable for him."

"Would you do that for me?"

"Babe, I will hold you the entire fucking time. Your pain will be mine. I promise not to let you go." He would step through the fiery gates of hell to help her. "There isn't anything I wouldn't do for you."

She licked her lips, tears gathering in her eyes. "You made that obvious when you flew to Mexico and took on an entire cartel just to rescue me."

He used his thumb to wipe away a stray tear. "And I'd do it again. I love you, Adri. You mean everything to me. Even if you hadn't wanted to become a vampire and be my mate, I'd still stay by your side until death parted us."

"I will always love you ... until the end of time." Adri drew her lower lip between her teeth. "I do have a question."

"What is it?"

"About how all this works. You said you couldn't get me pregnant because you were a vampire. Earlier you said vampires can have babies called true bloods?"

"You want babies?"

Adri nodded shyly.

"Nothing would make me happier than you carrying my child. Several of the Sons from Oregon have sons."

"So there really are no daughters born?"

"Yes, as I said earlier, vampires only conceive males. Only once that I know of did a woman become a vampire without the help of a male and that was because she was from a primordial bloodline, a brother of Vlad Tepes."

He definitely couldn't wait to get started if that's what she wanted. Hell, he'd gladly give her lots of sons.

"So, once I become a vampire I can get pregnant?"

He nodded.

"I've always wanted children." Adri grinned. "I want babies with you, Gunner. But even if we couldn't have had them, I still would've chosen to be your mate."

"And here I thought my biggest worry was you not wanting to become a vampire. Just how many babies are you thinking?"

"Maybe a half dozen…"

This woman would be the death of him, he thought with a chuckle. "How about we start with your change and talk about babies later."

"Will you give me your blood now?"

"Are you in that much of a hurry?"

Adri gripped the T-shirt she wore and attempted to pull it over her head. Gunner gripped her hands, stopping her. Her lips turned down as she looked at him in question.

"Not that I don't want you, babe, but we'll have plenty of time for that latter. This goes much deeper than making love for me. I'm giving you the most precious thing I have. This is about joining our blood for eternity. You need to tell me if you aren't ready for this."

"I've always been yours, Gunner, from the moment we danced in Mexico. I would have followed you then, even if you thought I was some sort of stalker. I've never wanted to be with anyone more. I'm ready if you are."

"Are you sure? There's no turning back once you accept my blood."

Adri ran a hand down the whisker scruff on his cheek. "I've never been more ready for anything in my life."

Gunner's vampire surfaced, more ravenous than ever. His gaze heated. The bones in his cheeks snapped and transformed. His fangs punched through his gums, elongating. The fact she didn't pull back in fear warmed his heart. Adri now accepted him as he was. Her gaze hooded with desire, as though she not only accepted the changes in him, but found him arousing. Gunner pulled her back against his chest and enveloped her within his embrace, holding her tightly against him. The pain would come fast and swiftly. Gunner used his fangs to tear a hole in his wrist. Blood ran down his forearm as he took the wound to her lips, holding it just inches away.

"Tell me again that you will be my mate. Pledge your eternity to me and I'll pledge mine to you."

She gripped his arm. "I love you and I can't wait to be yours."

"Mine and I am yours. I love you, babe."

Adri brought his wrist forward and sealed her lips over the wound. Gunner could feel the pull of her suckling all the way to his groin. But now was not the time to sate the desire sluicing through his veins. Now was about lessening her pain and holding her through the worst of her change.

Adriana was his for time without end. He'd not let anyone, or anything, come between them ever again. Gunner's mission in life would be to see to her happiness … even if that meant giving her half a dozen sons or more. Besides, he'd enjoy the hell out of their baby-making sessions. Now that Adri was bonded to him as his mate, there was no way he was ever letting her go again.

Taking back his wrist, Gunner sealed the wound just as he felt the spark of fire begin deep in her abdomen. Her soft groan carried to his ear, nearly decimating him. He tucked his chin into the crook of her neck, held her tightly, and whispered, "You got this, babe… We got this."

Adri's heart began to beat within him, making his own heart thunder against his sternum. Their blood unified in the fiery exchange. Adriana Flores had stolen his heart long ago back in Mexico and now the two had become one.

Forever.

EPILOGUE

A FEW DAYS HAD PASSED SINCE HER COMPLETE TRANSFORmation and each day her vampire seemed to get stronger. Adri found that she could now hear whispers from across the room. Her sense of smell had also improved, telling her when other vampires were in the vicinity. To her surprise, she had scented Gabby and Ryder before they had even disembarked from the motorcycles at the clubhouse.

Gabriela Trevino Caballero grabbed a bottle of wine and a couple of glasses from the bar, heading for the chairs where Adriana rested. The men, along with Ryder, had left for the Blood 'n' Rave moments ago, having heard that Draven and Brea were in town. Adri wasn't yet feeling up to partying, even though she'd gained strength daily. Besides, she had wanted to catch up with Gabby.

Adri had been thrilled when Ryder and Gabby had arrived, returning Gunner's motorcycle. Caitlyn had driven it home to Oregon from Helena, and Gabby had volunteered to bring it north to Washington. On the trip home, she'd ride on the back of Ryder's bike.

Now, Adri watched Gabby pull the cork from the bottle with a pop, then pour them each a glass of the deep-red Merlot. "How are you feeling?"

"Better than I was yesterday. That's for sure."

Gabby grimaced. "I still remember my own turning as if it were a mere day ago. It's not easy to forget."

"Being burned alive from the inside?" Adri took a sip of her wine. "I doubt I'll ever forget the fiery pain."

"Gunner held you through it, though, right?"

"He did." Adriana smiled, remembering how his arms had comforted her and lessened some of the pain. "I doubt I would've survived if he hadn't absorbed some of my agony. The few times he left to take care of his needs, the pain had become unbearable."

"I remember all too well." Gabby took a sip from her glass. "We have our men to thank for getting us through."

Adri thought of the time she saw Ryder as a vampire. "When did you know?"

"Know what?"

"That Ryder was a vampire. Was it before or after I picked you up in Todos Santos?"

"Before."

"You never told me."

Gabby smiled sadly. "I couldn't. It wasn't my secret to share."

"I saw Ryder one night ...with fangs." Adri toyed with the stem of her glass, looking at her lap. "After I moved to Oregon."

"You never said anything."

"I didn't know if you were aware of what he was. And since I wasn't one-hundred percent positive of what I saw, I kept it to myself." Adri shrugged, remembering trying to convince herself what she had seen wasn't real. "When I found out Gunner was a vampire, I told him what I knew now to be true about Ryder."

"What did he say?"

Adri chuckled, shaking her head. "He hypnotized me, making me forget it all. But later, when his vampire emerged again, I recalled my memory of Ryder, though it seemed more like a dream. How did you take it when you found out?"

Gabby raised a brow. "You actually witnessed my meltdown."

Adri recalled the moment, and her reaction. "I thought you were upset over your uncle being killed."

"Mostly, I was. But some of it was my freaking out over learning Ryder was a vampire. How did you take it when you realized what Gunner was?"

"I think having seen Ryder first somehow helped." Adri thought back to witnessing Gunner's fangs the second time, proving vampires existed, and being afraid of what he became but not fearful of him. "I was frightened at first. But in the long run, it didn't matter that he was a vampire. I had already fallen for him."

"How are you doing now?"

Adri smiled. "Other than feeling like I came out of the worst hot flashes of my life?"

Gabby laughed.

"None of the pain matters. All I'm feeling is happiness. I'm more in love with Gunner than ever." As she spoke, Adri turned toward the door, scenting the man who owned her heart before he even stepped inside. "What are you doing back? I thought you went to the Rave with the guys."

His smile made her pulse hammer, glad that he returned for her. Never could she love another. Adri thought without him she wouldn't be able to breathe.

"I remembered something," he said as he strode toward her.

Adri furrowed her brow. "What?"

"This."

He pulled her into his embrace, his strong arms wrapping around her, then he leaned down and slanted his lips over hers. He kissed her hard, one filled with promise for the night to come.

Gabby cleared her throat, gaining their attention, her smile twinkling in her eyes. "Mind pointing me in the direction of where you left my mate?"

Gunner laughed. "He's at the end of the drive waiting on you. We'll join you at the Rave in a bit. There's something I need to give Adri first."

"I bet there is." Gabby laughed upon her exit, leaving them blessedly alone.

Adri's eyes heated; Gunner's turning black. Her fangs punched through her gums as she was suddenly ravenous for more than blood.

"Damn, but you look sexy as hell with fangs," Gunner growled, baring his own razor-sharp canines.

Adri could actually scent his desire, starting a hunger deep within her belly. "You were saying?"

"That I had something to give you." Gunner swooped her into his arms and headed for their suite.

"Am I going to like it?"

Depositing her to her feet, he then pulled his shirt over his head. Lord, she'd never get tired of seeing his granite-like chest and abs.

Tossing the T-shirt aside, he picked her up and placed her atop the comforter, coming to rest between her spread thighs. The ridge of his hard-on nestled between them. "Babe, I think you're going to love it."

Adri smiled, knowing full well that she would. Suddenly ravenous and remembering Gunner's lessons on feeding, she bared her fangs and sank them deep into his neck. The sound of his groan carrying to her ears and the honeyed taste of his warm blood flowing over her tongue was damn near orgasmic. She'd definitely love what he was about to give her, but it was the man who had stolen her heart.

Forever ... and always.

ABOUT THE AUTHOR

A daydreamer at heart, Patricia A. Rasey, resides in her native town in Northwest Ohio with her husband, Mark, and her two lovable Cavalier King Charles Spaniels, Naomi and Buckeye. A graduate of Long Ridge Writer's School, Patricia has seen publication of some her short stories in magazines as well as several of her novels.

When not behind her computer, you can find Patricia working, reading, watching movies or MMA. She also enjoys spending her free time at the river camping and boating with her husband and two sons. Ms. Rasey is a retired third degree Black Belt in American Freestyle Karate.

Made in United States
Troutdale, OR
04/07/2024